Cold Winter in Bordeaux

ALLAN MASSIE

QUARTET BOOKS

First published in 2014 by
Quartet Books Limited
A member of the Namara Group
27 Goodge Street, London W1T 2LD

A catalogue record for this book
is available from the British Library

ISBN 978 0 7043 7328 0

Typeset by Antony Gray
Printed and bound in Great Britain by
T J International Ltd, Padstow, Cornwall

For Alex and Lizzie
with love

I

Sunday afternoon, and one of these October days when, as Lannes' mother used to say, October had given up on autumn and was opening the door to winter. The wind that had blown all week had died away, the weather had turned chill, and a freezing fog hung over the city.

He was alone in the apartment, except for Alain's cat, No Neck, who now leapt on to his lap, pushing his head between Lannes and his book, and digging his claws into his thigh. Marguerite was out, summoned by her mother. The old lady was complaining again of 'palpitations'. It probably meant nothing. It was her way of commanding attention. If Marguerite immediately responded, it was because her inability to love her mother as she thought she ought to made her feel guilty. Clothilde was also out, somewhere, with Michel. He hadn't asked where they were going or what they would be doing. The girl, at nineteen, was entitled to her independence, or such independence as could still be enjoyed. As for Michel, Lannes both liked him – the boy had charm and good manners – and distrusted him. His grandfather, the retired professor of literature who looked like a colonel, no doubt felt the same. Lannes respected him but the young people's relationship caused them both anxiety, the professor for the boy's sake, Lannes for Clothilde's.

He ran his hand along the cat's back, scratched it behind an ear, causing it to purr. Did it miss Alain? Had it forgotten him? Would it recognise him when he returned? When? If? He knew it was if, but had to believe it was when. It was nine months since his last postcard from Algiers. Did the silence mean he was now in England? 'It doesn't do to brood,' he said to the cat, 'or worry.' But it was inevitable that he did. There was after all nothing that really concerned him now but the children, the need for all three of them to survive what he thought of as 'all this'.

He picked up Dominique's last letter from the little table by his chair, and read it again. It was lyrical. An account of his work, of nights spent in the mountains sleeping under the stars, of labour in the forests, of the transformation in the health and morale of the 'kids from the city' with whose charge he and his friend Maurice de Grimaud were entrusted. 'It's astonishing, and richly rewarding,' he wrote, 'to see how they respond.' One of his colleagues had led his little troop into a village and the children had run away and hidden from them thinking they were Germans – 'because they were so smart and took such pride in their appearance as they marched along singing'. 'We really are doing great work for France and for the National Revolution,' Dominique wrote. 'Boys who used to hang about smoking in cafés now delight in fresh air, exercise and physical training.'

Perhaps they did. No doubt they did. Dominique had always been truthful, never one to engage in fantasy. Nevertheless, Lannes remembered that someone had once remarked to Napoleon's mother how proud she must be to see one son an emperor and others kings and princes, and the old woman had replied, in her broad Corsican accent, 'so long as it lasts'. Which, of course, it hadn't. The emperor had ended up a prisoner of the English on St Helena. And the Marshal, the hero of Verdun where Lannes had been wounded, how would it end for the old man?

He lit a cigarette, causing No Neck, who disliked the smoke, to jump off his lap. He returned to his book, a novel by Walter Scott which he had read once, years before, and enjoyed. But today the adventures of the young men on the Solway, which he understood to be a border between Scotland and England, could not hold his attention. He let it fall again and closed his eyes.

He wasn't quite asleep when he heard the door open, and Marguerite returning. There was less constraint between them now than there had been the previous year when he had betrayed her by leaving her in ignorance of Alain's determination to join de Gaulle and the Free French. Then his suspension at the request of the Occupying Power, and the cause of that suspension, had pleased her. She had been less happy when he was reinstated, but was resigned to it. In any case, as he had said, how would they live without his salary? Yet she still hated his work, and, though there was less constraint, he knew he hadn't regained her trust, and didn't deserve to.

'How was she?' he said.

'As she always is.'

He knew she wished she liked her mother more, though he thought it evidence of her essential goodness that she liked the old woman at all and took such trouble over her, responding to her demands, enduring her constant complaints without complaining herself. But that was one of the many things they never talked about.

'I hope Clothilde won't be late,' he said.

'Oh, but I trust her with Michel. I'm so glad she's got him.'

It wasn't only because the boy sometimes brought her flowers when he came to collect Clothilde. He even flirted with her, and Lannes had seen his wife blush – with happiness? – when Michel paid her a compliment.

'I made Mother an omelette with three of the eggs I found in the market yesterday. She insisted she had no appetite, but she ate it all.'

II

The fog was still thick and it was clammy and cold as he set off to the office. He wore his thorn-proof tweed coat and leant on his stick, because his hip ached as it always did in this weather. The ache was almost an old friend, souvenir of his war. 'Ils ne passeront pas,' they had said at Verdun, symbol of France defiant. For years he had told himself: you survived Verdun, you can survive anything. He wondered if the Marshal thought of Verdun when he woke in the mornings in Vichy. It was strange. He deplored Vichy in many ways, though aware there had been no good choices to be made in the summer of 1940; yet he had never lost his respect for the Marshal, respect and even regard.

Clothilde had returned home in good time, before the curfew, glowing with happiness.

'We met a friend of Michel's, called Sigi. He sent you his regards.'

'Did he now?'

'He said to say you have his respect.'

'Indeed.'

'You don't like him, Papa? I hear it in your voice.'

'Let's just say I doubt if he's a good influence on Michel.'

He had left it there. Perhaps he should have taken the opportunity to speak more strongly, to tell her he was a dangerous man, not to be trusted, a murderer and a Fascist. But he had said nothing. He had said nothing because to say anything would have required him to say everything, and . . .

He banged his stick against a lamp-post in irritation and self-reproach.

There was a pile of paperwork waiting for him. There always was, and it was rarely important, a reminder nevertheless that despite everything the business of functionaries went on. The less autonomy Vichy had, the more assiduously it deluged the police with paper in order to maintain the pretence of government. Little of it mattered, not much anyway, but it all required his attention, even if the attention he gave it was never more than perfunctory.

There was a knock on the door. Young René Martin entered. As ever Lannes was touched by something frank and unspoilt in the boy's expression. Somehow or other he retained his faith in the virtue and necessity of their work. Moncerre, whom they called the bull-terrier, said the boy was naive, and loved to tease him, but Moncerre was wrong. It was just that René Martin hadn't yet succumbed to the prevailing cynicism.

'I called you at home,' he said, 'but Madame Lannes said you were already on your way. There's been a death, a woman in an apartment in the Cours de l'Intendance. Her maid discovered the body when she came to work this morning. That's all I know.'

'Is Moncerre in?'

'Not yet.'

'Call him and tell him to meet us there.'

Was it reprehensible to feel his spirits lift? Undoubtedly. Nevertheless that's how it was. With luck, this would be ordinary police work, nothing to do with the war, or with members of the Resistance groups whose activity over the last year had occupied so much police time.

*   *   *

They stopped off at the Bar Jack, rue de Voltaire, for a coffee and Armagnac.

'The dead woman is called Gabrielle Peniel,' René Martin said, 'but that's all I know.'

He was impatient to get on, be at the scene of the crime. Lannes delayed, smoked three cigarettes, and ordered another Armagnac. The boy didn't understand that this was his way of preparing himself, that it was, as it were, a gear-change.

A delay of twenty minutes would make no difference, except to his mood. He almost said, 'She won't run away, you know.' If the maid had found the body on her arrival this morning, it was probable that her employer has been killed at any time over the weekend.

The concierge was waiting for them at the door of her lodge.

'I'd never have thought it,' she said. 'Poor Marie, that's the maid, was in a real state. Nothing would do for her but that I went up to see for myself. Well, there's no doubt to my mind. It's a murder, superintendent, and a nasty one. Nobody ties a silk stocking round their own neck. Of course you don't need me to tell you that. I settled Marie with a glass of the rum which I keep on account of my rheumatism. She was speechless, poor girl, well, not exactly, because in actual fact she couldn't stop talking. But when I say speechless, I mean that she was making no sense at all. She still isn't really. Anyway I've settled her in my lodge and I'll keep her there till she's recovered herself sufficiently for you to speak with her. Now do you want me to accompany you to Madame Peniel's apartment?'

'That won't be necessary,' Lannes said. 'I'll have a word with you later. Meanwhile I would be grateful if you would continue to look after Marie, and keep an eye open for the doctor and the other members of my team who will be arriving soon.'

'Very well, if that's how you wish it, superintendent. Here are the keys. Naturally I locked up the apartment, which is on the first floor right. I know how to behave in these circumstances, even though it goes without saying that we've never had this sort of thing here before, not in my time. You'll understand that this is a very respectable building; my tenants are all good people. As for Madame Peniel, it's hard to take it in, such a distinguished lady she was. A bit reserved, but always polite and well-spoken.'

It was an apartment with high ceilings. Someone, presumably the maid, had opened the shutters and pulled back the curtains to let the grey morning light in.

The salon was furnished in the style of the Belle Époque and there were three cases of stuffed birds. There was a smell of stale cigar smoke and an empty bottle of champagne stood with two glasses on an occasional table beside a grand piano, a Bechstein. The body was in the bedroom. It lay on the floor. The woman was wearing only knickers, which had been pulled down to her knees. As the concierge had told them, she had been strangled with one of her silk stockings – a suspender belt lay on the floor beside her. A bottle of scent – Chanel No. 5 – was there too, with its top off, as if it had fallen from the dressing-table. Some of it had spilt and the air was heavy with the perfume. The woman's face was swollen and it was impossible to say if it registered any expression.

Moncerre, entering, said good morning to them, took in the scene quickly, and smiled.

'Looks pretty straightforward, don't it? Nice pre-war crime of passion. All we have to do is identify the bastard.'

'Certainly what we are supposed to think,' Lannes said.

'Can't see how it could be different. They split a bottle of fizz. She goes through to the bedroom for a spot of how's your father, sits at her dressing-table to tart up. He comes up behind her, puts his hands lovingly on her shoulders, whips the stocking round her neck and goodbye lady-love. She tips over backwards. Bet you a hundred francs that Dr Paulhan finds a bump on the back of her head, and that the technical boys find no sign of forced entry but fingerprints everywhere.'

'Yes, that's what it looks like,' Lannes said.

'So, cheer up. This is a murder we'll be allowed to solve. Makes a change. A nice change, in my opinion.'

He looked at Lannes and smiled.

'All right then, chief, what don't you like about it?'

Lannes lit a cigarette.

'I don't know,' he said, 'but I don't like it at all. Let's wait to see what the technical boys find. Have you noticed,' he said, 'there are three photographs on the dressing table and another by her bed, all of the same woman? I think it's herself, though you can't tell with her face the way it is, but I'm sure nevertheless. No other photographs. What sort of woman surrounds herself with her own photographs?'

'A vain one, obviously,' Moncerre said.

'A vain one, and I would guess, a cold one.'

'I noticed two others in the salon,' René Martin said.

'So what do you have for me, Jean?' Dr Paulhan as usual spoke without removing the Boyard cigarette from the corner of his mouth. He laid down his medical bag to shake hands first with Lannes, then with Moncerre and finally with young René Martin. He knelt beside the body.

'Looks straightforward,' he said. 'I can tell you she wasn't killed this morning. Probably yesterday, but you'll have guessed that for yourselves. Cause of death obvious. Do you know anything about her?'

'Nothing yet. The concierge says she was a distinguished lady.'

'Nothing distinguished about the way she died,' Moncerre said.

'Well, when the technical boys have finished, send her over to me. I'll cut her up, but I doubt if I'll be able to tell you more than your own eyes can.'

'You can tell us if she'd just had sex,' Moncerre said.

'Oh yes, I'll be able to tell you that, which will help you only if you find the man.'

'If it was a man,' Lannes said.

'Any reason to think it wasn't?'

'Just keeping an open mind.'

'Let's hope it's not one of our Kraut friends,' Moncerre said.

'No reason to think it might be. Right, I'll have a word with the maid. Moncerre, you see if you can get anything more from the concierge, and René, start looking through her desk, will you? Set aside anything that's of interest.'

*　　*　　*

Marie was a thin pale girl with lank hair and rabbit teeth. She was still shivering, and when she spoke her words came sometimes hesitatingly, sometimes tumbling over each other. She had worked for Madame Peniel for nine months and been glad of the job, because her father was a prisoner-of-war in Germany, her elder brother too, and her mother was in and out of hospital, she didn't know why. No, she knew nothing about Madame Peniel's private life.

'Well, I wouldn't, would I?' she said. 'To tell you the truth, monsieur, I was scared of her, I don't know why, because she never raised a hand to me, or her voice indeed, but I was.'

As for this morning, well, she had never seen anything like it. Naturally she hadn't. Her family might be poor, but they were decent law-abiding people. That was how she had been brought up. Seeing Madame like that, her always so well-dressed, had given her quite a turn.

'But I knew something wasn't right soon as I drew the curtains in the salon. It wasn't how she would leave it, and I've never known her drink champagne. And the cigar smoke, well, I've never smelled tobacco there either. I'm surprised she allowed it. And to pull down her knickers like that, well, that's disgusting, don't you think?'

'Yes,' Lannes said, 'I agree with you there. Did she have many visitors, do you know?'

'Only her pupils, she taught piano, see. Only to girls, though, and only in the afternoons.'

*   *   *

'I didn't even bother to ask the usual question,' Lannes said. 'Can you think of anyone who might have wanted to kill her? The poor child knew nothing; that was obvious.'

'The concierge wasn't much help either,' Moncerre said. 'Madame Peniel was "always correct", but "not one to talk". However, she is sure, insists really, that she didn't open the door to any stranger over the weekend. Which must mean that the dead woman brought her murderer home with her. Assuming the concierge is speaking the truth, of course, which there's no reason to suppose she isn't.'

'What about the pupils?'

'Well-turned-out girls between the ages of twelve and sixteen, more or less. That's what she says, anyway. Can't see one of them wrapping a stocking round her neck.'

14

They had repaired, as so often, to Fernand's brasserie, and as usual there were more German officers there than Bordelais. Their mood and demeanour had changed. They were still 'correct' as instructed, but there was a difference, an edge to them, and one sensed their awareness that they were fortunate to be stationed here in France, while their Sixth Army was engaged in Stalingrad, and were uncertain how long their luck would hold. Lannes knew little of how that battle was going, nothing indeed for certain, but, since he had started listening surreptitiously to the BBC, he had begun to hope that Hitler had, as Fernand said, 'bitten off more than he can swallow'. Moncerre on the other hand was still sure that 'the Russkies will crack'. It was in his nature to expect the worst. Not that they talked much about the war, or indulged in speculation. What was the point? It was out of their hands.

Fernand's son Jacques brought them their dish of calf's liver and pommes lyonnaises.

'You're fortunate,' he said. 'That's the last of the liver.'

Even Fernand, who was on good terms with the men who ran the black market and had, moreover, farmer-friends who kept him supplied, was experiencing difficulties. Fortunately his cellar was still well-stocked and the St-Emilion he had recommended went happily with the liver.

Lannes could see that young René was eager to discuss the case, even though he had found nothing of interest among the dead woman's papers, only a list of her piano pupils and a timetable of their lessons.

'That helps us a lot,' Moncerre said.

'Their parents may be able to tell us something about the dead woman,' Lannes said. 'Anyway, that's the first thing we have to find out. What sort of person she was.'

It was always the same. Except for a killing in the course of a botched robbery, it was more often than not what you learnt of the victim that opened up a case.

'It's odd, though,' Moncerre said, 'the concierge is sure she never had a lover. I asked about men visitors and she said "certainly not"; only an elderly man, might be an uncle, she said. It's the sort of thing concierges usually know.'

'Usually,' Lannes said, 'but we've known them to be mistaken – and to tell lies. All the same the little maid was clear on one point. I mean about the champagne and cigar.'

'You get black market Havanas for the Alsatian, don't you?' Moncerre said. 'So let's put the boss in the frame.'

Lannes studied the list of pupils' names René had passed him. He put his finger on one.

'I'll deal with this girl,' he said. 'Divide up the others between the two of you and make a start this afternoon.'

'What about the uncle?'

'We'll have to find out who he was, if indeed he was her uncle. You got a description from the concierge?'

'A description, for what it's worth, but no name.'

'I'll have a word later with her myself.'

'Do you think the technical boys can tell us what brand of cigar it was?' René said.

'They've got to be good for something,' Moncerre said, 'but we won't solve the case by going round all the tabacs in the city. We should be so lucky.'

'We've got to start somewhere,' René said. 'It was only a suggestion. If it's an expensive cigar, that tells us something surely. And the champagne, Krug '28. There's not many people can afford to drink wine of that quality. What's wrong, chief? You think I'm barking up the wrong tree?'

'I don't know,' Lannes said. 'It's just that there's something about it I don't like. It was all a bit obvious, a stage set, pointing us in the direction the killer wants us to go in. And what the concierge said about the absence of men in the dead woman's life and the maid's evidence about the champagne and the cigar, it all worries me. That's why I want you to start with the names on the list. Find out as much as you can about Madame Peniel.'

'You do like to make things complicated,' Moncerre said. 'You always do, chief. It still looks simple to me, crime of passion, good old crime of passion. And what about the name you've reserved for yourself?'

'That's someone I know,' Lannes said.

III

Nevertheless, Lannes went first to Henri's bookshop in the rue des Remparts. The shop itself was closed, as it often was now, because since the boy Léon had left the previous summer with Alain and their friend Jérôme to try to join the Free French, Henri could rarely bring himself to attend to business. He was one of Lannes' oldest and closest friends, and at least he was no longer drinking himself into a stupor almost every day as he had for the year after his twin brother Gaston's murder.

They embraced – Henri was the only man Lannes greeted in this manner. The little French bulldog, Toto, sniffed his ankles, and then, satisfied, withdrew to curl up on a cushion.

'Is there any news of the boys?'

'None, I'm afraid.'

'I suppose there can't be. I miss Léon, you know. So of course does Miriam. I always deplored poor Gaston's perversion, as I suppose it was, but I came to understand why he loved the boy. Would you like coffee? It's not very good coffee, I'm afraid.'

'One of the minor penalties of defeat,' Lannes said. 'All the same, I'll say yes.'

'I came to think of him almost as the son I've never had, you know. Do you think they've reached England?'

'I don't know. We've had no word.'

It was the answer he had given Henri every time he put the question as indeed he did every time Lannes called on him. It was almost a routine now, a barren one.

'And Miriam?' Lannes said.

Henri passed him the coffee cup.

'I'll tell her you're here.'

It was six months since the publication of an order requiring all Jews to wear a yellow star, an order which followed other restrictions on Jewish businesses and on their free circulation in the city. Miriam had succeeded in transferring the licence for what had been her father's tabac to Henri, but, since the first deportation of

17

Jews from Bordeaux, at this time only those categorised as foreign ones, they had thought it better to put a manager in the tabac and for Miriam to take refuge in Henri's attic. She had been unwilling to do so at first, but, after the death in September of her sister, Léon's mother, from cancer, she had given way to Henri's plea which Lannes had supported.

Now, entering the room, she looked like an old woman. Two years previously, when they had first met – at the time of Gaston's murder when he was also investigating the anonymous letters sent to her husband, the old count, himself now dead, Lannes – had wanted to make love to her, and had been restrained only by his reluctance to deceive or cheat on Marguerite, and by Miriam's own good sense. Today he felt only pity, and admiration for her refusal to submit to despair. She had lost at least a dozen kilos, her face was deeply lined, and she moved with none of her former confidence.

'It's because I can't sleep,' she said, extending her cheek to him as she had only recently started to do. 'There's no word, I suppose.'

'I'm afraid not.'

'It's terrible that Léon doesn't even know that his mother is dead. And Alain? You must be as anxious as I am.'

'I'm anxious, yes, but there's nothing one can do.'

And really there was nothing to say. This was the terrible thing, that conversations all over France went round in circles, and said nothing. Of course there were those on the other side, as he had come to think of it, for whom that wasn't true, those who believed – who still believed – in Vichy and its National Revolution. But that 'other side' included Dominique and his friend Maurice who was, as it happened, Miriam's step-grandson and whom she had described to him at their first meeting as 'a sweet boy', which indeed he was. Dominique and he were both sweet boys – Alain had once said, 'Of course I realise that Dominique is nicer than I am which is why Maman loves him more.' He had denied only the second part of the sentence, and hadn't replied that it was Alain's dark side and capacity for discontent and anger that made him his favourite son. This was anyway something no father should admit to.

'And you, Jean?' Miriam said.

'And me? Crime goes on. And we have to solve crimes which seem petty, indeed unimportant, set against the criminal times we live in. I'd a murder this morning, a nasty murder, a woman, and nasty because she was humiliated in death' – these knickers wrenched down to her knees, which he wouldn't mention – 'and I'll work on it, of course I will, but . . . '

'But?'

'I think of these Jewish women forced into cattle-trucks.'

'Yes, of course,' Miriam said, 'and I feel guilty because I have a bed in Henri's attic even if I can't sleep.'

'No,' Lannes said, 'it's ridiculous for you to feel guilty because you haven't been arrested or deported. We are all entitled to do what we can to survive. Sometimes we are required to do things of which we might in other circumstances have reason to feel ashamed. But the circumstances are as they are. We have to live with them as best we can. At least that's how it seems to me.'

'I suppose you're right,' Miriam said. 'Nevertheless, that's how I feel.'

Lannes took a sip of his coffee which was as bad as Henri had said it would be, and lit a cigarette.

'The murdered woman, Gabrielle Peniel. The concierge called her "Madame", but there's apparently no sign of a husband. She gave piano lessons, but only to young girls. I don't know why I don't like the sound of that, because it doesn't seem unreasonable, but I don't. I suppose the name doesn't mean anything to you?'

'I knew a Peniel once, or rather knew of him,' Henri said. 'He was a friend of my father, an acquaintance anyway; they used to play bridge together at the club. There was some scandal, I can't remember what. He was a doctor, I think. As I remember, Jewish perhaps. Then I don't know, he dropped out, was required to resign from the club. Perhaps he had been cheating at cards. It's a long time ago, a few years after the last war. He might be some connection, perhaps the dead woman's father. Bordeaux, as we know, is a small town where there are so many connections, our Bordeaux, I mean . . . '

By which Lannes understood the Bordeaux of respectable people, the professional classes and perhaps also the Bordeaux of the wine barons, the Chartrons. That was the milieu into which Henri had been born, one which Lannes himself rarely encountered except in the course of duty.

IV

The wet cold was sharper as Lannes limped across the public garden which was all but deserted. A few off-duty German soldiers were taking photographs of each other by the fountain. They would send them home and their parents or wives or girl-friends would be happy to think of them safe in France rather than serving on the Eastern Front. How long would they be here? For the first months of the Occupation, he had sometimes thought that there might be a settlement, that the Armistice might be replaced by a Treaty, the Occupation end, and the prisoners-of-war return. Perhaps it had never been likely. The English remained defiant. Nevertheless, it had seemed possible then that Hitler and Churchill might each conclude that victory was unattainable, and that it made sense to engage in negotiations. He didn't know, couldn't tell even if he had really hoped for this. Now since the invasion of the Soviet Union, it was impossible; war to the death, millions of deaths – and the tightening of the German grip on France. For Vichy, collaboration was ever closer, more dishonourable, inescapable. The deportation of foreign Jews was only a start, the application of the anti-Jewish laws ever stricter, and there was talk of raising a legion of French volunteers to serve in the war against Bolshevism on the Eastern Front, while there was also the demand for more French workers to be dispatched to work in Germany. At least Dominique's post in Vichy meant he wouldn't be called upon.

The maid, correct, as if there was no war, in black dress, apron and mob-cap, admitted him. On the hall-table the brass bowl for visiting cards was empty, as it had been on his previous visits and would surely remain for ever. Professor Lazaire, who still looked like a colonel, but now with his yellowing skin like a colonel of colonial infantry, was in the same high-winged chair, and the little fox-terrier at his feet again jumped up, barking, before lying down satisfied that Lannes posed no threat. And again the maid offered him tea, and, without waiting for a reply, disappeared to make it. Lannes apologised for troubling him. The professor waved a deprecating hand, and for a couple of minutes neither spoke.

Then the professor said, 'It's not about Michel, I hope, and your daughter. He brought her to see me, or, more precisely, to show her off to me. I found her charming.'

'Thank you,' Lannes said. 'No, it's not about Michel. She's very fond of him and my wife thinks the boy equally charming.'

'And you?'

'I like him. I'm afraid for him. I don't like what I hear of his politics, but I'm afraid for all the young people. Even if we come through this, the divisions will survive. There will be recriminations, acts of revenge. It doesn't bear thinking on. But it's another matter altogether that brings me here.'

The maid returned with the tea and a plate of little cakes.

'My own baking,' she said.

'Gabrielle Peniel,' Lannes said. 'Your granddaughter, Anne-Marie, is a pupil of hers, isn't she?'

The professor took a cigar from a box on the little table beside his chair, sniffed it, rolled it in his fingers, clipped the end, lit it with a long match, and blew out smoke.

'A curious question for a policeman to ask, but I suppose you have your reasons.'

Lannes sipped his tea which was scented with bergamot, and laid the cup down.

'The worst of reasons,' he said. 'She was found dead this morning. Murdered, there's no doubt about that. Your granddaughter's name was on a list of her music pupils. I hope you may be able to tell me something about her.'

The professor drew on his cigar again. Lannes lit a cigarette and waited.

'She was a pupil, for a time. Then I withdrew her – at Anne-Marie's request, I should say, for I have never met the lady, the unfortunate lady, I suppose I should now call her.'

'At your granddaughter's request? Did she want to stop learning the piano or was there some other reason?'

A long silence, like the hush that comes over a theatre audience before the curtain goes up.

'No, she loves music and now has another teacher.'

'So?'

The fox-terrier put his paws on the professor's knees and was rewarded with a scratch behind the ear and one of the maid's little biscuits.

'I realise this may be difficult,' Lannes said, 'and you don't want to involve Anne-Marie in what is a nasty business or expose her to questioning. I fully understand that. But in a case like this it's only by understanding the victim and learning all that I can about her that I have any chance of finding her killer.'

'I'm seventy-five,' the professor said, 'and sometimes my memory plays tricks on me. Anne-Marie and Michel are all I have now, all I care for. I don't want any harm to come to them. It's dangerous loving someone, giving your heart to them, when you're my age. Does that sound feeble?'

'Not at all.'

You don't, he didn't add, have to be seventy-five to have learnt that.

'She said she was creepy. Madame Peniel. Just that, creepy. I didn't enquire further. The word was enough. She's an honest child and an intelligent one. She was – what shall I say? – uncomfortable with her. As I say, I didn't press her. That word and the look on her face were enough.'

'Yes,' Lannes said, 'I see.'

If it had been Clothilde, wouldn't he have behaved in the same way?

'You'll want to speak with her,' the professor said. 'I realise that. I'm sure I can trust you to be gentle. She'll be home within the hour. Meanwhile, would you like a game of chess?'

'I doubt if I can give you a match.'

'I'm sure you can. So much of your life must be like the game.'

'In life,' Lannes said, 'I try to avoid sacrificing a pawn.'

*   *   *

The girl was slightly-built, blonde like her brother, but with pale skin and milky-soft blue eyes. Lannes remembered that when they first met the professor had said that his dead wife had had German cousins, and indeed Anne-Marie looked like an illustration from the fairy-tales of the Brothers Grimm, Gretel perhaps. He had forgotten the young people's German ancestry, and it now occurred to him for the first time that Michel looked like the perfect Aryan poster boy for the Hitler Youth.

'This is Clothilde's father, darling,' the professor said. 'He is, as you may know, a policeman, and he has some questions to ask you.'

'Questions for me? What fun!'

'You won't mind if I remain, superintendent?'

'Not at all. I want to ask you about Madame Peniel, Anne-Marie.'

'Is she dead?'

'Why do you ask that?'

'Because I can't think of any other reason why you should ask me about her. Unless, of course, she's been caught out.'

'Caught out? In what? You told your grandfather she was creepy. In what way?'

She crossed to the professor's chair and perched on its arm. She smoothed her skirt, and said, 'You didn't ask me, grandpa, did you? I was glad at the time, but now . . . is she dead?'

'Yes, she's dead. She was found murdered this morning. Your name was on her list of pupils, that's why I'm here. I need to find out whatever I can about her.'

'I can't say I'm sorry.' She stroked the old man's cheek. 'I'm not being hard, grandpa, but she really wasn't a nice woman. She used to stroke me – just like this – and it was creepy when she did it. Then she said she knew someone who would like to meet a lovely girl like me – ugh, lovely girl indeed. It gave me the creeps, which is why I told you she was creepy. Does this help? I never saw her again after she spoke like that and stroked me in that way.'

'Do you know if she made any similar approaches to any of her other pupils?'

'No, but then I don't know any of them. But I'd be surprised if she didn't. Don't ask me why. I just know.'

V

A policeman would like to be able to work on a single case to the exclusion of other matters. But it was never like that. When Lannes went to report his preliminary investigation of the Peniel case to Commissaire Schnyder, the Alsatian's interest was perfunctory.

'It's quite clear it was a crime of passion,' he said, 'and I'm sure you'll solve it. As of course you should. But really it's not important, is it?'

'Investigating such crimes is our business,' Lannes said. 'It's what we exist to do. In any case I'm not persuaded that it is just what it appears to be.'

'Really? Is that so? Well, I've no doubt you will pursue the matter diligently.'

Schnyder flicked a spot of cigar ash from the lapel of his beautifully-cut pale-grey double-breasted suit.

'There's nothing straightforward,' he said. 'These days there's nothing straightforward. It makes life and our job difficult. You'll be aware that there is a stirring of Resistance activity, even here in Bordeaux. What's your opinion of that?'

'Nothing to do with us', Lannes said.

'Not the opinion of our masters. I've had a meeting with the Prefect. He's worried.'

'So?'

'So he wants it investigated.'

'I wouldn't know where to start. Resistance activity sounds vague. Is there a body? No? Then I don't see where we come in.'

'It's the way the wind's blowing,' Schnyder said. 'We're not going to be able to stand aside. You have to realise this.'

He got up and stood by the window looking out on the square. Even the good cut of his suit couldn't disguise his big fleshy buttocks.

'There's another thing, Jean,' he said, still with his back to him. 'I'm embarrassed to ask you.' He turned round. 'But there's a question I'm obliged to put. It concerns your son. Where is he?'

'Dominique's in Vichy. You can ask Edmond de Grimaud about him. You know de Grimaud, don't you? It's his son Maurice who arranged a job for Dominique there.'

'But you've another son, haven't you?'

'Yes.'

'As I said, I'm embarrassed. You'd better see this.'

He took a sheet of writing paper from his breast pocket, unfolded it and passed it to Lannes.

Ask Jew-lover Lannes where his pansy son Alain and his Jewish boyfriend are.

There was of course no signature.

'Malicious,' Lannes said.

'Yes,' Schnyder said, 'malicious. Nevertheless.'

'And untrue. Alain is not homosexual.'

'But he's not in Bordeaux, is he, and neither, I assume, is the Jewish boy? And you have Jewish friends yourself?'

'French citizens,' Lannes said.

'You remember that king in the Bible we talked about, the one who walked warily in the sight of the Lord?'

'Agag.'

'That's right. I always forget the name. Are you walking warily, Jean? I'm afraid you aren't, and I don't want to lose you, I really don't.'

It was probably true. Schnyder wasn't such a bad chap. It was understandable that he wanted to play safe, even if this meant his backside was creased from sitting on the fence. And he really was embarrassed and didn't want to lose him. All the same Lannes had no doubt that the Alsatian wouldn't defend or protect him beyond a certain point – a point from which they mightn't be far distant. Moreover, he couldn't pretend, even to himself, that Schnyder's position wasn't justified, didn't make sense. He was a servant of the Republic – or rather of the French State, now that the name of the Republic had been expunged – and he would do whatever was declared to be his duty. Lannes couldn't blame him. He wasn't entitled to expect him to be a hero, whatever a hero was in present circumstances. He wasn't after all a hero himself, far from it, just a middle-ranking cop trying to make the best of things at a time when any choice you made was likely to turn out badly. He lit a cigarette and held up the paper Schnyder had handed him.

'You don't want this back,' he said. 'Better perhaps if it never reached you. I think I know who wrote it. An old enemy. Meanwhile I've a murder case to pursue.'

*　　*　　*

He didn't, however, do so immediately. Instead he left the office and made his way to the Café Régent in the Place Gambetta. It was still cold, and threatening rain, and the terrace was deserted. He shook hands with the old waiter Georges whom he had known since he first frequented the café in the days long ago when he was a law student, and Henri, Gaston and himself would gather there with a few friends to talk and play billiards two or three evenings a week. How simple life had seemed then when he was happy because he had survived his war and the future was like a summer morning under a blue sky.

When Georges had brought him his Armagnac and coffee that was more chicory than coffee, and had shuffled off on his waiter's flat feet, Lannes took the note from his pocket and read it again. The reading wasn't necessary, he knew just what it said, but now it occurred to him that the second 'his' – as in 'his Jewish boy-friend' – might be intended to refer to him rather than to Alain. It wasn't improbable if the writer was, as he had first guessed, the advocate Labiche, who had once asked him in the rue des Remparts if he had been visiting his 'pretty Jew boy'. Yet the more he thought about it, the less likely it seemed that it was Labiche who had sent Schnyder the note. He couldn't say why. It wasn't out of character, and yet it didn't ring true. He wondered if Madame Peniel was indeed Jewish, and was disturbed that the thought had come to him. Miriam hadn't recognised the name. It was Henri who had spoken of a Peniel, who might have been a Jew, the mysteriously disgraced acquaintance of his father's. Nevertheless, the thought wouldn't go away, even if it was probably this note and the Alsatian's talk that had put it in his mind.

He made his way to Mériadeck. It was the Jewish quarter and the few people in the streets looked tired and pinched. The old tailor's sign had been removed. He would have been forbidden to carry on his business, but, when Lannes rang the bell and was admitted, there was cloth on the table and it was evident that he was still working, if only perhaps for a few old customers who relied on him.

'So, superintendent, and why do you come to see old Léopold? To check that I am still alive? Or to ask me questions? Of course you have come for that reason. So how can the old Jew help you?'

'Have you had any trouble?' Lannes said.

'Trouble? Why would I have had trouble? But then why wouldn't I? By the waters of Babylon we sat down and wept, when we remembered thee, O Jerusalem. You see, the old Communist can still quote scripture. Brandy or tea?'

'You told me once you drink brandy only when you are afraid.'

'So: tea then. What do I have to be afraid of? But for you, superintendent, I think brandy.'

There was mockery in his voice. There had been mockery in his voice each time Lannes had talked with him.

'Peniel,' Lannes said.

'Peniel?' the old Jew laughed. 'My wife's cousin. My very late wife's cousin. Second cousin or third cousin, I don't know. Is he dead that you come to me? Not that it matters. We shall all soon be dead. Isn't that so?'

'I don't know if he's dead or not.'

Léopold took a pinch of snuff and sneezed.

'So you don't know if he's dead, but you still come to me, and I tell you that I know nothing about him. Ephraim he was called, but he left the synagogue a long time ago. I left the synagogue myself but I found another faith, as you know. And that faith too left me long ago. So there we are. Ephraim became Édouard. He had ambitions to become a gentile and a gentleman. So who is dead, superintendent?'

'A woman who may have been his niece. She called herself Madame Peniel, but I suspect she was never married. She taught music.'

'And now she has been murdered.'

'Yes.'

'And you come to me. But I can tell you nothing. Except

this. Ephraim – Édouard – was no good. As for a niece, well, I can't tell . . . I know nothing of any niece. Nothing.'

'Miriam didn't recognise the name.'

'And why should she? We never spoke of Ephraim. Nobody did. We expunged him. He left the family, so the family chose to forget him. It was easy, he wasn't memorable. So I can tell you nothing. Drink your brandy, superintendent, and tell me in turn if you have news of young Léon and your son?'

'Sadly, I can't.' Lannes picked up his glass and said, 'Your health.'

'My health? That is good. In Spain they say "salud y pesetas!" That is better, yes? A good boy, Léon, but doomed. So: we are all doomed. He loves your son, I think, but your son doesn't know that, does he?'

'No, I don't think he does,' Lannes said.

VI

Lannes had had René collect the photographs of the dead woman. He spread them out on his desk. There were more than twenty of them. In most she was well, even stylishly, dressed. You might read a look of disdain on her face. Lannes was wary of such interpretation. He had known too many whose appearance and manner bore little relation to their character and behaviour. There were five portraits of her in the nude. Young René had found these in a locked drawer of her desk and had been embarrassed when he presented them to Lannes. The earliest showed her as a young girl; she was lying on her belly on a chaise-longue with her heels in the air and she was looking over her right shoulder at the camera; her lips were open but the expression on her face was grave rather than inviting. In another, taken perhaps in her twenties, she was sitting astride a chair and her chin was resting on its back as if the chair was a horse she was riding. The tip of her tongue protruded from the corner of her mouth. Two others showed her sitting on the floor with her arms wrapped round her knees. She was smiling in the first, looking fixedly at the camera in the other, taken some years later. In the fifth she was lying on a bed. Her hair had fallen over her eyes, a feather shawl was draped over her breasts and her hand lay between her legs.

'She certainly fancied herself,' Moncerre said. 'Don't know that I do.'

'And there were no photographs of anyone else in the apartment?'

'Not that we've found,' René said.

'Anything else of interest?'

'Her bankbook. Regular sums paid in, some of them quite large. Always in cash. Music teaching must be more profitable than I'd have thought.'

'Interesting. Either of you get anything from the pupils you've spoken to?'

'Nothing at all,' Moncerre said. 'They say she was a good teacher, but strict. It doesn't surprise me' – he picked up a photograph – 'that she was strict. Probably enjoyed rapping their knuckles with a ruler when they played a wrong note. She looks a proper bitch if you ask me.'

'Two of the mothers wouldn't let me speak to their daughters,' René said. 'It would upset them, apparently, because they had been so fond of Madame Peniel and were distressed by the news of her death. I must say' – René pushed a lock of hair off his forehead – 'that surprised me. None of the other girls claimed to like her, though they all said she was a good teacher and they had learnt a lot from her even if they didn't enjoy their lessons.'

Lannes said, 'I'll speak myself to the mothers who wouldn't let you question their daughters.'

He told them what Anne-Marie had said.

'This is getting interesting,' Moncerre said. 'But the set-up, the champagne and the cigar smoke. You can't wish away evidence like that.'

'It's evidence, certainly, but the importance of evidence depends on how you read it.'

'If I understand you, chief,' René said, 'you suspect that she was procuring girls for perverts who like them young.'

'I like that,' Moncerre said, 'and so one of the fathers knocks her off.'

Lannes said, 'I've only one sentence to go on, and Anne-Marie's reaction. It's no more than a possibility that we'll find that this is the explanation for the murder. As I said, we need to know much more about her. Meanwhile we need to get hold of the so-called uncle. Have another word with the concierge, will you? And, René, you might see if you can get anything more from the maid, Marie. She was frightened of me, as well as suffering from shock. She may be more forthcoming with you.'

*   *   *

He couldn't get the photographs out of his head. Who took them and who were they taken for? Only the woman herself? How often did she look at the nude ones? And when, in what circumstances?

A maid admitted him to the apartment in the rue Michel-Montaigne and showed him into the salon. High ceilings, Second Empire furniture, paintings, mostly landscapes of no particular quality. The airlessness of a room in which the windows were never opened, Venetian blinds drawn, and vases of artificial flowers. 'Madame will be with you in a moment,' but it was at least a quarter of an hour till the door opened and a tall woman came in. She wore a brown velvet dress and her dark hair was pulled back in a bun.

'I'm surprised to see you,' she said. 'I assume your visit is on account of the sad death of Madame Peniel, but I have already told your young officer that we have nothing to say. She taught our daughter the piano, very well too, but we had no other dealings with her and I cannot see that her death concerns us.'

'I am sure it doesn't,' Lannes said. 'Nevertheless, I should like to speak with your daughter. You told Inspector Martin that she was fond of Madame Peniel and is distressed by the news of her death. It's possible that Madame Peniel may have said something to her which might help us find the killer.'

'Impossible. It's ridiculous to suppose that Charlotte can say anything that would help you. She knows nothing about that.'

She smoothed her dress over her bottom and sat down, quite heavily, in a high-backed chair. She sat very straight and sniffed, loudly, twice.

'But I should like to speak with her, and I would rather do so here, in your presence if you prefer, than summon her formally to my office. You will understand, Madame Duvallier, that I have the authority to do so. However, I have no wish to exercise that authority.'

The fencing continued for several minutes. Then Lannes, who had not been invited to sit down, said, 'I understand your reluctance, and this is indeed a delicate matter, no doubt upsetting for your daughter. Moreover I have no wish to report to the examining magistrate that you have been obstructing me in the performance of my duty, which is nevertheless what I may have to do. Now will you fetch your daughter, or shall I ask the magistrate for a warrant summoning her to a formal examination? It's one or the other, and the choice is yours.'

She sniffed again and got up and left the room. Lannes waited. He wanted to smoke but hesitated to do so. If she isn't back in five minutes, he thought, I'll either light up or walk out and send them a summons. What a futile business it was. He was sure now the girl would tell him nothing. Her mother would be making certain that she didn't. Well, he would see about that, if they came back. He felt very tired, extricated a Gauloise from the packet and tapped it on his thumbnail.

The door opened. Madame Duvallier resumed her seat, her back stiff with antagonism. The girl stood a little apart, twisting her handkerchief in her hands. Her mother told her to stop doing that and stand up straight. She was a plump girl with black hair, dark eyes and a big, full-lipped mouth.

'Your mother will have told you why I'm here,' Lannes said. 'Did you like Madame Peniel?'

'She was all right.'

'A good teacher?'

'All right, I suppose. I'm sorry she's dead. At least I suppose I am.'

'Charlotte!'

'Well, I haven't really thought about it, Maman. I mean, why should I? She was only my music teacher. Actually,' she turned towards Lannes for the first time, 'to be honest, I didn't much like her.'

'Why was that?'

31

'Well, she was sarky, you know what I mean?'

'Yes, I know what you mean. Now, Charlotte, I've an important question for you. I'm afraid it may embarrass you, but I hope you can bring yourself to answer it. One of her other pupils has told me she made unsuitable suggestions to her. Did she ever make any to you?'

'Superintendent, I can't allow you to put such questions to my daughter. She's an innocent child. She doesn't know what you mean.'

'Did she?' Lannes said.

The girl flushed. Her lower lip wobbled. She looked as if she was about to cry.

'Yes,' she said. 'She put her hand into my blouse and felt my breast and said she knew men who would like to do that. It was disgusting. She was disgusting, I'm glad she's dead, really glad, but it wasn't me, really. It wasn't my fault, Maman.'

She fell to her knees, clutching her mother and burying her face in her lap.

'I hope you are happy, superintendent.'

'Not happy. Not at all. But I am grateful. You're a brave girl, Charlotte. Thank you.'

Well, it was perfectly clear, or at least partly clear. He had no doubt that other girls, if pressed, would confirm what Charlotte and Anne-Marie had told him. But would any go further? Would they admit to being introduced to 'men who would like to do that'? Not when their mothers were present, surely, and it was unlikely that any had already confessed to their parents. But if they hadn't, then the motive for murder which Moncerre had advanced evaporated. It was going to be a wearisome business, questioning all the pupils, and it was probable that such questioning wouldn't take them further and might indeed give rise to complaints from the parents. It was more urgent to find the elderly man who used to call on Madame Peniel and whom the concierge suggested was her uncle. He knew that sort of uncle. And there was another possibility: that they were pursuing a scent that had never been laid, that she didn't procure girls, and that when she thrust her hand into their breasts or up their skirts, she was doing no more than what pleased her, and that talk of the men who might enjoy it was a blind which also excited her. When he thought of the photographs this seemed quite likely. Nasty woman either way. Unhappy one too perhaps.

*   *   *

Clothilde and Michel were playing piquet. The boy rose at once to shake his hand. He was always polite but there was some reservation in his manner when he addressed Lannes. Probably Sigi had told him to be wary. Or perhaps he had spoken of Lannes with contempt. Now Michel pushed back his hair and said, 'I hope you don't object, sir. Madame Lannes has invited me to stay for supper and spend the night here.'

'Why should I object? As Clothilde's friend you are always welcome.'

Had he put that badly? Implying that in other circumstances he would have been quick to show him the door?

'I take it you've told your grandfather,' he said. 'He worries about you young people, as we all do, and must, in these times.'

Marguerite didn't look up from the sauce she was making when he came into the kitchen.

'Are you happy about this?' he said.

'It's good for Clothilde to have company of her own age, and he's a charming boy. I like having him here in any case. With the boys away and their room empty. It feels like a reproach whenever . . . '

Her voice tailed off. They had got into the way of not completing sentences when they spoke to each other. The unspoken words were an accusation: he should have prevented Alain from running into danger. He remembered the look on her face, both stricken and angry, when he had said he was proud of Alain's decision to set off to join de Gaulle, and that she should be proud too. They had scarcely spoken since about where he might be, what he might be doing. She protected herself with silence. Well, that was her way. His too, he had to admit. They both feared that he might be dead and that they would never learn how, where or when. That was part of the horror with which they lived. He gave himself a glass of marc and said, 'I've a case that troubles me.'

33

She didn't lift her gaze from the pan.

'What would you do,' he said, 'if Clothilde told you that one of her teachers had made advances to her?'

'But they're nuns,' she said.

'Quite,' he said. 'I was just wondering how you would react, as a mother.'

'As any mother would,' she said. 'But you're talking nonsense.'

'Of course I am.'

He wondered if Anne-Marie had spoken to Michel about Madame Peniel. Wouldn't Clothilde have confided in Alain if one of her teachers had behaved in that way? And wouldn't she have said things to her twin brother that she would have been too embarrassed to say to her parents?

Conversation was sparse during the meal – macaroni with tomato sauce, and with Marguerite apologising for its inadequacy. What was there to talk about? So many subjects were barred. Clothilde was nervous, tried to keep the ball rolling, without success. Marguerite had nothing to say, having on previous occasions asked Michel about his family. Lannes was sure that the young people were eager to be left alone, and looked at him hopefully when Marguerite retired to bed immediately after the meal of which she had eaten very little. But instead of following her he asked Clothilde if she would make coffee. Did she look anxious, as if afraid that he was going to speak sharply or firmly to the boy? And was there a flicker of apprehension in his face too? And indeed he might have said something like 'Clothilde's very fond of you – you will take care not to hurt her, won't you.' The words were there in his mind, all the more so, because once again the thought came to him that Michel in his blond beauty really did look like an Aryan poster boy.

Instead he said, 'I don't suppose you ever met your sister's piano teacher?'

'No, of course not.'

'Of course not, why would you have, but you'll have heard of her murder and you probably know I'm investigating it. I've spoken to your grandfather and to Anne-Marie. I wonder if she said anything more to you than to either of us. It would be natural if she had.'

He lit a cigarette and pushed the packet towards the boy who took one and held his face towards Lannes for a light.

'From what Anne-Marie said, she's no loss.'

'That may be true. Nevertheless, murder is murder.'

'There are people being killed everywhere. Why bother about a woman like that, of no importance?'

'It's what I do,' Lannes said, 'what I'm required to do.'

He drew on his cigarette.

'Did you know she was a Jewess?'

He despised himself for putting the question, despised himself not only because of the implications of asking such a question at any time, in any circumstances, but, more particularly, because it was an appeal to the ugly prejudices which might not be natural to the boy, but which he had almost certainly imbibed from Sigi and his political associates.

Michel leant back in his chair, his chin tilted and the hand holding the cigarette raised high.

'She was filthy,' he said. 'No, I didn't know she was Jewish, Anne-Marie never said, not that I was interested before, not interested at all, not till she told me what the woman had been up to and what she said, which was disgusting. So I'm not surprised, not surprised at all. So you see why I think she is no loss.'

Clothilde came back with the coffee. She handed them each a cup. For a moment her fingers rested on Michel's.

'You both look very serious,' she said. 'You haven't been quarrelling, have you?'

'Not at all,' Lannes said. 'We've been talking about murder, that's why we look serious.'

'Oh,' Clothilde said. She smiled at Michel. 'You're privileged, very lucky. He never speaks of his work to me. I suppose it's about Anne-Marie's piano teacher. She sounds like a right cow. Are you going to find who killed her, Papa?'

Lannes said, 'I rather think Michel thinks I shouldn't bother.'

'Oh, but you must. People shouldn't be murdered, not even a woman like that.'

'Yes, I rather agree with you.'

He drank his coffee, stubbed out his cigarette.

35

'I'm for bed. Don't sit up too late.'

Marguerite was already asleep. That was how it was nowadays. She slept earlier and longer than she used to. It was a sort of denial. He was happy to think that he could trust Clothilde to go to her own bed and send Michel to Alain's. He wondered who had told her Madame Peniel was 'a woman like that', Anne-Marie or Michel himself? How little he really knew of the young, even the daughter he doted on. What would they be talking about now? It worried him that Clothilde could scarcely take her eyes off the boy.

VII

'I think you've been looking for me.'

'So?'

'I'm a friend of Madame Peniel.'

He was unwilling to come to Lannes' office, would explain why when they met. Meanwhile . . .

'All right then,' Lannes said, and suggested they meet that afternoon in the Café des Arts, Cours de la Marne.

It was all but empty at that hour, and Lannes recognised his telephone caller from the description the concierge had given of the man she called Madame Peniel's uncle. He was sitting in the far corner of the room with an empty glass before him. His lank grey hair was still wet from the rain, his bony face was dark; he wore a soiled raincoat and fingerless gloves. He didn't look up as Lannes approached. Lannes stood there a moment, eyeing him.

'We've met before,' he said. 'Some years ago, wasn't it?'

'Then you will understand why I chose to ask you to come here. I have no happy memories of police headquarters. Or of your cells. Not that the case ever came to court. As it shouldn't have, since I was innocent.'

'You were?'

He sat down. The waiter approached. He asked for an Armagnac.

'And you?'

'A small Vichy water, please.'

What had it been? Blackmail? Procuring? Abortion? Something sordid anyway. He himself had been only a junior inspector then, like René now. It surprised him that he remembered the man, who now for the first time raised his head, and he realised why he was memorable: one of his eyes was brown and the other blue. Yet he had recognised him as an old customer before he had seen this. Strange.

'So you were a friend of Madame Peniel,' he said. 'The concierge suggested you were her uncle.'

'No, not that. She was my daughter actually, or so I was told, for I don't mind confessing that I was never married to her mother, so she may not have been, but I came to regard her as such. Are you surprised that I called you?'

'It's what happens when people have something to tell me . . . '

The man flexed his fingers, which he couldn't quite straighten.

'All right then,' he said. 'I hesitated, you know. Why shouldn't I leave you to find me – which you might not have done, since I'm not in any way remarkable. But then Gabrielle was the only woman I've ever cared for. I don't usually like women – you may remember that – but I was fond of her, in my way, and somebody has murdered her. So I would like her killer to be found. Would have liked, rather. Only he can't be, mustn't be. That's what I've got to tell you. That's what I've been instructed to tell you.'

He sipped his Vichy water without visibly lowering the level in the glass, and licked his thin lips.

'She was doing good work, you see, important work, for us.'

'I don't understand what you're talking about. Instructed? Who has instructed you? And who is your "us"?'

'I can't tell you that. I've been deputed to give you a warning. Lay off.'

'You're either an idiot or think I'm one,' Lannes said. 'You've no happy memories of our cells? Well, you're going to find yourself in one again very soon. Let me make things clear. I have evidence that Madame Peniel – what did you call her? Gabrielle, wasn't it? – was engaged in procuring underage girls for men who like that sort of thing, and now that I've met you and recognised you I'm inclined to think I've reason to believe you were her accomplice. Enough reason to book you. So that's just what I'm going to do unless you explain yourself.'

He lit a cigarette and looked the old man in the face. It was quite without expression. Then he licked his lips again.

'You're being foolish, superintendent,' he said. 'Do you think I would have called you if I didn't have protection? All I will say is this: I'm a patriot, whatever you think you know of me in the years before the war. My poor Gabrielle was a patriot too. Yes, I don't deny that she was engaged in the activities you speak of. But who do you think were her clients? Meanwhile I've a letter for you.'

He pulled it out of his inside breast pocket, and got stiffly to his feet. He lifted his glass of Vichy water, and spat into it.

'I've another reason to dislike you, superintendent, but I'll say nothing of that. Some day I'll want something from you and you'll give it me, I assure you. Meanwhile, as I say, I'm protected. I'm not going to see the inside of your cell again. You may be certain of that, believe me. Now read your letter and do as you're told.'

Lannes watched him moving with small steps out of the café. He moved only from the knees, as if his thighs were tied together.

It was a cheap envelope, greyish paper, such as some cafés supply to their clients. He was reluctant to open it. To have that wretch proclaiming himself a patriot and speaking of the protection he enjoyed – it was disgusting – disgusting and, he had to admit, disquieting. He ran his fingers over the envelope. There was something stiff there, as it might be a photograph. And which sort of patriotism had the old man boasted of? Edmond de Grimaud was a patriot – so was Sigi – to their minds, anyway. And the Resistance group who had set off an explosion which derailed a train near Bergerac, killing two elderly women, because they had made a mistake and their device was intended for a goods train, not a passenger one – they were patriots too, of course they were. Patriotism was a licence to lie, a licence to kill, a licence for murder.

He slipped his thumb under the flap of the envelope. Two snapshots and a sheet of the same cheap grey paper. The first photograph was of himself, sitting at a café table with Léon and smiling at the boy; the second showed Léon with Schussmann, the German liaison officer. The typewritten message was brief:

I need to see you. You need to see me. So stay where you are. Or these photographs go to the Boches.

Lannes knew he was trapped. The cards had fallen badly. The photographs were compromising. It was true that Kordlinger, who had taken over as liaison officer after Schussmann shot himself, had managed to arrange his transfer only a couple of months after Lannes had been supplied with information that gave him a hold over the German, but there was no reason to suppose, or hope, that his successor would no longer be interested in Schussmann's case. It was the spook who called himself Félix who had used Léon as bait to catch the sentimental fool, and Lannes had no doubt that it was Félix whom he was now instructed to wait for.

Who do you think her clients were, the old man had asked, with a note of contempt or perhaps mockery in his voice. The implication was clear. Clear and disturbing. Not the Boches – that was too much to expect – but men of position, what they had become accustomed to recognise as untouchables. Again he thought of the advocate Labiche with his perverted taste for young flesh and his membership of the body set up to 'deal with' the Jewish Question. Even in his mind he put the words deal with in inverted commas.

The waiter approached. Lannes asked for another Armagnac. The waiter collected the glasses, held up the one into which the old man had spat, and said, 'A dirty type, superintendent. I don't envy you a job that brings you in contact with such vermin.'

'You have to serve them yourself,' Lannes said.

'True enough, and I do it with disdain. But I'm not required to do more than put a glass in front of them and take their money. I don't know how much you know of him – of course I don't – but I would advise you not to believe a word he says, not even if he swears by the Virgin. That one would sell his grandmother for a sou. Perhaps I don't need to tell you that.'

'No, Marcel, you don't, but thank you for your advice.'

Lannes waited, smoked and waited. A white cat with a black face crossed the floor, rubbed itself against his legs. Three men in blue overalls, work clothes, came in, their hair wet from the rain which the briefly open door revealed as a thin persistent drizzle. One of them called, loudly, for three large reds. He rolled a cigarette, leant with his back to the bar, stared at Lannes and turned away again. He was a big fellow with a swollen nose and a bruise on his left cheek. They began to talk about football.

The telephone rang. Marcel answered it. Lannes watched him; he nodded, hung up the receiver, came over and said, 'It was a message for you. No, he didn't want to speak to you, just said he would be with you in an hour's time.'

Lannes slipped the envelope with the photographs into his pocket.

'I don't know who he is,' he said, 'but I can't wait any longer. When he arrives, tell him I had another appointment. Tell him to call me at headquarters. Meanwhile I'll drop in tomorrow morning and you can give me a description of him.'

The rain was falling harder now. Lannes turned up the collar of his coat. The gutters ran yellow. He thought: he won't do anything with the photographs because he wants something from me. So it's cat and mouse, but which of us can play the cat better and make the other the mouse?

VIII

Michel stood, poised, on the balls of his feet. The instructor blew his whistle. Michel hesitated a moment, came lightly forward, leapt, landed both hands on the wooden horse, somersaulted high, and landed secure, both feet together, chin raised, hands clenched by his side.

'All right, not bad.'

The instructor almost smiled. He was a small man in his sixties, bald, wiry, one-eyed, a veteran of the Foreign Legion. He had lost the other eye in the war against the Rif, almost twenty years ago. He still spoke with a Russian accent, all the stronger when he inveighed against the Bolsheviks. In the Legion he had been known as Ivan, but he had told the boys to address him as Count Pierre. Michel knew himself to be his favourite. Once the Count had told him he had had a hand in the murder of Rasputin – 'That filthy lascivious monk, a German spy. But it was that bastard Lenin I should have shot,' he said.

'Did you ever have the chance?'

'Alas, no. And now I believe that it was God's will I was denied the opportunity, which I would surely have taken.'

'But why?' Michael said. 'Why should God have willed that?'

He didn't believe in God. Sigi had told him Christianity was a slaves' religion, but there was no reason to pass this judgement on to the old Russian.

The Count had made two glasses of tea from the samovar he kept in the little room where he changed from his shabby suit into the white cotton high-necked jersey and drill trousers he wore in the gym. He added sugar and a slice of lemon and handed a glass to Michel.

'You're a good boy,' he said, 'but you can't be expected to understand these things. You have no knowledge of the Russian soul. When they murdered our poor Tsar – not that he was much of a man, I don't pretend that he was – the Almighty decided that Holy Russia should endure a time of suffering, so that she might expiate her sins, and he gave the land to the Bolsheviks and the Jews, first to the intellectual Lenin and then to the Georgian cobbler who calls himself Stalin, that the people should know the meaning of Hell and repent. And now he has sent Adolf Hitler to cleanse the land, after which Russia will be reborn. This is how it works. This is how History unfolds.'

Sigi laughed when Michel recounted this conversation and said that the old man was 'mad, loose in the top storey'.

'Nevertheless,' he said, 'he's on the right side, and you can learn from him; not from his ideas, certainly, but from what he knows of struggle. He will make you hard. Do you know why Stalin adopted that name which is not of course his real one? It is because he thinks of himself as a Man of Steel, which is what it means. But he will be melted in the flame of battle. There's no doubt about that.'

Michel loved the gym. A dozen of them, his colleagues in the Légion des Jeunes de l'Aquitaine, went there two afternoons a week. Sigi approved: you must build your body so that your mind and soul will be strong when the hour of trial comes, he said.

Michel wondered at his use of the word 'soul', but, on reflection, concluded that he didn't mean what the priests meant by it. Five years ago, he had been devout, attending Mass regularly, confessing his sins – before, he now thought, he had really had any sins to confess, not real sins. He had observed Lent faithfully, denying himself chocolate and all sweet things. Now Sigi assured him that there was no such thing as sin; it was an invention of the Church to keep even the strong in chains. 'We have freed ourselves of such nonsense,' he said. When he spoke, Michel believed him. Afterwards, alone, he wasn't so sure. But in any case his religious enthusiasm had faded. Boxing took its place, boxing and girls. He decorated his bedroom wall with posters of boxers – Georges Carpentier, Eugène Criqui, and his favourite, Charles Ledoux.

He was at home in the ring. Count Pierre called him 'the most beautiful of boxers'. There were few things he liked better than matching Michel against a bigger boy, and watching him dance and jab till his opponent turned away in embarrassed anger at being made to look a fool. This afternoon he had sparred with his friend Philippe, who was taller, heavier, and slower. Philippe was powerful, with a swinging right hand which, however, he was incapable of landing on the light-footed Michel. Afterwards, Count Pierre applauded and rubbed embrocation into Michel's thighs, muttering endearments in Russian.

Philippe said, 'I'm not going to fight you again. You always make me look a fool.'

Michel smiled. Boxing was not only good fun. It was preparation for the war against Bolshevism in which, as Sigi assured him, he was destined to engage. The future of France was at stake. He said nothing of this to his grandfather. He loved the old man and respected him, but knew he was out-of-date, with no understanding of the reality of the world today – a reality which Sigi explained to him.

'Every man has a choice,' Sigi said. 'He is either a slave or a master. I have no doubt to which category you belong. We are creating a New European Order and there is a place for you in its Orders of Knighthood.'

Michel glowed with pride.

Then Sigi said, 'And your girl, Clothilde? She must not distract you. Nevertheless I approve of your relationship. Keep close to her. Yes, I approve. Her father is a man whom I respect, a man in whom I have long taken a close interest.'

IX

'Nobody came asking for you, superintendent. I'm quite sure of that.'

The waiter, Marcel, looked up from running a wet cloth over the zinc counter.

'Not of course that he might not have looked in and gone away immediately, seeing no sign of you. But nobody asked, that's certain.'

He gave Lannes an Armagnac and himself a cup of coffee.

'On the house.'

'What would your boss say to that?'

'He'd say, always keep the police happy. That's what he'd say.'

'You'll let me know if anyone comes calling?'

'But certainly.'

'Thanks.'

It was unlikely. Whoever wrote the note – Félix? – was playing with him. Cat and mouse. Cat and mouse.

The weather was still filthy, colder and with a sharp wind blowing heavy rain up river. Clothilde had gone to class. He had left Marguerite in bed. She had a headache and complained of being shivery. He had brought her a tisane which it was probable she wouldn't drink. 'All I want to do is sleep,' she had said as he leant over to kiss her goodbye. She had turned her head away so that he kissed only her hair, not her cheek as he had intended.

It must be Félix. No one else – surely – would have these photographs. The one of him with Léon had been taken outside that café in the rue de l'Arcade. They had met there a couple of times and on the last occasion Léon had said that for the first time he was able to think of Lannes as something other than a policeman. But what was Félix doing back in Bordeaux? The chap in the Travaux Ruraux office in Vichy had assured him Félix was out of favour, deemed a security risk, and had been sidelined, given a desk job in their headquarters in Marseille. Perhaps he should ring him to enquire. Lannes had liked him. Pity his name had slipped his memory. But it would return.

And was it Félix who had sent that anonymous letter to the Alsatian?

At least the Armagnac had warmed him. Bloody weather.

*   *   *

Old Joseph had a cold too, sneezed twice.

'You shouldn't have come in,' Lannes said. 'Should be at home in bed.'

'Might not get up again. You're in luck, superintendent. There's a girl to see you. Same one as came when she was beaten up last summer. At least I think she's that one. Can't really tell these days.'

*   *   *

'Yvette,' Lannes said, 'and what brings you here?'

'Pining for you,' she said. 'Aching for you.'

'I believe you.'

Lannes settled himself at his desk. She perched on its corner, hitching her skirt up.

'Honest,' she said. 'I really thought you would have come to see me.'

'Well, I haven't, and you know why.'

'Course I do. You can't trust yourself, can you? You do fancy me, don't you? A girl always knows.'

She leant across the desk and kissed him on the cheek.

'See,' she said. 'Two o'clock, any afternoon. There's no one at the desk, old Mangeot takes his kip then, and his missus puts her feet up in the kitchen, resting her bunions, she says. You know my room number.'

'Stop it, Yvette, and tell me why you are here.'

'Give me a cigarette then.'

She held his wrist and looked over the flame.

'It's the old Jew,' she said, 'old Léopold. He wants to see you.'

'I didn't know you knew him.'

44

'Course I do. We look after each other in Mériadeck. Thought you'd have known that. No one else will if we don't.'

'I suppose you're right there.'

'He really wants to see you. Urgent, he says. I'll walk there with you if you like. Wolfie's gone. Thought you might like to know.'

Wolfie had been her German customer. Lover really, perhaps, the way she spoke of him.

'Sent to the Eastern Front,' she said. 'He may be dead already. What do you think?'

'You were fond of him, weren't you?'

'Oh, fond,' she said. 'There's fondness and fondness, but he won't come back from there, not likely I'll see him again.'

'All right then.'

He shrugged himself in to his coat, picked up his stick.

'You're not shy to be seen with me in the street?'

'I'm seen with all sorts, Yvette.'

'Oh good.'

She hooked her arm into his.

'What about your wife?' she said. 'Or your daughter?'

'What about them?'

*   *   *

The old tailor was sitting in a chair by his stove which gave out only a feeble heat. He had a fleecy shawl round his shoulders and didn't get up to greet them. The air was chill and dusty and the light poor. He told Yvette to make tea and took a pinch of snuff.

'Cousin Ephraim,' he said.

The orange cat that had no name but Cat jumped on to his knees.

'He called you, didn't he, superintendent? I hadn't seen him myself for twenty years, but he came here.'

'It's because of me,' Yvette said, spooning tea leaves into a pot. 'He said he needed me, but spoke to me as if I was dirt. That was a month ago, or more. So I came to see old Léopold here, like I do when I've a problem, like lots of us do here in Mériadeck.'

'They think I'm wise,' the old tailor said. 'I tell them they're fools, which they are. But this girl isn't altogether foolish.'

45

'Thanks a lot. Nasty bit of work he was, with his eyes of different colours.'

'Abortion, wasn't it?' Lannes said. 'I couldn't remember when I met him, but that's what it was. We couldn't hold him, not enough evidence. That was years ago. Now he's interested in my murder, involved really. He said the dead woman was his daughter, or passed as such. She took his name anyway.'

'He doesn't like women,' Yvette said. 'He's that sort of type. I could tell that straight away. You always can.'

She handed Lannes a cup of tea.

'What did he want of you? I mean precisely.'

'He said he knew a woman who staged entertainments. That was his word, entertainments. I didn't like the sound of it, but money's scarce. So I came to consult old Léopold.'

'You knew this when I was last here,' Lannes said, 'but you said nothing about it.'

The old tailor poured tea into the saucer and drank from it. His hand shook a little and some of the tea spilt on his waistcoat.

'It was Yvette's business, not mine. I gave you his name, didn't I?'

'Yes, you gave me his name. What about these entertainments? Was he more specific?'

'Oh yes, he was specific, if the word means what I think it does. His friend – that's what he called her – had a client – that was his word – who wanted to see a girl of my age put on an act with a younger girl.'

'How young?'

'Twelve or thirteen, he said. That's when I told him to bugger off. He didn't like it . . . '

'And then . . . ?'

'Then he said, I know you go with Germans – though there's only been one or two besides Wolfie, a girl's got to live – and then he said he had friends who don't like this sort of thing. I didn't care for the sound of that, but I still told him to bugger off. Pretending to seduce a kid, going through the motions, that's not nice. So when I thought it over I came to ask Léopold here for advice.'

'I told her to have nothing to do with it, which is what she'd already decided, and that his threat was probably empty. I may have been wrong there. So after you'd been here, I got word to him and he came here at my request. He threatened me too, but I told him I'm too old to be afraid. So here we are.'

'And what else did you say to him?'

'Just to leave the girl alone, and that I knew things about him that his so-called friends would not like. But I can't protect her, an old Jew like me. So we've turned to you.'

Yvette perched on the corner of the old tailor's worktable and again, in an accustomed and practised movement, hitched up her skirt.

'He scared me,' she said. 'I'm still scared really, though I don't know quite why, except that now it's the friend he spoke of that's been murdered, isn't it? And that frightens me. So you'll speak to him, won't you, and come to let me know how it goes. Two o'clock's the best time, like I said.'

'I'll see what I can do, but . . . '

He got to his feet.

'But . . . ' he said again. Then, 'What are these things you know about your Cousin Ephraim?'

The old tailor smiled.

'I know nothing, but he doesn't know I know nothing.'

* * *

There are crimes, lots of them, which are straightforward. The solution is staring you in the face and it requires no detective skill to solve them. Most murders were like that, in Lannes' experience. But there are others which are like a maze. You have to find your way to the centre and often you take wrong turnings, and the further you go, the more you are baffled and lost. Lannes turned up the collar of his coat against the rain. Why was the woman killed? Nothing that he had learnt pointed to a solution. Nothing made sense. Everything he had learnt seemed to confirm his immediate suspicion that the set-up, with the empty bottle of champagne and the cigar smoke was a blind. He couldn't believe that Madame Peniel – Gabrielle – had had an assignation with a man. It simply didn't ring true. His instinct revolted against the idea. Ephraim – her father, as might be – evidently her accomplice

47

or collaborator, as pimp or procurer, director perhaps of her 'entertainments', had hinted that she was engaged in some form of Resistance activities; and his association with Félix – if it was Félix, and he had little doubt that it was – pointed to the form that these might have taken – the same game Félix had tried to play with Schussmann. But if so, why was she killed, and by whom? Was it possible she was double-crossing him? But if she was, what then was Ephraim's role? Ephraim who had arranged to meet him in order to tell him that the murder of the woman he said was his daughter, and for whom he proclaimed affection, must not be solved.

He would have to speak to Bracal, the judge of whose own loyalties he was unsure, and call Félix's colleague in Vichy, Bracal's friend, Vincent he'd called himself, though that certainly wasn't his real name, Vincent who had assured him that Félix had been relegated to push paper in the Travaux Ruraux' Marseille office. But how much could he reveal to Bracal?

Marguerite looked worn, tired, exhausted, might indeed have been weeping.

'It's not Clothilde, is it?'

No matter how he spoke with approval of Michel, and tried indeed to trust him, there were elements of their young love affair that worried him, and he feared that it would end unhappily.

'Clothilde? No, she's in her room, writing an essay, she said.'

'So?'

She turned her face away, and he thought, how lined it is, has become in the last year.

She hesitated, then, 'I lay down for an hour in the afternoon, and had a horrible dream, a frightening one. I dreamt that Alain was dead, I don't know how, but there was his body laid out, unmarked but his face white as a sheet. And I thought how we hadn't said goodbye and never would, and how he slipped away without telling me he was going. You knew but I didn't and I have never been able to forgive either of you. It was as if he felt nothing for me, and now there he was dead . . . '

'That wasn't why,' he said, 'it was rather because he felt too much for you, because he loves you and didn't know how to say something to you that would cause you anxiety. You must believe this.'

But it wasn't true, or was, at best, what they call a half-truth. He hadn't told her because he didn't trust her, didn't at any rate trust her to understand why he felt he had to go. But of course this couldn't be said.

He put his arm round her and kissed her on the cheek.

'It was only a dream, a bad dream. Bad dreams mean nothing.'

But that wasn't so. They speak of the dreamer's fears and guilt.

X

Things were moving, though it wasn't yet clear to them how or in what direction. They had been in England for six months, being trained at a Free French establishment, a manor house and camp somewhere in Oxfordshire. They were still together – the Musketeers – but this wouldn't last. It had been intimated to them that they weren't all suited to the same role in the movement.

Two weeks previously Jérôme had been summoned to an interview with the Colonel who went by the name of 'Cinna'. (How they loved noms de guerre – and how necessary they were, especially for those who had wives and children in Occupied France.)

Jérôme clicked his heels and saluted, striving to appear military. Colonel Cinna smiled.

'You can forget that,' he said. 'Sit down. You're not going to be in uniform much longer.'

Jérôme said nothing. He bit the underside of his lower lip.

'You're willing, I've seen that,' the Colonel said, 'but all the same,' he rapped his fingers on the desk. 'All the same. Why did you join us?'

'To fight for France, sir.'

His voice was too light, he knew that, and now there was a tremble in it.

The Colonel nodded. He took a cigarette from a packet of

Player's, rolled it in his fingers, fitted it into a holder, and lit it. He pushed the packet across the desk, said 'take one', and rang a little hand-bell for an orderly.

'Bring us some coffee,' he said.

'English coffee,' he said to Jérôme. 'No good, vile stuff, but better than nothing. I tell myself so anyway, though I can't say I succeed in convincing myself. No, my boy, you'll never be a soldier. Coming here does you credit, but you're useless. You must know this yourself; I've no reason to think you a fool.'

Years later, when he wrote a memoir, Jérôme would say that he wanted to think this the worst moment of his life, but that wouldn't be true. He was ashamed, but he was also relieved because he feared that he was a coward and knew he was afraid. As a small boy he had been bullied at school and had a painful memory of wetting himself when one of his classmates twisted his arm behind his back. Nevertheless, hearing the colonel's judgement, he coughed and nearly choked when he drew on the cigarette, and this was because he was so close to tears.

The coffee was as bad as the colonel had said it would be.

'You know that we broadcast to France. It's important. Wars are won by words as well as by arms. The French people must be informed. They must be encouraged. They must be given hope, the assurance that the war will turn, the Occupation end, and France resume its rightful place as a Great Power. I've listened to you in our discussion groups, in the debates we stage. Much of what you have said is nonsense – that's understandable, you're very young – but you've a nice voice. It's a light one, admittedly, but even when you are speaking nonsense your sincerity rings through. I like that. So this is how we shall use you: to address the youth of France. Do you write poetry?'

Jérôme felt himself blush.

'It's not very good, I'm afraid.'

'Just as I thought. Still: a young poet speaks to his generation. That sounds all right.'

*   *   *

Alain had an appointment in London. Alerted by a comrade he had volunteered for missions in France and been summoned to the BCRA (Bureau Central de Renseignements et d'Action).

And for Léon? Nothing, though he had volunteered for the same service.

'It's because I am a Jew,' he thought. 'Even here this pursues me, though there are many Jews in the Free French. Where else should we be?'

First, however, they had three days' leave in London. They stayed at a YMCA, within sight of the Palace of Westminster and the sound of Big Ben. They went to the theatre, the Old Vic where they found Shakespeare's language incomprehensible, even though all three had read, even in Jérôme's case studied, Hamlet. Then they crossed the river and walked up Charing Cross Road through Leicester Square and on to the Café Royal for supper.

'Oscar Wilde used to drink here,' Jérôme said. 'Just think of that.'

*　　*　　*

Alain presented himself at the office in Duke Street. The sentry checked his name, told him he was early and showed him into a waiting room. There were pre-war French magazines on the table. He chose the *NRF* (*Nouvelle Revue Française*), but found himself unable to concentrate on the text, and turned to the English humorous paper, *Punch*. A couple of the cartoons made him smile, but the articles he skimmed seemed feeble. If I was English they might make me laugh, he thought; what a strange people they are.

'Colonel Passy will see you now,' the sentry said, and introduced him.

Alain saluted with brio. The colonel, who seemed middle-aged but nevertheless had something boyish, even mischievous, in his expression, did not rise from his desk, but waved a hand indicating that Alain should sit down.

'So,' he said, 'you've volunteered for missions in France. Very well, there are some things I must tell you, and you must consider them carefully. You are wearing a uniform, an honourable uniform, but the secret war isn't the one you've been training for. And first, I must tell you that the lives of others will depend on your conduct; you don't have the right to put them at risk. You'll be alone and without the protection of the uniform you are wearing now. If a soldier in uniform is captured, he's sent to a prisoner-of-war camp. That wouldn't be your fate. You would be questioned and tortured. We'll supply you with a cyanide pill, which you can bite on if you think you can't endure the torture. Do you understand? You'll work alone, no contact with comrades except when the service demands it. And it goes without saying that you must not look up old friends or your family. Absolutely not your family. No contact, no communication, that's the rule. I repeat: you'll be alone, live alone, take your meals alone. No days off, no Sundays, no Saturdays, no leave. You'll be in the front line, twenty-four hours a day, because the Vichy police and the Gestapo work round the clock, and you will always be in danger of arrest. As for that, if you withstand torture and don't take the poison, you'll either be shot or sent to a labour camp in Germany where you'll probably die in any case. Do you understand what you are letting yourself in for?'

'I understand, sir.'

'So think about it, reflect on it. If you don't think you're up to it, you can withdraw your application. There would be no shame in doing that. It would show you are clear-thinking and intellectually honest. We can't afford to have people who are not up to it. Right?'

'Right, sir. I shall reflect, as you advise, but I don't think I shall change my mind.'

'Very well. Reflect, and meanwhile au revoir.'

Alain said: 'I have a comrade, a friend who has also volunteered.'

The colonel opened a file and consulted it.

'Léon Fagot? Jewish, yes?'

'On his mother's side, I believe, sir, but a French patriot.'

'No doubt, no doubt, and we can make use of Jews. But it would be even more dangerous for your friend, you understand? As it happens, I have a report on him, an interesting one.'

Afterwards, Alain said, 'I can't say anything, but I think you'll hear from him. Indeed I'm almost sure you will, Léon.'

XI

Bracal leant back in his chair, his eyes closed. The silence prolonged itself. It was four o'clock in the afternoon and the light outside was already fading. Lannes lit a cigarette. The headache which had begun just after lunch was worse. A bluebottle buzzed round the electrolier that hung over the desk. Bracal sighed.

'He hasn't been to see me,' he said. 'I rang Vincent as you asked.' He opened his eyes. 'As far as he knows the man is still in Marseille. This doesn't mean anything of course; I don't need to tell you that. Vincent's all right, old friend of mine as I told you, trustworthy, reliable, but these spooks don't let their right hand know what their left one is up to. Still, I don't like it, any of it, and these photographs . . . '

'They're intended to compromise me.'

'Undoubtedly. But the boy, you tell me, is no longer in Bordeaux.'

'That's correct.'

'I won't ask you where he is. I don't want to know.'

'I couldn't tell you even if you did.'

'Good.'

Bracal pushed his chair back and got to his feet. He took a bottle of cognac and two glasses from the cupboard, and poured them each a drink. He splashed soda into his own one.

'The Resistance,' he said. 'Do you believe the dead woman was working for them?'

'It's possible.'

'Or did they kill her?'

'That's possible too.'

'We're public servants,' Bracal said. 'We take our orders from Vichy. No question about that. But what is Vichy? Is everyone there of the same mind? This chap you call Félix, for example. Is he working for the Resistance on the sly, or is he trying to compromise it and undermine it? These spooks love playing for both sides. Half of them are as twisted as a corkscrew. What do you think?'

Lannes tilted his glass, watched the brandy swirl round, took a sip; good brandy, not the sort of stuff you should put soda in. But Bracal might be one of those who preferred to make his drinks last, and indeed he was even now topping his up with more soda. A careful man. Likeable too. Trustworthy – the word he had applied to his friend Vincent. Lannes had no reason to think he wasn't, and yet, these days, who could be sure of anything?

'I've no idea,' he said, 'but these entertainments.'

'Yes?'

'The story's credible, no matter which side he's playing for.'

'But then, why kill her?'

'Perhaps she'd been turned.'

'Perhaps.'

'I was told not to pursue the investigation. That was the message. From Félix, as it appears.'

'From Félix?'

'So it would seem. But . . . '

'But what?'

'I don't know. It's complicated and I admit that I'm confused. At a loss, really. On the other hand, if I hadn't got that message, I'd have pursued a quite different line, nothing to do with the war, the Occupation, the Resistance.'

Bracal's fingers began a little dance on the desk.

'The question,' Lannes said, 'is: do I obey? Do I drop the case?'

'I can't advise you to do that. If, as it may be, it's the Resistance – let's call it the Resistance – that killed the woman, abandoning the case would look suspicious. Suppose you're right, and the dead woman had been turned, then either the Boches or someone in the administration must be curious. At the very least they would want to know why the investigation wasn't being pursued. You and I, we'd both come under scrutiny. I don't have to remind you that your own sheet isn't completely clean – in their eyes. You have to give at least the appearance of activity. But it would be a good thing if this Félix was to disappear. He's evidently an awkward customer. That's the impression you've given me. An awkward fellow, but I have the feeling that he's worse than that; that he's a fool. I'll have another word with Vincent. Meanwhile it might be a good idea if you were to arrest someone. This chap Peniel, who claims to be the dead woman's father, perhaps. Haul him in for questioning, bang him up in a cell for a few days, and see what you get from him. You can manage that, can't you? Have a word with Vice too. Perhaps charge him with living on immoral earnings, procuring minors for purposes of prostitution. That might be best, don't you think?'

XII

'It's quite simple,' Lannes said. 'I want to know who her clients were.'

Peniel shifted in his chair.

'I don't know why you've brought me here. You were told to lay off.'

Moncerre, standing by the window, filling his pipe, laughed.

'You've got a nerve,' he said, 'I'll give you that. But I've had a word with a couple of my friends in Vice. They've had their eye on you for some time. They'd like us to give you to them. What do you say to that?'

'It's absurd.'

'Absurd, is it?' Moncerre said. 'Then why are you sweating?'

Peniel looked at Lannes.

'I just passed the message to you,' he said, 'that's all I know.'

Lannes pushed a couple of the nude photographs of Gabrielle Peniel across the desk.

'Did you take these?'

'What if I did?'

'Your own daughter . . . '

'Perhaps.'

'Actually,' Lannes said, 'I couldn't care less about the photographs. They don't interest me, except for what they tell me about her, and more immediately about you. Which isn't nice, admittedly, but then you've never been nice, have you? I've spoken to Yvette by the way. She told me about the little show you wanted to stage with her and a younger girl, no more than a child really. She was disgusted of course because she's a nice girl.'

55

'I don't know what you're talking about. Or who.'

Moncerre had his pipe going. He crossed the room and stood behind Peniel and put his hand on his shoulder.

'He doesn't know what you're talking about, chief,' he said. 'Suppose I take him down to the cells and give him a going over. His memory might return. What do you say?'

Lannes smiled and shook a Gauloise from the packet and lit it.

'I don't know about that. He's protected, you see. That's what he told me. Protected. So protected that he doesn't want us to find out who murdered his daughter. What do you think of that?'

Moncerre bent down, took hold of the leg of Peniel's chair, and flipped it so that both chair and man fell over.

'That's just a taste,' he said. 'Protected, are you? Get up.'

Peniel obeyed, slowly.

'I'm an old man,' he said. He rubbed the side of his face. 'You're a brute,' he said to Moncerre.

'You're beginning to get the message,' Moncerre said. 'Give me ten minutes with him, chief, and he'll spill everything.'

'I don't think we're going to need rough stuff,' Lannes said. 'He's going to want to talk very soon, aren't you, Peniel? Now sit down and tell me where Félix is to be found.'

'Félix? Don't know anyone of that name.'

'The man who gave you the envelope for me.'

'Met him in a bar.'

Lannes sighed. There were interrogations you could enjoy. He'd experienced many such, usually with professional criminals. They were like a game of chess. But there was nothing to relish in this one. Peniel was a repulsive object, a man who disliked women, as he himself had said and as Yvette had twigged, and also one who had been happy to assist in procuring young girls for men with depraved tastes and in setting up spectacles – sex shows between girls – to excite voyeurs and perverts. But he was also an old man, now caught in a trap – a well-deserved trap – and not knowing who he should be most afraid of: the police, Félix, or his daughter's clients, whoever they were. Even his defiance was pitiful.

'I think he thinks he's in the Resistance,' Moncerre said. 'Maybe the Gestapo would like a word with him. Mind you, old man,' – he leant towards Peniel and patted him on the cheek – 'with the Gestapo it doesn't often stop at a word, or so I've heard. What do you say, chief?'

'I think he needs time to reflect,' Lannes said. 'Take him to a cell and leave him there. There's no need to knock him about.'

'As you say. And what then, chief?'

'I'll see you at the brasserie for lunch. Tell young René. Meanwhile there's someone I want a word with.'

*   *   *

A Mercedes was standing outside the house in the rue d'Aviau. As Lannes approached, the old count's eldest daughter, Madame de Thibault de Polmont, came down the steps. She was wearing a fur coat and fur hat and was escorted by a middle-aged German officer with several lines of ribbons on his chest. The driver held the car door open for her. Both got in and it drove away. Lannes waited till it was out of sight before approaching the house and ringing the bell. As on his first visit – more than two years ago now – it was several minutes before the door opened.

'Oh, it's you again,' old Marthe said, and sniffed. 'Since you've come to the front door this time, I suppose it's not me but his lordship you want. You may get some sense out of him and then again you may not.'

'How are you keeping, Marthe?'

'What's that to you, or anyone? I live as I've lived since the old devil was killed, and you did nothing about that.'

The 'old devil' was the Comte de Grimaud, whose mistress she had been more than half a century ago and who even in their old age would have his hand up her skirt. They had bickered like cats on a rooftop and neither would have admitted what Lannes believed to be the case: that each was the only person the other had ever truly loved. She had a right to be disagreeable, and Lannes respected her sour temper, even liked her for it.

'Madame de Thibault de Polmont looks well,' he said. 'I just saw her leave with one of her German friends.'

'The silly old bitch. I've no time for the pack of them.'

Jean-Christophe, who was now the Comte de Grimaud, was

sitting in the high-backed, winged chair in which his father had first received Lannes, and which he had, as it were, annexed as soon as the old man was buried. He wore a plum-coloured velvet smoking jacket and black-and-white checked trousers and his yellow shirt was open at the neck. A decanter of port and a half-empty glass stood on the little table by his side. He was already bleary-eyed and, perhaps because Marthe hadn't troubled to introduce Lannes but had merely opened the door for him, it was a moment before he recognised his visitor. When he did so, he drained his glass and said, 'I've done nothing. You've no right to disturb me. You've no right to be here.'

Each time he had met him, Lannes had felt both pity and repulsion. It was more than ten years since the man had narrowly escaped a prison sentence on account of his sexual tastes which were directed towards young girls. His father had employed all his influence, which was considerable, to get the charges dropped; influence and money, for he had paid off the parents of at least three girls. He already despised his son, and perhaps it was the harsh contempt he had always shown him which prevented Jean-Christophe from ever coming to maturity. Lannes didn't know whether there was indeed an explanation for such tastes, or whether viciousness was innate. Perhaps you could never be certain about such things. Perhaps indeed men like Jean-Christophe were to be pitied. That didn't, to Lannes' mind, make their behaviour forgivable or less repulsive. To take advantage of children. Well, he thought of Clothilde as she had been at the age of eleven or twelve . . .

'I'm investigating a murder,' Lannes said. 'That gives me the right. But it's information I want. I'm not accusing you of anything.'

It would have been ridiculous even to pretend to do so; he knew very well that the wretch in the chair was incapable of the act of self-assertion which murder so often is. It was no surprise to see him refill his glass and take a gulp of the wine.

'A woman called Madame Peniel has been killed. You knew her of course, you and your lawyer, Monsieur Labiche.'

'I don't know what you are talking about. I've never heard of the woman.'

58

The count dabbed his temples with a red and white spotted handkerchief.

'I've spoken to the man who says he was her father. Édouard Peniel, formerly known as Ephraim. He's in one of our cells now.'

'I'm glad to hear it, but he's a liar. Whatever he says will be a lie.'

'Undoubtedly he's a liar,' Lannes said, 'nevertheless . . .'

'I hadn't seen him for years and then he came here one day.'

'And so?'

A tear trickled down the count's fat cheek and when he reached out for his glass his hand was shaking and he didn't dare take hold of it.

'You despise me, don't you? But you don't understand, nobody understands what it's like to want something so much and to be afraid. Afraid of myself and of . . . do you know what comes between me and sleep? Night after night? I run my hand up a young girl's skirt and stroke her soft thighs. That's what I do in my mind and for a moment I'm happy. But that's all it is, I can't help myself, and then when I do fall asleep I have nightmares. I told him to go away. I haven't touched a girl, a real girl, for years, and I told him to go away. You must believe me.'

'I'm ready to believe you, but there's something else, isn't there? He didn't go away, did he? He wanted more.'

It was a hunch, no more than that, but then it was a hunch that had brought him here, to this house which reeked of corruption, where there had long been, as old Marthe put it, much wickedness.

'He wanted something from you, didn't he? And he came with an invitation, I think.'

Jean-Christophe wiped his eyes, but the tears continued to flow, and it seemed as if his whole body was shaking.

Lannes said, 'It's best if you tell me.'

'I don't know. I don't know anything. She was a terrible woman. Once, years ago, she . . . she supplied me with what I wanted, and it was wonderful, and then, and then . . .'

'She blackmailed you, didn't she?'

'She said she would send photographs to my father if I didn't pay. So I paid, what else could I do, and it went on and on. She's dead now of course and I don't know who has the photographs, but till I

59

learnt of her death I had thought it was all over because she couldn't send them to you people without questions being asked about how she came by them, and my father is dead. So I was, I won't say happy, because I don't know what that means and haven't for years, but at least safe. And then he came with what he called a proposition. Have you noticed his eyes? Only the brown one has any life in it, the blue one is dead. And this proposition . . . '

'Yes?' Lannes said, no more than a mild prompt, for he realised what a relief it was for Jean-Christophe at last to speak of what he had fearfully hidden for so long, the relief of confession; so often over his life as a policeman Lannes had known such moments when the dam breaks and what has been repressed floods out.

'He said they were staging a show. I knew what he meant. I'm not a fool whatever you may think, and for a moment I was tempted, excited. You find that disgusting, I suppose, but that's because you don't understand what it is to be like me. To be walled up, because that's what I've been for years. But then what he said next frightened me. There's a German officer lodging here, he's a cousin, some sort of cousin of my sister's late husband, and he said he knew he would be interested, so would I please bring him along. How could he know that – that he would be interested, I mean? I told him, again, to get out, because I was afraid. I don't mind admitting that to you now. I was afraid. And then he said it was my patriotic duty to do as he asked, and his brown eye glittered. I wouldn't have thought a brown eye could glitter, but it did.'

'And then?'

'Then she was dead, I heard she was dead, and I was so relieved that the bitch was dead and I hadn't had to speak to Colonel von Feidler.'

'But you would have done so?'

'I don't know. I thought I had no choice and then I thought if I did nothing, nothing would happen.'

I thought if I did nothing, nothing would happen. The words sounded in his mind as he crossed the public garden, a chill wind in his face. For the first time he felt sympathy for Jean-Christophe: I thought if I did nothing, nothing would happen. Hadn't that been the attitude of the French politicians to Hitler and the Nazis in the years before the war, the attitude of the English too, and wasn't it, shamefully often, his own response to difficulty? Least said, soonest mended is an old proverb and can often seem to be a wise one. When he thought of the silence of their apartment whenever Marguerite and he were alone there, didn't they both prefer to live in this silence because each feared what might be said if they broke it, and so chose to trust that if neither said anything, nothing would happen? And perhaps this was indeed wise, this conspiracy of silence.

Fernand greeted him with a warm handshake, as usual.

'That bastard, the advocate Labiche, is here today. It would give me pleasure to turn him away, tell him he's barred. But you know how it is, Jean. No matter, I've put him at a table on the other side of the room from your boys who are already here, and close to the door from the kitchen so that he is in a draught. That's the best I can do. Meanwhile there's a nice gigot of lamb for you.'

Moncerre was drinking beer.

'I needed to wash my mouth out after our session with that fellow,' he said. 'What a type! Do you know what he said to me when I shoved him into the cell? He said I'd regret it, once his friends heard about it. Friends! That type over there's one of them, isn't he?'

'Labiche. Of the same stamp, certainly, but not, I think, the particular friends he was speaking of,' Lannes said. 'Untouchable, however. So you needn't hope to have the chance to knock him about.'

'Maybe the day will come,' Moncerre said. 'It can't come soon enough for me.'

'On the other hand,' Lannes said, 'if Peniel can be believed when he says – or implies – that he was working for the Resistance, Labiche and he are on different sides.'

'If,' Moncerre said. 'It's a big if, with a type like that. Furthermore, if the Resistance is made up of that sort, there's bugger-all hope for France.'

'Keep your voice down,' Lannes said.

Jacques, Fernand's son by one of his mistresses, brought them the lamb.

'It's very good,' he said. 'From the Landes. The old man's been keeping it for you.'

He leant over, and said, very quietly, 'Can I have a private word with you, sir, before you go?'

'Of course,' Lannes said.

Fernand had once spoken of the boy's wish to join the police. If this was what he wanted to speak about, he would certainly tell him to do no such thing.

As usual they drank a St-Emilion with the lamb which was every bit as good as Jacques had said it was. Lannes felt himself relax. Now wasn't the moment – and this wasn't the place – to recount his conversation with Jean-Christophe. In any case he needed to mull over what the count had said of Peniel's attempt to get him to lure that German officer into the dead woman's young honeytrap. He would speak to Bracal first; see if he knew anything of this Colonel von Feidler.

Young René said, 'I've got some news, chief. The technical boys have at last reported.'

'What took them so long?'

'Well, I asked but they just shrugged their shoulders and said, pressure of work and that they were short staffed, people off with flu.'

'The usual excuses,' Moncerre said. 'Truth is, they're bloody lazy.'

'And?' Lannes said.

'Well, it's interesting even if we have had to wait for it. There were no fingerprints on the champagne bottle or the glasses, none in the apartment except for those of the dead woman and the little maid who is hardly a suspect. And others on the piano which are probably those of some of her pupils. And, most importantly perhaps, she hadn't had sex. Doesn't sound like a crime of passion to me.'

He smiled as he said this, and Lannes thought that the smile might be directed, mockingly, at Moncerre, though perhaps even the bull-terrier had already given up his hope that this was what he had called an old-fashioned pre-war crime, without complications, and one which they might quite easily solve.

'So we're getting nowhere,' Moncerre said. 'I'd be as well to go home if my wife wasn't there.'

'Not quite nowhere,' René said. 'Eliminating possibilities is progress. That's what you've always told us, chief, isn't it?'

'Bloody negative progress,' Moncerre said, 'when you find you're arrived in a dead-end street.'

They had a second bottle of St-Emilion with the cheese which was a Cantal in perfect condition – the black market again, of course. The coffee was undrinkable. Even Fernand's coffee was undrinkable now.

Lannes said, 'I'd like you to talk again with the mothers of her piano pupils. Do it together this time. Be tactful, though I don't mind, Moncerre, if you glower a bit and look suspicious.'

The brasserie was emptying. Lannes lit a cigarette and, having made sure that Labiche had already gone from the table by the door into the kitchen, went through there to hear what young Jacques had to say. The boy took off his apron and suggested they step outside into the narrow alley where they kept the rubbish bins.

'It's Karim,' he said, 'you know, the young Arab you had the old man get out of town. He's back, said he couldn't stand life on the farm he was sent to, for safety, wasn't it? Maybe they didn't want to keep him any longer. I don't know. And I don't know that I would believe anything he said. Anyway he's back and came to see me.'

Even in the dim afternoon light in the alley, Lannes could see that the boy was embarrassed. He remembered how Fernand had told him that Karim had made a pass at Jacques and Jacques had smacked him in the kisser.

'He wants to see you,' Jacques said. 'Insisted it was important. Urgent too. He was in a bit of a state, I thought, said he didn't dare to come to you at headquarters. Well, that doesn't surprise me, him being what he is, so I said I'd pass it on next time you came in which I didn't expect to be long.'

'Did you arrange to meet again?'

'Well, yes we did, but only because I thought that he might really have something important to tell you. Otherwise . . . not that he's such a bad chap, really, only . . . you understand, don't you?'

'I understand. All right then, if you can get in touch with him

63

today, tell him to come to the café near the station where we talked before. Tomorrow afternoon, four o'clock. Can you manage that? If you like, I'll tell him not to trouble you again.'

'It's all right,' Jacques said. 'He's not such a bad chap, really, but . . .'

XIII

Michel lay back in bed, sweating a little and panting. He shouldn't have, but he couldn't not, he thought. Years ago his grandfather, embarrassed, had warned him off. 'It's not that it leads to madness, that's an old wives' tale,' he had said, 'or rather the theory of doctors who are probably ignoramuses. But it's degrading. It's making an object of anyone whose image you are imagining, and this is wrong. Moreover it's not only a sign of weak will to indulge in the practice, it weakens your will further every time you give in to the temptation. So it's a bad habit.'

He wiped himself with the hand towel he had kept between his legs. It was one he had brought from the gym, and he would take it back there and soak it in a basin. Perhaps his grandfather was right and it was shameful. But he couldn't not, and he couldn't take Clothilde to his bed, and when he had yielded to Philippe's urging and accompanied him to the brothel in that street behind the railway station, it had been disgusting. Not at first, admittedly. It had been all right when the woman sat beside him on the bed and stroked his cheek and said he was a lovely boy and told him to be easy and even when she began to unbutton his flies, but then it was all wrong, not just the scent she wore, though that reeked of he didn't know what but something cheap, pervasive and nasty. So what was it? She was like an animal – that was it. No, not an animal, a machine. Anyway it was too much and all wrong. He had stammered that he couldn't, which made him feel a child and ashamed, and he had fled. She didn't even laugh. Somehow that made it worse, as if he didn't matter at all.

When Philippe asked him how it had gone, he had lied. Naturally he had lied and he didn't like lying.

'Mine was quite something,' Philippe had said. 'I don't usually like niggers, but she was hot stuff, believe me. I've arranged to have her again next week. What about you?'

He had made some excuse, and Philippe didn't ask him again. So he wondered if he had been told how it had gone, or hadn't gone, and whether he despised him. All he had actually ever said was, 'Your Clothilde won't thank you for keeping yourself pure. That's what girls pretend they want, but really they like a chap who knows what's what, and that takes experience. They don't ask how he came by it.'

He was a fool, really, Philippe, and jealous too, because he knew that Michel had always found it easy to get girls to kiss him, and he had seen Clothilde fall for him in no time at all.

He turned over in bed, pressing his cheek into the pillow.

There were times he had had enough of Philippe, more than enough, to tell the truth, because though he was rich and well-born, there was something vulgar about him. 'A bit hairy at the heels' was a dismissive expression of his grandfather's, and though he didn't exactly know what it meant, he was happy to apply it to Philippe. It just seemed right.

Yes, he was intolerable really. The other day, for instance, when he had been going on about Count Pierre, and told him, 'You should be careful. Anyone can see that he fancies you. He's a ridiculous old aunt, everyone knows that.'

'So why do you come to his gym then?' he'd replied. 'Anyway you're being absurd. He's a veteran of the Legion and won the Croix de Guerre in Morocco. They don't give that medal to aunts, you know.'

And then there was politics. They'd argued about that too, and the war.

'It's nothing to do with us now,' Philippe said. 'We just have to live through it, prepare for a career after it, and meanwhile enjoy ourselves as best we can. Anything else is futile. As for your Marshal, he's a senile old goat, and I don't mind who hears me say so.'

For a moment he had had no reply. It was true that Sigi had told him the Marshal was only good to serve as a flag, and that something more was needed. Still it was no way to speak of the old man, the Hero of Verdun, especially if you were only a rich lout like Philippe.

'So do you want the Communists to win?' he had said. 'Because that's the alternative.'

'They won't,' Philippe replied. 'The Americans will win the war, believe me, my friend.'

'The Americans! You have to fight to win a war and they're doing precious little fighting, as far as I can see. Anyway America's run by Jews and all they are interested in are their profits and their investments. They're paying the Reds to fight Germany, and if the Reds win, all the Americans will do is call in their debts. There are three powers in the world: Communism, the Money Power, and Germany. The first two are hateful and that's why France must be Germany's ally, taking our part in building a New Europe.'

Philippe had laughed, but that's what Sigi had said, and Sigi knew about these things.

Yes, he would like to drop Philippe, only Sigi had said, 'Keep close to him. I know he's an idiot, but he's a useful idiot, or rather his father is. I've got my eye on him. So make Philippe your best friend, never mind if he talks a load of cock and irritates you.'

He would obey, of course he would obey. Whatever Sigi said, whatever. Meanwhile he couldn't sleep. He turned over again and banged his face on the pillow. Clothilde, she was so sweet, just the thought of her, the picture of her turning towards him and smiling with her lips parted and dying to be kissed. Yes, I really am in love, he thought, we're really in love. I so want her. Oh God in whom I don't believe. Oh God . . .

He leapt out of bed, hands and feet on the cold tiles, and did twenty press-ups.

XIV

At last it had stopped raining. There was just a touch of pale blue in the western sky, even if the sun itself was still hidden by heavy cloud. Lannes' headache had gone too, and though the sharp breeze from the river nipped his cheeks and his hip ached, he felt better than he had for days. All the same he wished he had suggested another meeting place. He wouldn't be able to enter Chez Gustave without remembering the champagne they had drunk there on the morning Alain and his friends had left.

There was no sign of Karim, and indeed the café was deserted except for a couple of railway porters in the uniform of the SNCF. Gustave greeted him with a handshake, and without waiting for him to order picked up the bottle of Armagnac and poured them each a drink.

'How are things?' Lannes said.

'Not good, of course they're not good – what's good nowadays? – but they could be worse. Young Paul's engaged to be married, you'll be glad to hear.'

Paul was his son whom Lannes had arrested for an inept burglary, given a dressing-down, and told to go off and make sense of his life.

'Yes, you really straightened him out,' Gustave said. 'I'm grateful and so's the missus. We could see he was going to the bad, mixing with scum, and wouldn't listen to a word we said. Now he's again like the boy he was when he was little.'

'He would probably have come right in his own time,' Lannes said. 'I did no more than give him a shove in the right direction. I hope she's a nice girl.'

'A nice girl and good as gold. They're a real pair of lovebirds. Our only worry now is this talk of making the labour service in Germany compulsory.'

'That's bad,' Lannes said. 'But isn't he registered as war-wounded? He got a bullet in his knee, didn't he?'

'I'm afraid they'll pass him as fit.'

'Tell him to walk with a limp. More to the point, if there's any real danger of him being conscripted for service in Germany, have him come to see me and I'll find him a job which will ensure he's exempt. Meanwhile, pass on my good wishes and congratulations on the engagement. Ah, here's the boy I arranged to meet. May we use your back room again?'

He picked up his glass, and jerked his head, indicating that Karim was to follow him. Even so, the boy hesitated in the doorway.

'Come in and sit down. What the hell are you doing back in Bordeaux?'

Karim shook his head and sat down on the edge of the wooden chair. He picked at a scab on the back of his left hand. Despite the cold, he was wearing only a singlet, dirty-white, under his thin jacket, and cotton trousers. No wonder he was shivering.

'You'd better have a drink to warm you.'

'No, I'm all right. Anyway I don't drink alcohol. That's not for the reason you may suppose because though my father was an Arab and I've got an Arab name, I'm not a Muslim. I'm not anything actually.'

He pulled up his singlet and scratched his belly.

'But that farm. I couldn't stay there. Don't think I didn't thank you for arranging to get me out of Bordeaux once you explained the danger I was in here, because I did. But I couldn't stay there. These peasants, they're no better than animals, filthy animals.'

What would the farmer and his wife have thought in their turn of this half-Arab boy who prostituted himself to middle-aged men, some of them members of the Occupying Army?

'Besides,' Karim said, 'I was worried about my mum. She's an old sow, I know that, but she can't do without me.'

She had certainly told Lannes that she couldn't do without the money her son brought in, taking over her bed to let the Boches stick it up his arse, as she put it.

'I try to keep her off the drink, or ration her at least. She's killing herself, otherwise. That's the other reason I don't drink myself, I've seen what the stuff can do to you.'

He scratched his belly again. A pink spot flared on the café-au-lait skin.

'So. Young Jacques said you had something for me.'

'Yeah, that's right.' His tongue flickered over his lower lip. 'He's all right, Jacques, I like him, could like him a lot, you know. Look, this is difficult. Maybe I will have something to drink. An orangeade, that OK?'

When Lannes returned with the bottle and glass and another Armagnac for himself, Karim had taken one of his cigarettes from the packet on the table, and was leaning back, smoking and frowning. The cigarette was stuck in the corner of his mouth, gangster style, and there was something pitiful, even ridiculous, in the assumption of toughness by this skinny boy whose soft skin and dark liquid eyes made him look vulnerable.

He doesn't even shave yet, Lannes thought.

'How old are you, Karim?'

'Old enough.'

Certainly old enough to have assumed responsibility, in some fashion anyway, for that drunken wreck of a mother.

'You know what I am,' Karim said, 'what I do, sort of. I'm not ashamed, I tell you that. The way things are, the way I am, I don't reckon I got much choice. Leastways, that's how I see it and it's my business, no one else's. Understand? So I'm not apologising for nothing. I'm not dirt, I want to make that clear. I don't see myself as dirt and I'm not dirt. Got it?'

'I understand.'

Lannes lit a cigarette, drew the smoke deep into his lungs and exhaled. Karim stubbed his out, reached towards the packet of Gauloises, hesitated, and looked Lannes in the eye for the first time.

'That's all right,' Lannes said, 'take one.'

He flicked his lighter to the boy who moved his face forward and looked at Lannes over the flame.

'Thing is, I like sex, see, and I'm good at it, give satisfaction, usually anyway, most times really. But now I've a problem and I don't know, it doesn't seem right. Well, it's worse than that, really. It's a lot worse. Which is why I asked Jacques to tell you I wanted to see you. Understand?'

'Go on.'

Again Karim scratched his belly. The sound of laughter came, muffled, from the bar.

'There's this geezer,' he said, 'old guy, been with him three, four times. I don't like him much, something creepy about him, he has eyes of different colours, but that's not it. I can't say what it is, not exactly, but . . . anyway, I raise my price for him and he pays. Well, he came round in search of me. The old woman told him I wasn't in Bordeaux – she can't stand him either, says he's a bad smell, though how she can tell one smell from another beats me. Eddy, he calls himself. You interested?'

'I might be. Go on.'

'Well then, it so happens I come in while he's there. Bad timing because he was on the point of buggering off, and he comes over all smarmy and says he's so happy to see me again, but he hasn't come for sex, not today, which I was pleased about because I don't like what he likes, which is the other reason I make him pay through his Jewish nose. There's a friend of his, he says, wants to meet me, is eager and pays well. So I say, fine, because I need the cash and the old woman's slate at the Alimentation for her rum is sky-high, astronomical. So I go with him, and he leaves me with this chap, thickset, oily hair, smoking a cigarette through a holder, who looks at me like I was dirt, and like I say, I'm not dirt, so I think I don't have to stay here and do anything with this guy. But then he hits me, smack in the belly, and knocks the wind out of me, and picks me up and hits me on the chops, and holds me by the hair, and says, you're an Arab and a pretty boy, and I don't like Arabs and I don't like pretty boys, and then he throws me down so that I'm lying across the table and he's grabbed me again by the hair, and then . . . then . . . it's degrading. You can guess what then, I don't want to speak of it.'

He had been speaking faster and faster, his words tumbling over each other, and now he stopped and looked at Lannes and there were tears in his eyes.

'You don't have to spell it out,' Lannes said, 'but there's more, isn't there?'

Karim nodded and drank some of his orangeade. Lannes passed him another cigarette, took one for himself and lit them both.

'He said he'd a job for me and I'd no choice. I was his boy now and if I disobeyed him, he'd have me carved. He'd take pleasure in carving me himself so that nobody would say I was a pretty boy ever again. Or he'd kill me. He didn't care which.'

'And the job?'

Lannes knew what the answer was going to be, but he had to hear it from the boy. The bloody fool, he thought, the bloody brutal fool, the demented fool.

'And the job?'

'There was a German officer, he said. He would introduce me to him, dangle me – his words – before him. He's a degenerate, you see, he said, has a taste for brown boys, and you're going to satisfy it. Well, in ordinary circumstances, I wouldn't mind, you know that. But I didn't like this, there's something nasty about it, and I was frightened, I was shit-scared, I don't mind telling you that, shit-scared. So that's why I told Jacques I wanted to see you. Can you help me, will you?'

Lannes leant back in his chair, looking hard at the boy who had averted his head.

'You've done right,' he said. 'You've had it tough and you're right to ask for my help. Which you'll get. I can't say, don't worry, because that would be foolish, nobody's free from worry, or from fear, not these days, but you can worry less, a bit less anyway.'

XV

It was still dark on a day that might never be light. Fog hung heavy. Léon, hovering in the doorway of the hut, felt the chill penetrating his bones. It was a morning made for goodbyes, and what made it worse was that he knew Alain was eager to be off. Would he give him another thought once they had said 'au revoir' and the car, the headlamps of which barely penetrated the gloom, had rolled out of the estate? Doubtless he would, often – they were each other's best friend, weren't they? – and yet he would soon be caught up in the action he yearned for, while Léon remained in limbo. And there was the too awful possibility that 'au revoir' might really be 'adieu', that they would never see each other again.

Alain came out, wearing his greatcoat, the beret at an angle pulled down over his right ear, and a kitbag slung over his shoulder. The light in his eyes didn't belong to this grey hour before dawn.

'So,' he said. 'You're not to worry. I know there will soon be something for you.'

'Of course there will,' Léon said, denying his misery.

'I'm sure of it.'

'Well, then, we'll see. Meanwhile . . . '

But there was nothing he could find to add to that 'meanwhile'. To wish Alain 'luck'? The notion was inadequate, therefore preposterous.

'We'll meet again,' Alain said, speaking in English the first line of the song they heard everywhere.

'Don't know when, don't know where . . . ' Léon obediently responded, a tremble in his voice.

'Under the Arc de Triomphe, as we agreed, on the day of Liberation,' Alain said, 'if not before. You're not to worry,' he said again.

'Of course not,' he lied, and thought of the cyanide pill which his friend would never be without from the moment he boarded the aeroplane that would take him to France.

Someone rapped out an order. They embraced. Léon, for the first time – the only time ever? – let his lips brush Alain's.

Alain stepped back, then forward again, put his hands on Léon's shoulders, hugged him to himself, and kissed him on each cheek.

'That's it,' he said. 'They're waiting for me. Best be off. Aux armes, citoyens! Vive la France!'

'Vive la France!'

He watched the rear lights of the car till the fog swallowed them up. Alain had tried, for his sake, to disguise his excitement, his exhilaration even, but when he had put his hands on Léon's shoulders, it had felt like an electric charge. He turned back into the Nissen hut and lay down on his bed, his face pressed into the pillow. He remembered how he had left Bordeaux without a word to his mother. Had she sat in her chair weeping when she learnt of his departure and feared for him? And how seldom he had given her a thought since! This too was something of which he had to be ashamed. Not of course that he was ashamed of what he felt for Alain, which he had acknowledged only to Jérôme and the nature of which he believed Alain didn't suspect.

Two nights previously they had listened to Jérôme's first broadcast to the Youth of France. He had spoken well, even movingly, they had agreed on that, though Léon thought the script he had been given to read was poor stuff.

He kept that opinion to himself, like so much else.

Alain said, 'You see, they've found the right role for Jérôme. They'll do the same for you. You're not to worry about that. They assess us pretty carefully, you know, and not without insight.'

But what if their assessment of him was negative?

Then Alain surprised him.

'We're not d'Artagnan and Athos, really. I know that it's not like the Musketeers, not really. My father brought me up on Dumas and still reads him whenever he feels low, which is quite often, poor man. But there's no colour in our world today and no romantic exploits either. I'm well aware of that, and I realise I may be killed any day after I am parachuted into France. We may neither of us survive this war. There's no glory in it either and if we are killed it will most probably be like a rat caught in a trap. I don't even know if I'll die bravely or if, at the moment of death, it will be a matter for consolation or pride that one has done the right thing. But there it is: we'd be ashamed of ourselves if we had made any other choice. So if I don't survive and you do, I would like you when you're back in Bordeaux to tell my father – and my mother – that I did what I thought I must do and was happy. Don't say that I died for France, because that would make my father look sceptical – he detests the big words and high-flown rhetoric – and my mother would dissolve in floods. And I'll do the same for you of course, tell your mother and your Aunt Miriam, and old Henri too – if things should turn out the other way. I think that's all.'

'Don't be morbid.' Léon forced himself to smile. 'It's natural what you say when you're about to go into action, but I'm convinced we'll both come through. We'll meet in Paris, as we've agreed, at the Liberation, on the Champs-Élysées or under the Arc de Triomphe. I've never been to Paris, you know, and I've no intention of dying without seeing Paris.'

'All right then,' Alain said, 'that's a deal. And in any case I too am determined to see Paris before I die.'

That evening was the only time Alain had ever spoken of death as a real possibility, though the idea of it was never far from Léon's mind.

There came a cheer and a babble of conversation from the far end of the hut where people were gathered round the wireless.

'What is it?'

'Wonderful news!'

'It's the turning point of the war!'

'What news? What's happened?'

'American forces have landed in North Africa, near Algiers.'

'You call that wonderful? It's outrageous, an invasion of French territory, an act of aggression.'

The speaker was their sergeant, in peacetime a Parisian lawyer who, despite his membership of Action Française, had joined de Gaulle in 1940, one of the comparatively few French soldiers evacuated from Dunkirk who had declined the chance to be repatriated and chosen to remain in England. He now pulled at his moustache and said, 'I hope Vichy throws them back into the sea.'

It was with difficulty that Léon prevented himself from laughing out loud. Whoever said the French were a rational people? But he couldn't help smiling and the sergeant turned on him, angrily.

'Are you mocking me, little Jew?'

'Certainly not, my sergeant, but we are engaged to fight against Vichy, aren't we?'

'You don't understand, young man. You don't begin to understand, Vichy is France too.'

So do you cry 'Vive de Gaulle' or 'Vive le Maréchal'? Léon wondered, and then it occurred to him that it might be possible, quite sincerely, to do both. Moreover, if the American landing succeeded, there might be some in Vichy who cheered it, and were ready to adjust their political position accordingly.

XVI

'So what do you make of it?' Bracal said.

Lannes had no immediate reply to offer because, quite truthfully, he really didn't know what he thought. There had been rumours that the Americans were preparing a landing in North Africa, but he had discounted them as he discounted so many of the 'on dits' which people had bandied about since 1939.

Bracal smiled.

'I'm not surprised that you decline to commit yourself, Jean, even in a private conversation. What I am sure of is that it will make your work – our work – even more difficult, not to say dangerous.'

This was doubtless the case, but what struck Lannes was that this was the first time Bracal had addressed him by his Christian name. He couldn't respond in kind, even if etiquette permitted him to do so, because he didn't know the judge's one. Indeed he knew very little about him, not even whether he was married and a father.

'It may be the turning point,' Bracal said. 'Or it may not. What I'm sure of is that things will get worse before they get better. The word is that Laval has gone to Germany to meet Hitler – gone of his own accord or been summoned, I don't know. When I say that's the word, I mean it's information a friend in Vichy has passed on to me. It's not public knowledge.'

Lannes thought, why are you sharing it with me?

He said, 'And the Marshal?'

'Well, as I'm sure you realise, since Laval returned as Prime Minister in place of Darlan in the spring, the old man isn't much more than a figurehead. Apparently he says that Laval knows how to talk to the Boches, and Darlan doesn't. He might be right there; Laval's a politician to his fingertips and the Admiral is really a bureaucrat. My friends say he is never happier than when drafting a memorandum which most of the time nobody reads. They don't like Laval but they respect him even if they also deride him as an Auvergnat peasant.'

And who were these friends, Lannes wondered, and what was their position in Vichy? Did they blow with the wind? Was Bracal alert to any change in its direction? He lit a cigarette.

'I don't understand politics,' he said, 'I'm only a cop.'

'Oh, quite.'

'But if you ask me, the Marshal should fly to Algiers. The Americans still recognise him as Head of State, don't they?'

Bracal's fingers tapped out a tune on the desk, his habit, Lannes had noticed, when he wanted time to think or was uncertain what to say. The sound of a horn blared from the square.

'That's the Gestapo,' Bracal said. 'I've come to recognise their note. This news will have made them edgy, though they'll never admit to that. You're right, Jean. The Marshal should indeed do as you suggest. It's the only way to save his honour and perhaps his life. But he won't. He has his own idea of honour, you see. It's one of his lines, you know: I made the gift of my person to the French People and I will never desert them. You're a reader, aren't you? There's a character in Dickens who keeps saying that – that she will never desert her husband. She's absurd of course, and not only because her husband is an idiot. Do you know how many sensible people deserted in 1940? Save your skin if you can and all that. It made sense, didn't it, sense of a sort anyway.

'My son was taken prisoner,' Lannes said, 'and I've never read Dickens. My English novelists are Walter Scott and Stevenson. So you think the Marshal will stay?'

'I'm sure of it.'

'Poor man.'

'You have a regard for him?'

'I was at Verdun.'

'Of course. A long time ago.'

'There are days it seems like yesterday, and days it seems another life. For the Marshal too, doubtless.'

'Perhaps. But there's another thing. Admiral Darlan is himself in Algiers. Pure chance. His son is ill in hospital there. But he is still the Marshal's Dauphin, and the word is, he's determined to resist the Americans to demonstrate his loyalty to the Axis. It's a question of course whether the Army there obeys him. But all this is a distraction from what you have come to report to me. Are you any closer to finding the killer of that wretched woman?'

'There are days,' Lannes said, 'when I feel further away than ever.'

'Do you find it strange that we concern ourselves with such questions at such a time?'

'Strange perhaps, but what else can we do? It's our métier, just as clerks go to their offices and the wine barons still make wine.'

He outlined all that he had learnt of the case and the course of his investigations, and finished by saying, 'Nevertheless, it's a case I want to solve. The dead woman was not admirable, I grant you, a procuress and, I believe, a blackmailer, but . . . '

'This fellow you have in a cell who claims to be her father, Ephraim Peniel, isn't it?'

'Or Édouard – he goes by both.'

'From what you say, he has to be broken. I'll interrogate him myself. That's not a criticism of you, Jean, or of your methods, but I've found in the past that there are criminal types who defy the police because, if you forgive me, they live in the same milieu, but who are – what shall I say? – less at ease with the judiciary. Have him brought to me tomorrow. At eleven? Right?'

He stood up to indicate that their conversation was at an end, but, when Lannes remained seated, said, 'There's something else, isn't there?'

'Yes,' Lannes said, and recounted his conversation with Karim.

Bracal crossed the room to his drinks cabinet and poured two brandies. As before he topped one up with soda water and passed the other to Lannes.

'This is worrying,' he said. 'You believe the boy?'

'Yes.'

'He sounds a disreputable type.'

'Yes.'

'But you believe him.'

'Yes. He's frightened, very frightened, and that often leads people to speak the truth. Besides, though he is indeed, as you say, disreputable, and what many would call degenerate, he has, odd as it may seem, a certain sense of honour. I don't think he's lying about this, though I've no illusions that he wouldn't lie about other matters when it seemed prudent or necessary to him to do so. This fellow, Félix, he's quite out of control. I think he may be mad, he's certainly dangerous, and it's the same nasty game he played before, which led to Schussmann's suicide and all sorts of trouble.'

'You hate him, don't you?' Bracal said.

'I don't hate people.'

Bracal raised an eyebrow.

'You're a strange one yourself, Jean.'

Lannes shook his head.

'I don't know about that,' he said, 'I hate what people do, often. I think he has to be stopped.'

'Unquestionably. Do you plan to see him?'

'I think I must.'

'Very well. Keep me informed. We may have to take drastic action. I don't know. By the way, have you spoken of this to Commissaire Schnyder?'

'No, I haven't.'

'Why not? Surely you should have? As a matter of duty?'

Lannes stubbed out his cigarette, drank his brandy, and made no reply. Bracal smiled again.

'I think you are wise,' he said. 'I have every respect for Commissaire Schnyder, as a diligent officer. But I think you are wise. Please keep me informed.'

It was only when he was descending the stairs that he realised he had said nothing about Colonel von Feidler. Well, it could wait, like so much else.

XVII

Even though Bracal had said he would interview Ephraim Peniel, Lannes wanted another go at him first. It wouldn't, for one thing, be a bad idea to let him know the judge was interested, and give him a night to sweat on it. So he had him brought up from the cells.

Peniel at once began to complain. He had a delicate stomach. The food here didn't suit him. It was cold in the cells and he couldn't sleep.

'You've brought it on yourself,' Lannes said. 'So don't look for sympathy from me. I've been talking to a couple of friends of yours. I say friends, though neither of them seems to care for you. I don't care for you myself if it comes to that. You say the dead woman was your daughter, but I've never met a man less distressed by finding his daughter had been murdered. Except one – and he had killed her himself. What do you make of that? What should I make of that?'

Peniel made no reply. He hunched into his jacket. For a moment Lannes saw the years fall away from him to reveal a delinquent schoolboy who knows he has done something beastly but still hopes he may escape punishment.

'Tell me about Colonel von Feidler.'

'Never heard of him.'

'Don't be stupid. Who put you on to him?'

Peniel shook his head.

'All right,' Lannes said. 'You don't want to speak. I think you're making a mistake but you're entitled to say nothing. The converse is that I'm – we're – entitled to draw conclusions from your silence. The first of course is that you're guilty – not necessarily of murder, for I don't really believe you killed your daughter. You might kill if you were afraid, kill in panic, anyone can do that, but not this sort of crime, not that theatrical set-up. But you're certainly guilty, guilty of procuring young girls for sex, or sex shows, or both. Well, that's a matter for the Vice Squad who will undoubtedly be interested when we've finished with you. By the way, your case is almost out of my hands. You've an appointment with the examining magistrate, Judge Bracal, tomorrow morning, eleven o'clock. He's going to want a list of the girls you procured and of your daughter's clients. You realise what this means of course. When you refuse to satisfy him, he'll sentence you to preventive detention. That'll last for months. I could let you go tomorrow, but you are making that impossible for me. So it's your decision. Fine.'

He lit a cigarette, crossed the room and poured two tots of Armagnac. He passed one to Peniel, who said, 'I don't drink alcohol.'

'As you like.'

Lannes downed his and left the other on the desk in front of the hunched figure opposite him.

'Shall I tell you what I think?' he said. 'I think you're quite happy to be locked up, relieved anyway. That's because you're more frightened of Félix – or whatever name you know him by – than you are of me. I know what he did to Karim and what he has planned for him. Nothing to say to that? Oh yes, I know Karim.

He doesn't much like you either. Just takes your money and submits or whatever. That's right, isn't it? No affair of mine what you have got up to with the boy. But handing him over to Félix, that's different. Now tell me about Colonel von Feidler.'

Peniel shifted in his chair. Shifted? Squirmed.

'You approached Jean-Christophe who is an old client of your daughter's. Fine. But what made you think this Colonel von Feidler would be interested in your little shows? What put you on to him?'

For the first time Peniel raised his head to look Lannes in the eye. His own brown one was watering, but the blue one remained dry. He twisted his fingers round each other.

'Ask Félix,' he said, 'if you find him. I've nothing to say to you. Except this. I'd almost forgotten I was a Jew. I decided long ago not to be one. But now, I find I can't escape it. You know what that means today, to be Jewish. Gabrielle's mother was a Jewess too. We did it only once. It disgusted me – woman's smell, revolting. But she held me responsible, and, when she died, Gabrielle came to me and told me she was my daughter. I don't know if she was, as I told you, her mother was a whore. All the same, I did what I could for her. I don't like people. I never have. But I felt something for her. I don't know just what. Perhaps because she had no morals. Does that shock you? It shouldn't. You're a policeman after all. Perhaps it was Gabrielle who forced me to be a Jew again. I don't know. But now, the world being as it is, I've no choice, do I? So when Félix approached me, I said yes. Because I'm a Jew. Not that he knows that, he hates Jews himself. And now it's got Gabrielle killed, and I know nothing about that. So if your judge locks me up, I won't complain. And as for that filthy Arab boy, he'll come to a bad end without my help.'

* * *

When he was alone, Lannes opened the window wide. It was a steel-grey afternoon, but the bitterly cold air felt good. He breathed in deeply. Then he leant there, smoking, looking out at the people coming and going in the square. A man was roasting chestnuts on a brazier, and the scent rose to him and this also felt good. Something in Peniel's speech had moved him, the sense that he knew he was defiled and nevertheless kept going. There was misery and desolation everywhere. He thought of Schussmann, the poor fool, and of Léon, now of Karim whom Félix was planning to use as he had used Léon. Then he thought of Clothilde and Michel as he had surprised them sitting side by side on the couch yesterday evening, holding hands and with faces flushed, both looking for a moment guilty, before each smiled a welcome to him, and covered their dismay at his return with a show of good manners. He picked up the brandy Peniel had refused and drank it, slowly. He would buy a poke of chestnuts and go to see Henri and Miriam. These landings in North Africa? He had always discussed the news with Henri.

*   *   *

As soon as he had settled him with a cup of bad coffee, Henri went up to the attic to call Miriam.

'We've got news,' he said, 'she'll want to share it with you.'

She greeted him with a kiss. Were the lines on her face deeper each time he called?

'This life in hiding doesn't suit me,' she said. 'I've always been energetic, accustomed to walk every day. Sometimes I'm tempted to go out, but then I think this might bring trouble on Henri. I suppose it's illegal to give shelter to a Jew.'

'Not illegal,' Lannes said, 'at least I don't think it is, not yet anyway, but . . . '

'Dangerous?'

'Perhaps.'

She sat on a high-backed chair, smoothing her skirt as she settled herself.

Henri said, 'I apologise for the coffee. It's undrinkable, isn't it? I'll open a bottle of wine. No, it's all right, Jean. These days I manage to restrict myself to a glass or two.'

Lannes leant back. He had been at ease with Miriam since they first met, that ease disturbed only briefly when he wanted to make love to her, and now that he no longer did so, the ease had returned and he was happy to sit with her without talking as Henri busied himself with corkscrew and glasses.

'It's a light Graves,' Henri said, 'poor Gaston's favourite, as you will remember.'

He stuffed tobacco into his pipe while Lannes and Miriam lit cigarettes. Toto, the little French bulldog, woke up and sniffed Lannes' trouser legs, then, deciding as usual that he was a friend, turned away to sit by Henri's feet. Henri, having got his pipe going, emitted little puffs, and said, 'I'd a visit yesterday from Madame de Balastre, Jérôme's mother. She's an old friend, but she came here because she knew that Léon used to work in the bookshop. She had news. Since the boys left she has taken to listening to Radio London. That surprised me since she and her husband are staunchly maréchaliste, but there it is, I suppose the maternal instinct is stronger than political allegiances. We live in confusing times, don't we? I'm sure she still thinks of the Resistance as – I don't know what – nothing good anyway, criminal types perhaps. No matter. She said she had heard Jérôme speak on Radio London the previous night. Of course the speaker wasn't identified by name, but, as she said, she couldn't mistake her son's voice. She was almost in tears. But I assume this means that the three of them are in England, and that's good news surely.'

'It's a relief, certainly,' Miriam said. 'Don't you think so, Jean?'

What could he do but agree? What was the point of saying that they knew nothing of how the Free French – the Gaullists – operated? The boys might have been separated, given different roles. Alain and Léon might never have got further than North Africa, and, if that was the case, what position would they be in now that the Americans had landed there? Far from reassuring him, the news tightened the knot of fear in his guts. It was no surprise that – if Madame de Balastre was right, as she surely was, for what mother would not recognise her son's voice? – Jérôme had been assigned to propaganda work; you had only to look at him to see he wasn't suited to combat, to danger. Alain was different, Léon too perhaps.

Henri said, 'The American landings. Do you think this might be the beginning of the end, Jean?'

'The end of the beginning, perhaps. But we don't yet know how Vichy is responding. Are they resisting the Americans or greeting them as Allies? The word is that Laval has gone to meet Hitler. My fear is that there will be pressure for France to re-enter the war on the German side.'

'Surely he'll resist that?' Henri said.

'He may want to. I don't know. He's a deep one, Laval, but if he still believes that Germany will win the war, what sort of choice does he have?'

It was already dark when he left the rue des Remparts.

XVIII

There was a new mood in the city. You could sense it, even if nobody put it into words: an undercurrent of nervous excitement, whether that sprang from hope or apprehension. There was no certain news from North Africa. Some said the Vichy forces were resisting the Americans, that they had even repelled the invasion, others that they had laid down their arms and were welcoming the Americans as liberators. Lannes inclined to the latter view because there was more German activity in the city, staff cars and troop carriers hurtling through the streets, deserted of all other traffic except for bicycles and municipal buses. Then came firm undeniable news. Laval had returned from Germany empty-handed. The Free Zone was being dismantled and the French army commanded to disarm. All France would now be subject to Occupation. Yet Vichy remained in being, the shadow government of a shadow state. And the Marshal remained there, obedient to his promise not to desert the French People. Poor man, poor deluded old man. Still it appeared that Laval had resisted any German demand that France should declare war on the United States and Britain. Nevertheless, as Lannes said to Moncerre and young René, 'Things will get worse before they get better.'

'If they get better,' Moncerre said.

There was a letter on his desk from the Comte de St-Hilaire, Jérôme's godfather, requesting that Lannes would do him the favour of calling on him. He telephoned and spoke to the Count's butler, making an appointment for the afternoon after the butler had assured him that the Count had said a visit would be convenient at any time.

The sun had come out and it was a bright cold afternoon with only a few delicate fleecy clouds in the sky when he left the office, but there was still rainwater in the gutters and his shoes were spattered with mud well before he had reached the Count's 'hôtel particulier' in the Allées de Tourny. It was an address which, even after more than twenty years in the police, still left him, to his irritation, feeling abashed. When he was a young inspector, much like René Martin now, his boss had remarked on his feeling of social inadequacy and sought to rid him of it. 'Always remember, Jean,' he had said, 'that when you go to one of these grand houses, you are there as an officer of the Republic, either because its occupants have need of you, or because they or theirs have stepped out of line. Whichever way, you're the man in charge.' It was no doubt good advice, and it irked him to think that he had never had the confidence to act fully upon it. He smiled at the thought now, threw his cigarette away, and rang the bell.

The butler showed him into a salon where the Louis Quinze furniture and the portraits of what he took to be the count's ancestors might have been calculated to sharpen his sense of social unease. There was also a Fragonard of nymphs bathing, which was not to his taste, and a still life of bread, cheese, wine and fruit, which he took to be a Courbet, and which pleased him, because it was as ordinary as it was beautiful. He was still admiring it when the Count came into the room.

There was a moment of constraint. That was no surprise. It couldn't be otherwise. At their last meeting the Count had let him understand that the actress and star of the Bordeaux theatre, Adrienne Jauzion, whom the world took to be his lover, had been responsible for the killing of her father, Professor Aristide Labiche, the brother of the advocate whom Lannes detested; Lannes had already been ordered to abandon the investigation into Aristide's death, but now, the memory of that conversation hung trembling in the air between him and St-Hilaire. He had done nothing with the information, as the Count had known he would do nothing, and not only because he was in debt to the Count for having facilitated the escape from Bordeaux of Alain and his friends. He respected St-Hilaire, was grateful to him, might even like him; and yet he still resented, as he had then, his patrician certainty that Lannes would not act on the information he had given him. There had been extenuating circumstances, certainly; nevertheless, if a shopkeeper had told him that his mistress, in a moment of anger and bitterness, had killed her father, would he have done nothing about it? He could be sure of the answer and felt soiled.

'Have you word of your son?' the Count said.

For a moment Lannes hoped – feared – that it was to give him news about Alain that St-Hilaire had invited him, but this was absurd; the question would have been framed differently.

'None at all,' he said, 'but I gather Madame de Balastre has recognised Jérôme's voice on Radio London. So I hope they may all be in England.'

'Yes, I suppose mothers can't be mistaken about their son's voice. It must be worrying for you.'

'Given his sentiments, it would be worrying if he was still here.'

'Ah yes, the Resistance, an admirable cause, but perhaps not always admirable people.'

Lannes made no reply, and hoped the expression on his face was neutral.

'And now North Africa,' the Count said. 'A turning point.'

'Perhaps. Who knows?'

St-Hilaire took a box of Ramon Allones cigars from an occasional table, and offered it to Lannes, who declined, saying he preferred cigarettes, and was invited to light one. The Count clipped the end off a cigar and held a match to it.

'Oh, there can be no doubt,' he said. 'The Germans are a remarkable people, magnificent warriors, but now that the Americans have bestirred themselves, they're doomed. Between the pincer of the United States and the Soviet Union, a German victory is unthinkable. It's only a matter of time. Which is why I would wish that your charming son and that clever Jewish boy – was his name Léon? – were safe in a broadcasting studio with my godson. But now the Resistance, most of whom I suppose are Communists, are determined that France should become a battlefield, with Frenchmen killing Frenchmen. I have a certain regard for Monsieur Laval: a scoundrel, but an intelligent one, and a man who prefers peace to war. As we all should, don't you think? You fought at Verdun yourself, if I remember?'

'I did.'

The butler brought in a tray with a carafe of red wine and three glasses. He poured them each a glass, and when he had closed the door behind him, St-Hilaire said, 'I asked Mademoiselle Jauzion to join us. I hope this doesn't embarrass you. It was at her request that I wrote to you. She has something to say to you, some information, I gather, to impart – when she has repaired her maquillage, as she is, I presume, doing now.'

She was wearing a trim dark suit – costume, Marguerite would have called it – beautifully cut – Chanel, perhaps, though the name came to his head only because she was the only designer he could think of. But it was certainly à la mode – or à la mode of 1939 anyway, he was sure of that. The shirt below it was cream-coloured with a high lace neck, and whatever repairs she had been making to her face had given her a mask which expressed nothing. He wondered if she was nervous, and yet it was she who had invited this meeting. She settled herself in a high-backed chair, crossed her silk-stockinged legs elegantly, and met his gaze, then looked away. St-Hilaire gave her a glass of wine which she placed on the little table beside her chair without bringing it to her lips. She took a cigarette from a silver case, fitted it in an amber holder and waited for the Count to light it. She inhaled deeply, and then, blowing out smoke, said, 'She was my dresser for five years, Gabrielle I mean. She was efficient and orderly, and I relied on her. I never liked her but she had my respect, and then I found it necessary to dismiss her. Does this interest you, superintendent?'

'Assuming you are speaking about the murdered woman, Gabrielle Peniel, anything you might have to tell me about her interests me. We know so little.'

'Please sit down, superintendent. You unnerve me, standing there.'

He didn't believe this for a moment; yet did as she asked.

'Why?' he said. 'Why did you find it necessary to dismiss her?'

'Good dressers are hard to come by, and important for someone in my position. Nevertheless, I couldn't keep her after I learnt that she enjoyed a certain relationship with my uncle the advocate. I believe Monsieur de St-Hilaire' – she turned towards the Count with a smile – 'has spoken to you of my uncle and . . . '

She paused and St-Hilaire intervened.

'There's no need, Adrienne, to say anything about that. I'm sure the superintendent understands perfectly what you refer to, and how you suffered.'

'Certainly,' Lannes said. 'But this relationship between Gabrielle and the advocate. What do you imply by the word?'

'Not what the world might suppose,' she said. 'That wouldn't have been her way. Gabrielle was a lesbian.' She smiled. 'Perhaps you have already learnt that?'

'Perhaps.'

'That didn't concern me. Why should it? The tendency, if I may call it that, is quite common in the theatre. Elsewhere too, I suppose. She had a particular friend, a young dancer. Kiki she was known as. It was a passionate relationship; they used to have terrible quarrels which, I may say, rather amused me. But that wasn't why I dismissed her. What she and Kiki did together was no concern of mine. I hope that doesn't shock you, superintendent?'

'I'm a policeman.'

She picked up her glass and sipped the wine, a small delicate sip. She ran her tongue over her lips.

'Yes, of course,' she said, 'you must be hard to shock. There's another policeman in my story by the way. But I'll come to him later. This is more difficult than I had supposed it would be, even more difficult . . . ' – she turned towards St-Hilaire as if looking for support.

He said, 'I'm sure Superintendent Lannes is happy for you to take your time, tell the story in your own way.'

'I'm accustomed to speaking other people's words,' she said. 'I know how to deliver an author's lines. But this . . . Kiki was a nice girl, a silly little fool who didn't know what she wanted or who she was, which perhaps wasn't surprising since she was an orphan raised by nuns in a convent where they cared for abandoned children. Perhaps that is why I felt a tenderness for her. Being abandoned in childhood is another form of abuse, isn't it? The world is a rather horrible place, you know. That's why I have the reputation of being aloof. I have steeled myself against it, and the face I present to the world is a cold one. I display emotion only on the stage. Off stage I wear a mask. Do you understand?'

'Please continue,' Lannes said, 'when you feel able.'

'There are horrors everywhere,' she said, 'but you must know that. You know my uncle, don't you?'

'I know your uncle.'

'One day I found Kiki in tears. She was distraught, shaking with sobs. It was embarrassing. I thought she and Gabrielle had quarrelled again. They did, quite often; Gabrielle had a quick temper, a vile one. I think she hit her sometimes. But Kiki usually shrugged it off, with a laugh even. 'I'm a child of the streets,' she would say, 'I don't take things like that too seriously.' But . . . she had a sister, she told me, several years younger than herself, also being reared by the nuns. Kiki used to take her out for the afternoon. One day, at Gabrielle's suggestion, she brought the child to her apartment, for tea and cakes. They never got cakes in the convent and the child, I can't recall her name, was happy, and Gabrielle at her most charming. She was charming, when she chose. She played the piano and the little girl danced for her. Kiki too, I suppose. I'm sorry, I'm not telling the story well. It's because I'm embarrassed. Fortunately there's not a lot more of it. Gabrielle made much of the girl, and she was delighted by the attention. Kiki insisted she wasn't jealous. Why should she be? Her sister was only a child. Then one day when she collected her from the convent and suggested they might visit Gabrielle, the child began to scream. It was terrible, Kiki said. She never wanted to go there again. Kiki pressed her, and it came out. Gabrielle had taken the child out one afternoon, without telling Kiki, given her cakes and orangeade, and introduced her to my uncle. Need I say more? Naturally I dismissed her. In truth I couldn't bear the sight of her after I heard what she had done. I was trembling myself. She laughed at me. It was intolerable.'

The previous year when he was investigating Aristide's death, Lannes had summoned the advocate to his office, and had shown him a horrible and compromising photograph he had been sent of Labiche sitting on a couch with a naked girl who must have been no more than twelve. 'This means nothing,' the advocate had said, 'and in any case she gave what she would be giving to any young lout in the back streets in a couple of years.' Or something like that. Lannes had done nothing. There was nothing he could do. The advocate was, as the Alsatian said, 'one of the Untouchables', a man of position, honoured by the regime with a post in the Commission set up to deal with what they called the Jewish Question.

He had been ashamed. Of course he had been ashamed. Now, for the first time in their acquaintance, he warmed to Adrienne Jauzion. She was gripping the arm of her chair hard, her knuckles white. They were comrades in shame. He glanced at St-Hilaire whose face registered nothing, but who now rose and laid his hand very gently on Adrienne's shoulder.

'But there is more?' Lannes said.

She shook her head. He got up, walked over to the window. The light was dying in the deserted street.

'I have to ask you this,' he said. 'Do you know what became of the little girl?'

'No.'

The word was so quietly spoken that the sound was little more than a breath.

'And Kiki?'

'She went away. She said she couldn't bear to be in the same city as Gabrielle. But she's back. I saw her last week, in a café in the Place de l'Ancienne-Comédie. She was with a German officer. She pretended not to recognise me when our eyes met.

'I'll have to speak with her. You realise that, don't you?'

'Yes, I realise that. But I don't know where to find her. Perhaps I shouldn't have spoken.'

'No,' Lannes said. 'You were right to do so. You know you were right. But you mentioned a policeman?'

'I did? Yes, of course I did.'

She turned round to face Lannes again, glanced towards the Fragonard painting and murmured, 'So beautiful, if only . . . the policeman. I don't recall his name. Kiki knew him. I can't remember why or how, perhaps he was a neighbour. She told him what she believed had happened and he promised to make inquiries. Then he came to her a few days later, and said there was nothing to be done. It would be useless to lodge an official complaint, he said. It would be only the child's word that anything untoward – that was his word, I recall – had happened. Kiki would be liable to have an action for slander brought against her if she repeated the accusation she had made to him. He was sorry, he said, but that's how it was. For your own sake, he said, keep your mouth shut. Those were his precise words, I remember them well.'

'There may be something in the files,' Lannes said, though he doubted if there would be. 'I'll need to speak to Kiki. What was her real name?'

'Haget, Catherine Haget. But I'm sure she didn't kill Gabrielle.'

'I've no reason to think she did. But I'll have to speak to her.'

'And my uncle?' she said.

'And your uncle. Eventually. Finally, did you ever meet Gabrielle's father?'

'She never spoke of him, to my knowledge.'

XIX

'You must be waiting for someone. A pretty boy like you, sitting alone here. I'm astonished you haven't been snapped up already.'

Léon looked up from the marble-topped table. The speaker was a stout middle-aged man in a charcoal-grey double-breasted suit. There was a pink carnation in his buttonhole and he gave off a whiff of an expensive Cologne.

'Yes, I'm expecting my friend,' Léon said.

'As I feared, but perhaps you will have a glass of champagne with me while you wait.'

He waved vaguely, and a waiter appeared to take his order.

'I'm meeting someone myself,' he said, and settled himself on the velvet-covered banquette beside Léon. 'He's always late of course, the privilege of the young and beautiful.'

Perhaps Léon looked puzzled, for the words were repeated in French.

'Perhaps it's better that we speak your language and a pleasure for me too, since I have a great affection for your country. Allow me to introduce myself. My name's Edwin Pringle, Sir Edwin actually, and I am a Member of Parliament, for my sins. And you are?'

'Léon.'

'And serving gallantly with the Free French. Have you met de Gaulle? What do you think of him?'

'He's a great man.'

'Undoubtedly, though one with atrocious manners.'

He laid his hand gently on Léon's thigh.

'I confess,' he said, 'to having a certain sympathy for the Marshal. But I'm afraid he's doomed, poor old man. Ah, here's the champagne. It's in short supply, you know, but they are kind enough here to keep some bottles for me. I'm sure you will find it more agreeable than that doubtless atrocious coffee you have ordered. And are you excited by these North African landings?'

At the moment Léon was more embarrassed than excited. Was it etiquette to ask a Member of the British Parliament to take his hand away? Or to remove it himself? But could you do that and still drink the champagne he offered you? Fortunately the matter resolved itself, Sir Edwin taking a leather case from his inside breast pocket, extracting a cigar, and occupying himself in clipping its end.

'Sorry,' he said, 'it's the last survivor.'

'I prefer cigarettes,' Léon said, relieved. 'We don't know much about what's happening there yet. There are all sorts of rumours.'

'De Gaulle was in the same boat, you know. He had been kept in ignorance of the Americans' plans – they don't care for him in Washington, you know – which between you and me and the bedpost is a point in his favour. I'm not greatly enamoured of our American friends myself, since they are determined to destroy our Empire – and yours too, dear boy – just as soon as they have finished with little Adolf. I'm told that when de Gaulle learnt of the landings, he said he hoped Vichy would throw them back into the sea.'

'That's funny. Someone in our barracks said exactly the same thing.'

'You're a contrary lot, aren't you? Winston had to calm the General down over lunch. Otherwise, Lord knows what sort of trouble he'd have made. And what do they have planned for you, dear boy? Nothing too dangerous, I hope.'

Léon hesitated. He had an interview with Colonel Passy fixed for the following morning, but he mustn't say anything about that. He shrugged his shoulders, said 'it's not clear yet', and was relieved to see Jérôme standing at the door and scanning the room. He waved a hand to him.

'Why, your friend's little Jérôme,' Pringle said. 'How delightful! We met at a party last week. He's really charming. You're a pair of charmers.'

Jérôme made his way between the tables, leant forward to peck Léon on the cheek, and extended his hand to Sir Edwin.

'I'm so sorry,' he said, speaking in English 'I'm late, and we can't stay. We've an important appointment and we're already late for that too.'

'You've time for a glass of champagne, surely.'

'I would love to, but I daren't, we'll be in trouble if we are any later. Another time perhaps. Come on, Léon.'

Out in Regent Street, he hooked his arm into Léon's.

'It's so good to see you.'

'What's this appointment we have?'

'There isn't one. I made that up to get away. He's a notorious old pederast.'

'So?'

'Well, yes I know, but . . . we met at a party last week and I hadn't been there ten minutes before he was proposing bed. I tell you, I had the greatest difficulty in escaping from him. Fortunately he was distracted by the arrival of a gorgeous boy in RAF uniform.'

'He told me he was a Member of Parliament.'

'Oh yes, he is, but out of favour. They say Churchill can't stand him. He was a fervent Munichite and had lots of German friends. Or so they say. I'm told he's very rich, but all the same . . . oh, it is good to see you.'

'And you. Where are we going?'

'A Soho pub first, I think.'

'I don't want to drink much. I've got this appointment in the morning, remember.'

'Of course.'

'Is there any word of Alain?'

'No. None. But there couldn't be, could there?'

'I know, but I can't help hoping. And worrying.'

'Me too.'

'And after the pub?'

'Well, we'll see, won't we?'

*　　*　　*

Hours later, Jérôme turned on his side, and leant on the point of his elbow.

'I don't suppose we will ever do this again,' he said, 'but I wanted to just once. You don't regret it, do you?'

'Regret it? Why should I?'

'Because we're not each other's type.'

'I don't know what my type is.'

'Yes, you do, it's Alain.'

'That's crying for the moon.'

'I suppose we all cry for the moon, people of our temperament. I know I do and it's unattainable. You remember that Fascist boy back home in Bordeaux I told you I was crazy about? I still am. I think of him every day. Stupid, isn't it? Ridiculous really. All the more so because far from giving me any encouragement he made it clear he had no time for me. Quite the opposite indeed. Which doesn't stop me from dreaming about him.'

'So we're both stupid,' Léon said.

It was strange, lying there, with Jérôme's leg resting on his, and listening to the night near silence of London. He knew Jérôme was right. They would never do this again. It was a sign of affection, nothing more except perhaps loneliness, though he couldn't believe Jérôme was lonely – so many people had greeted him and chatted with him and been evidently pleased to see him in the two pubs they had visited; the one Jérôme had told him was known as the French, because its proprietor was indeed a Frenchman called

Gaston, with huge moustaches, and it was frequented by other members of the Free French because it always had stocks of Algerian wine and Pernod or Ricard; and the other called, he thought, the Fitzroy, which was said to be a haunt of poets, and where everyone had been drunker than he found comfortable. Jérôme had been at home in both of them, and he hadn't. He didn't belong anywhere, that was the truth.

Jérôme leant over and kissed his cheek.

'I must tell you,' he said. 'De Gaulle came to the studio the other day. He was about to broadcast to North Africa. I was introduced to him. He's so tall that he made me feel as if I was back in primary school. When he heard my name, he said he had been at St-Cyr with my father, in the same class actually. "A very gallant officer," he said, making me feel even more inadequate as the pansy son of a heroic father.'

'You shouldn't think of yourself like that. Would your father have been here, do you suppose?'

'I've no idea. I was only five when he was killed. Actually, from what I've heard, I suspect not.'

'Well, then, that makes you more adequate than he might have been.'

'That's kind of you,' Jérôme said, and kissed him again. 'But sadly it's not true. We both know that really.'

*   *   *

Léon was early for his appointment with Colonel Passy, but half an hour after the time he had been given he was still waiting and had smoked five cigarettes. There were only two left in the packet – Woodbines, he didn't much like them but they were cheap. Jérôme had made him a cup of coffee on the gas ring in his room, delicious real coffee – 'Smuggled, of course,' Jérôme had said – but he had been too excited to eat anything, and now felt sick with apprehension. The waiting room was cold and stuffy at the same time, and the other occupant was a middle-aged man in a brown suit, rather than uniform, who had a head as round as a cannonball and a neck as thick as a Prussian's. He looked at Léon as if he knew him for what he was and didn't like it. Somewhere, along the corridor, a door slammed. Léon twisted his fingers round and round. A pigeon landed on the window ledge and pecked the glass.

At last an orderly appeared and the man in the brown suit got to his feet, but it was Léon who was summoned.

He saluted Colonel Passy and was told to sit down.

'You look very young. Did you lie about your age?'

Léon swallowed.

'Not by much, sir.'

'Doesn't matter. Lots of people do. Your report's good, but I'm not happy about sending children over there.'

'I'm not a child, sir, whatever I look. I'm the same age as my friend Alain Lannes and you . . .'

'Alain Lannes. Ah yes, he spoke to me about you.'

'Have you any news of him? Is it permissible to ask, sir?'

'Permissible to ask, yes, but you don't expect me to answer, do you? You've been trained as a radio operator. That's why you're here. We need one in Paris. Have you friends or family there?'

'I'm afraid not, sir.'

'Good. You'd be no use to me for this job if you had. You'll be on your own and any contact with family or friends is forbidden. We can't rely on young men to observe that rule if we send them to their own city or home province. The temptation is too hard to resist when they're lonely. And you will be lonely, very lonely. I hope you understand that, because being in danger sharpens the feeling of loneliness even though you have comrades in your own little cell. Still, this report' – he tapped the papers on his desk – 'this report on you is positive. It says you're tougher than you look and know when to keep silent. So I'm satisfied, ready to take a risk on you. Don't take that phrase personally, as a criticism. I take a risk on every agent I send to France. We can't really be certain of anyone, of their capabilities, that is. Anyway you've passed all the tests set you. So you're in. My colleague will brief you, tell you what's what. You're Jewish, aren't you?'

Léon hesitated.

'Does that matter?' he said.

'Only if the Gestapo get hold of you.'

XX

There was no difficulty in finding Catherine Haget. She had correctly registered her residence: rue Belle Étoile, off the Cours de la Marne, the same street where poor Gaston had had his rooms, where he received his students and boyfriends, and where he had been so horribly murdered. The concierge told Lannes she was in an apartment on the third floor left, 'Though I'd be surprised if you find her up. She keeps late hours, that one, as her type usually does. Not that she's a bad girl, not really. I must tell you I'm a good judge of character, having seen all sorts in my time, and she's always well-mannered and polite and gives me the time of day with a lovely smile. I hope she's not in any trouble. She'll have to go if she is. This is a respectable house and my people won't like having the police here.'

'It's just a matter of routine,' Lannes said. 'Nothing important.'

He had no wish to get the girl into difficulties.

There was sleep in her eyes when she answered his knock; she wore only a towelling robe and her feet were bare. He showed her his badge and she stepped aside to let him enter.

'I wondered when you would get round to me,' she said.

She was a pretty girl with a wide mouth, dark eyes and curly hair, and, when she turned away to lead him into the small sitting room, the loose robe didn't prevent him from remarking her strong dancer's buttocks.

'Make yourself at home,' she said, and settled herself on a couch. 'Not that it's much of a home, I only rented this place last month, and it's not what I would have wanted, but there you are.'

It was certainly meanly furnished, and the half-dozen photographs of scenes from ballets that she had propped up on the shelves of an almost empty bookcase, and the vase of white chrysanthemums on the table beside a couple of coffee cups and a wine bottle, did little to give it a lived-in look. Lannes laid his hat on the table, lifted a newspaper from a wooden chair and sat down. He didn't remove his coat.

'So you're not surprised to see me?'

'Have you got a cigarette? Thanks. No, I knew that Adrienne Jauzion recognised me when our eyes met the other day even though I looked away almost at once, and the only question was whether she would want to get herself involved. I more than half thought she wouldn't because she's such a cold fish, but if you people got round to questioning her about Gabrielle, well then I wouldn't have expected her to keep quiet. It is Gabrielle you have come about, I suppose, for I can't think of any other reason why you should be here.'

'It's Gabrielle. Madame Jauzion said you were in the company of a German officer when she saw you.'

'And if I was . . . we're supposed to collaborate, aren't we?'

'Up to a point,' Lannes said.

'You have to yourself, don't you?'

'No more than is necessary. All I would say, Kiki, is that things may not stay the way they are, and you should bear that in mind.'

'Meanwhile the Boches are still here.'

'They are indeed. How long have you been back in Bordeaux?'

'A couple of months. I had a job in Paris; it came to an end, so I came back. It's my home town, after all, though to tell you the truth I've little enough reason to think of it as home. So, yes, I was back here before Gabrielle was killed. That's what you wanted to know, isn't it?'

She stretched out her leg and scratched her thigh. The skin was pale in the winter light of the room that wouldn't get the morning sun even if there was sun.

'I didn't kill her. If I'd been going to kill her I'd have done it five years ago. Do you believe me?'

'There's no reason why I shouldn't.'

It hadn't seemed probable, from what Adrienne Jauzion had said of the girl: that melodramatic set-up. It didn't ring true.

'But you had an affair with her?' he said.

'Yes, if that's what you choose to call it. She made a set at me and I was crazy about her. Crazy's the word, I think I was mad.'

'And now, this German officer?'

'That's different. He's a nice kid. He doesn't even want to be here. He's an innocent. These flowers there – chrysanthemums –

what kind of flower is that to give a girl? They're for the cemetery, aren't they?'

'Did you go to see Gabrielle when you came back to Bordeaux?' She got to her feet, lightly.

'It's no good,' she said. 'I told myself I wouldn't have a drink till evening, but I need one, badly.'

She opened the wine, took two glasses from a shelf, rubbed them with the corner of her robe, poured the wine and passed a glass to Lannes. She downed hers in one and refilled it. The rough red ordinaire left a smudge on her upper lip. She sat upright on the couch now, placed the glass on the floor, and hugged her knees.

'Did you?'

'Did I what?'

'See Gabrielle?'

She shook her head.

'I'm a mess,' she said, 'a real mess. I must look a fright. Yes, I went to see her. I hated her – there's a motive for you – but I was broke and I went to ask her for money. I thought she owed me.'

'And?'

'She made it clear that she didn't. She offered me a job, work. Her kind of work. I told her to stuff it, and I left. She was full of life when I left her. You know what? It amused her to have me begging. That's the sort of woman she was. I don't say she was asking for what she got, but don't expect me to be sorry she's dead. The world's a better place without the bitch. So there. Make of that whatever you please. I hope you never find whoever did for her. Does that shock you?'

'Madame Jauzion told me about your little sister. So, no, it doesn't shock me that you feel like this. Is your sister still in the orphanage with the nuns?'

The girl looked at him open-mouthed. Then her eyes filled with tears, and she buried her face in the cushions and sobbed, her whole body shaking. Lannes waited without speaking. There are girls and women who can make themselves weep at will; he had known many do so in the course of an interrogation, enough for him to be sceptical. But this distress seemed genuine.

He waited. Eventually the body stopped shaking. She sat up,

wiped her eyes as she had wiped the glasses with the corner of her robe, picked up her wine and held it a moment in both hands which were trembling, and drank it.

'She's not with the nuns. She's dead. She hanged herself. Five years ago. The poor fool, the poor innocent fool. The Ice Queen didn't tell you that?'

XXI

Instead of going home for lunch as he had intended, Lannes went to the Bar Météo, rue Fénelon. It was where he had met Félix, at the spook's invitation, the previous year, and, though it wasn't likely that the man made it his regular haunt – for it was surely the practice of his type to eschew any such routine – he felt obscurely that simply being there brought him closer, even though there was no evidence that Félix was still in Bordeaux. Vincent, Bracal's friend in Travaux Ruraux, had said that Félix had been ordered to return to their head office in Marseille, but had not yet, to his knowledge, reported there. 'It seems he's regarded as a lone wolf,' Bracal said.

The proprietor greeted him, a touch warily.

'You're not here on business, superintendent, I hope?'

'That depends. Meanwhile you can give me an Armagnac and a demi.'

'Depends on what?'

'Your memory perhaps.'

'My memory's terrible.'

'That's a pity. I met a chap here last year, in May I think it was.'

'Long time ago.'

He drew the beer and poured out two glasses of Armagnac.

'On the house,' he said, 'your health.'

'And yours. You'll remember him,' Lannes said. 'I've no doubt of that really. You let him have the use of your private room for our meeting. I don't suppose you do that for just anyone.'

The proprietor pulled at his moustache and downed his Armagnac. Lannes offered him a cigarette which he accepted. Two workmen in blue overalls came in and asked for big glasses of red. They began to talk about rugby, addressing the proprietor as Gaspard. Lannes took his drinks to a table in the corner of the bar, sat down and waited. Kiki's story had disturbed him. It was his duty to find Gabrielle's murderer but the more he learnt of the woman the less, it seemed, her death was to be regretted. He pictured that little girl dangling from the end of a rope and felt sick. There was a difference, doubtless, between guilt and responsibility, but the girl had been driven to it because Gabrielle was what she was. There came a burst of laughter from the bar. One of the workmen leant forward and punched Gaspard lightly on the shoulder.

'You old bastard,' he said, 'you really were an old bastard in those days, up to all the tricks.'

'If you say so,' Gaspard replied, laughing too. 'You were up to a few yourself, weren't you?'

He came out from behind the bar, crossed the room to join Lannes, pulled out a chair and sat down.

'They're old mates,' he said. 'We used to play in the scrum together. Good days they were. I'd like to help you, superintendent. I don't want any trouble; this is a respectable bar I run, so I'd like to help you. The chap you're asking about. He was in here just the other day, with a couple of other types I didn't like the look of. Tell the truth, I was happy to see the back of them when they left. He asked for the back room again and I didn't like to refuse him. There's something about him. I won't say he alarmed me, because I'm not the sort to be alarmed. I can look after myself, as you'd expect. In this line you have to be able to do that, and in any case, as my mates there would tell you, in the old days if there was any dirty work in the scrum or at a line-out, I gave as good as I got and usually better. But I can smell danger, and that type gives off a stench of it. That's all I know.'

Lannes took out his card and said, 'Your nose doesn't deceive you. If he comes in again, give him this and tell him to call me.'

*　　*　　*

It didn't make sense. Félix had sent Peniel to him – with the photographs – and had even arranged to meet him. Then he hadn't turned up, and there had been no further approaches. What had happened to make him change his mind? Was it because of what he had planned for Karim?

He left the bar and had walked some distance in the cold bright sunlight before he admitted to himself where he was going. It was probably a mistake; nevertheless . . .

*   *   *

The desk of the Pension Bernadotte was deserted, as she had said it would be at that hour, and so he went straight to her room and knocked on the door.

The radio was on, Charles Trenet singing 'Le Soleil et la Lune', and Yvette was lying on the bed, as on his first visit when he was investigating the murder of the professor, Aristide Labiche, whom she called 'the old gentleman'; and again she was naked but for a negligee which disclosed her generous breasts and was rucked up to the top of her thighs.

'Hello stranger,' she said, 'I knew you'd come some day. Needing?'

He was close to saying yes. She was a nice girl and a desirable one and he wanted her, and what would it matter? A half-hour in bed would mean nothing to her. She would give him pleasure, and he might even manage to please her in turn.

'You're playing games again, Yvette. It's pointless and you know why. I don't say that if things were different, I mightn't, but they're not. So put some clothes on and I'll take you out for lunch.'

She sighed. He knew it for a theatrical sigh. Then she smiled and eased herself off the bed, letting the negligee fall away. She leant forward, put her arms round his neck and kissed him on the mouth. She put her hand between his legs and giggled.

'You are silly,' she said. 'We both know that, don't we? Still, a girl never says no to a free lunch. Not this one anyway.'

*   *   *

The little brasserie used to be Jewish, and that might have deterred Lannes from entering it, on account of a certain delicacy of feeling, but the family who ran it had left Bordeaux before it became an Occupied City, indeed before the Battle of France. Old Isaac, the grandfather who had come there as a boy from the Ukraine before the turn of the century, escaping from a pogrom in Kiev – and who had served in the French Army as a cook throughout Lannes' war – had told him that everything would soon be up, and that they were off to North Africa. Lannes had been dismayed by the old man's defeatism. Well, it had been sadly justified. No doubt they had opened another restaurant in Algiers or Oran.

'I wish they'd all had as much sense as old Isaac,' he said. 'I wish they'd all gone while they had the chance.'

'So what is it you want to talk about?' she said when they were settled at their table and had ordered the plat du jour, which was a lamb stew that would be short on lamb, and a half-litre of the house Médoc.

'So?' she said again, laying her hand on Lannes' thigh. 'I'm a good listener. At least I can be.'

He spoke to her as he should have been able to speak to Marguerite, spilling out his anxiety, frustration and discontent. He told her about Gabrielle and the dancer and the little girl who had hanged herself – she took tight hold of his hand when he spoke of the child; about Félix and the photographs, and Karim and his fears for the boy; about Clothilde and Michel and his certainty that it must come to a bad end, on account of Michel's politics and his corrupting relationship with Sigi; about Dominique in Vichy and the worry this caused him now; about Léon who was old Léopold's great-nephew; about Alain and his pride in the boy, ignorance of his whereabouts, and the gnawing terror that this occasioned and kept him awake at night. He spoke of the difficulties of his position, of how he sensed that his immediate boss was coming to distrust him and of how he was sure that the Germans had their eye on him. And then he told her that there was a wall between him and Marguerite which he couldn't breach.

So he exposed himself and was ashamed, and ordered another half-litre.

'I'm sorry,' he said.

'For what?'

'For inflicting all this on you.'

'You are silly,' she said, and kissed him. 'It would have been easier for you to say all this in bed – you've no idea of the sort of confessions some of my clients come out with – but all the same I'm flattered that you've chosen to speak of it over lunch. It makes me think we're friends, that I'm not just a convenience, which is what I mostly am, I realise that. We are friends, aren't we?'

'I suppose we are.'

'Only suppose?'

Lannes picked up his glass and clicked it against hers.

'It would be simpler if you didn't love your wife. But you do, don't you?'

He supposed he did. Or was it because he no longer did that he was so reluctant to say or do anything that might hurt her?

XXII

Lannes had had few dealings with Lieutenant Schuerle, Kordlinger's replacement as the officer charged with liaison between the Occupying Forces and the PJ. He took this as evidence that Kordlinger's report had placed a black mark against his name. So it was a surprise when old Joseph knocked on his door and ushered the German in; even more of one when Schuerle did not greet him with that ridiculous Hitler salute, which even the unfortunate Schussmann had usually remembered to give, but instead offered a handshake which Lannes accepted. He was younger than his predecessors, no more than in his middle or late twenties it seemed, blond, and surprisingly quick to smile. He had been wounded on the Eastern Front; he wore a black leather patch over his right eye, and his left arm hung useless or almost useless, shattered, Lannes supposed, by shellfire, which was doubtless why he had been assigned to liaison duties.

'I have a problem I wish to discuss with you, superintendent,' he said, and he gave that quick smile which might have been intended to be disarming, but was also perhaps a sign of nervousness.

'Certainly,' Lannes said. 'Do sit down.'

'It is rather a delicate matter, and, if you don't mind, I would prefer not to speak about it here, in your office. As it happens, the sun is at last shining. It's a beautiful afternoon, even if a cold one – though the cold is nothing to what I was accustomed to recently, or indeed back home in East Prussia. Would you care to take a walk with me, superintendent, perhaps to your delightful public garden?'

'As you like,' Lannes said; he heaved himself into his thorn-proof English tweed coat, and collected his stick.

'That is kind of you. I was so hopeful that you would agree.'

The walk was passed in near silence, Schuerle making only the occasional remark about the beauties of Bordeaux or asking about particular buildings. Reaching the garden which was almost deserted despite the fine weather, they settled on a bench. Schuerle looked around, as if to assure himself, unnecessarily, that no one was near enough to overhear them.

'Charming,' he said, 'quite charming. You find my approach unorthodox?'

'Unusual, certainly.'

'Good, good. You wonder why I am behaving in this manner, especially since Lieutenant Kordlinger advised that you were not to be trusted. Does that surprise you?'

Lannes lit a cigarette.

'Not greatly.'

'He described you as obstructive and ill-disposed to the require-ment that the French police collaborate with us. He went so far as to request of your superiors – would that be the Prefect? – that you be dismissed, then appears to have withdrawn his request. I find this strange. Don't you, superintendent?'

'No doubt he had his reasons.'

'No doubt.'

Schuerle took an envelope from his briefcase and passed it to Lannes.

'This makes me feel as if I was engaged in espionage,' he said. 'I'm sure you've already seen the photographs. I suppose it is the boy who was employed to incriminate poor Schussmann and you with the boy. You wonder how they came into my possession? Evidently you have enemies, superintendent. Kordlinger required you to find and deliver the boy – the degenerate boy, I believe he said. You failed to do so, and yet evidently you knew him. What do you have to say?'

Lannes turned his head to look Schuerle in the face. He was smiling again – perhaps it was a nervous tic, consequence even of his war wound, not a genuine smile. But it looked like one.

'Kordlinger threw me into a cell,' he said, 'and had a couple of heavies beat me up. I'd nothing to tell him then. Now we're chatting on a bench in the public garden, and I'm wondering why.'

'I looked up your dossier. You were wounded at Verdun, decorated too. The Médaille Militaire, wasn't it? My father fought there also. He was not so fortunate. He was killed. I was a child, never really knew him. My hero father.'

He stretched out and took the photographs from Lannes. He put his finger on Léon's face.

'Nice-looking boy. Where is he now?'

'I've no idea. He got out of Bordeaux.'

'With your help?'

'If you say so. As you like.'

Schuerle began to tear up the photographs. His damaged left arm made it difficult, but he tore them across again and again, into tiny bits, put them back in the envelope, tore that across too, got up and stuffed it all into a rubbish bin, thrusting the compromising evidence out of sight under the newspapers that someone had discarded there.

'We don't need these. There will be other prints of course, and the negatives, but we don't want these ones to fall into the wrong hands, do we?'

Lannes dropped his cigarette under his heel and lit another. He was surprised to find that his hands were steady.

'The boy is Jewish, isn't he?'

'If you say so.'

'I was brought up by my grandfather, my mother's father,' Schuerle said. 'A Prussian of the Prussians, a Junker, with an old-fashioned sense of honour. He's dead now too. He shot himself, like that wretched Schussmann. He was ashamed, you see. He was a hard man, hard on himself and others, hard on me when I was a child, but he knew right from wrong, good from evil, and he was ashamed. He was proud of our family history which goes back a long way, to the days of the Teutonic Knights actually. He disliked the Jews, you would call him anti-Semitic, but nevertheless he said that many of them had fought bravely for Germany in the last war, and he detested the anti-Jewish laws and Kristallnacht – you know what Kristallnacht was, superintendent? of course you do – and he shot himself on the day the Wehrmacht marched into Poland. He left me a letter saying, "Fight for Germany, not for these scum" – a difficult instruction to follow. Well, I've done my fighting for Germany' – he touched his left arm with his right hand. 'Who do you think will win the war, superintendent?'

Lannes experienced a surge of happiness.

'Germany – the Nazis – will lose it.'

He had never supposed he might say such a thing, openly, without hesitation, in such circumstances.

'Indeed,' he said, 'they may have lost it already.'

Schuerle turned his face towards him. There was a dampness under his right eye, as if a tear had trickled from behind the leather patch. Lannes wondered if there was an eye still there, and then, absurdly, if an empty eye socket could weep.

A little dog ran past them chasing a ball, and a small boy followed, laughing.

'There are many in Germany who have arrived at that conclusion. I know some of them well, friends of my late father, brave men and German patriots like my grandfather, some also who were fellow students of mine. They would like to act, but whether they can . . . '

He broke off, leaving the speculation hanging.

'You wonder why I am telling you this,' he said.

'It would be surprising if I wasn't,' Lannes said.

'I'll come to that in a moment. Let me just say now that I want to avoid trouble. You're investigating a murder, I understand, the killing of a woman called Gabrielle Peniel. That is so, isn't it?'

'It's no secret, no secret either, that I haven't got very far. Do I take it that you have an interest in the case? That the German Army has an interest?'

'That would be a reasonable supposition.'

'Which invites the question: do you want the case to be solved or would you prefer that it was abandoned?'

Schuerle smiled again.

'You may not believe me but my superiors have no answer to these questions. I assume you know more about the dead woman than we do, but I would also guess, superintendent, that you have decided that the motive for the murder was political – using that word in the broadest sense. She was engaged – you will know this already – in activities that were discreditable.'

'I know about these activities and I have reason to think that they compromised people in high places, even, perhaps – I say no more than perhaps – German officers. Is that what you are afraid of?'

'Shall we say that my superiors would not wish . . . I don't need to spell this out. On the other hand you will, I'm sure, understand that this murder – the style of this murder . . . you see what I mean?'

Lannes did of course. Had the Boches decided to get rid of Gabrielle, there would have been no need of that elaborate stage set. They would simply have arrested her and she would have disappeared into a concentration camp. And if they knew about her activities and ignored them, then it was because they had indeed turned her, and she was spying for Germany. Which led him straight back to Félix – except that he couldn't understand why he in his turn had stage-managed that charade; it would have been so simple to shoot her. He lit a cigarette.

'There,' Schuerle said, 'I've delivered the message with which I was entrusted. You will doubtless act on it as you think fit. If I may express a personal opinion, it is strange for me after what I have seen in the East to find so much time being spent on the death of a loose woman. Strange, yet also oddly comforting. It suggests that something worthwhile may survive this terrible war.'

'You speak French very well, lieutenant.'

'My mother adored France. We often spoke French when we were together. On her mother's side she was descended from Huguenots expelled from France by your Louis XIV. Perhaps you know that two hundred years ago a third of Berliners belonged to Huguenot families and still spoke French among themselves rather than German? Some day our two peoples must be reconciled in a Europe that has turned its back on war.'

'There are many in Vichy who agree with you, Monsieur Laval for one. He is eager for France to take a leading role in your Führer's New Order of Europe.'

'My Führer's? Not that Europe, his Europe, you understand. Nevertheless, in my opinion, superintendent, any French Resistance now is a mistake. It will cause suffering and it will divide France deeply. Perhaps you think it is not my part to make such an observation.'

'I don't think anything,' Lannes said.

Schuerle got up, held out his hand which Lannes took, and turned away.

*   *   *

He didn't think anything . . . well, if by that he meant only that he preferred not to respond to Schuerle's observation, it was true enough. Truer, certainly, to say that he preferred not to think about the day of reckoning. If St-Hilaire's analysis was correct, and if, as he had – rashly? – told Schuerle, Germany – the Nazis – might already have lost the war, there was worse in store for France and the French people than anything they had yet experienced since 1939. It had been hard in the summer of 1940 and the months that followed to know how to act. His own difficulties and the opposing loyalties of his sons were evidence of that. But now Resistance was stirring and would provoke a Counter-Resistance, just as the Revolution of 1789 had provoked a Counter-Revolution, the Red Terror a White Terror.

He rubbed his hand over his brow, and realised how cold it had turned when he felt the skin of his palm against his forehead. Yet he could not summon up the energy to move. There was a rustle of wind; a few last leaves from the chestnut tree floated past him. The light was beginning to fade. They would soon be closing the garden. Yet he continued to sit there, smoking. He had liked Schuerle, a decent type, probably doomed; how close was he to those friends of his who 'would like to act'? He had no doubt, it was clear, what that action might be.

The park attendant approached him.

'We're about to close, sir. It's time to leave the garden . . . sorry, superintendent, I didn't recognise you. You remember me? I was the one who found that body in the bushes over there last year. I never heard if you discovered who killed the old gentleman. There's been no word of a trial.'

'I know who killed him,' Lannes said, 'but there won't be a trial. There's no case for one.'

'Like that is it, sir? It's a sad world we live in. Things were different when I was young.'

'So they were,' Lannes said, getting to his feet and leaning on his stick. 'And you're right. It's a sad world we've survived into.'

XXIII

Fernand's son Jacques was in the waiting room when Lannes arrived the next morning. He got to his feet as soon as he saw him and then hesitated as if he was nervous of being thought presumptuous. Lannes shook his hand and led him into his office.

'I'm surprised to see you here. I hope it's nothing bad. Your father's all right?'

'Yes of course, no reason why he shouldn't be, is there?'

This wasn't true. There was every reason why anyone might be in trouble, or at least difficulties.

'Then I suppose it's Karim? Yes?'

'That's right. He came round to the kitchen door yesterday, just when we were about to close, and said he had a note for you which he didn't dare deliver himself. I don't know why and I didn't ask him. No business of mine, I thought. But I hope he's not in the shit. I quite like him, you know, though I wouldn't trust him round the corner. Anyway, I promised I'd hand it to you – in person, he said, make sure it's in person – which is why I'm here. Is he in the shit?'

He handed Lannes a grubby envelope.

'He's in trouble,' Lannes said, 'because of what he is. But it's not really his fault. Give my regards to your father.'

'Of course. I have to say he wasn't pleased to find Karim hanging about. Do you want me to keep a table for you today?'

'Thank you. Do that, though I can't guarantee.'

'There'll be blanquette de veau. One of your favourite dishes as I remember.'

'We'll try to be there.'

The note was brief.

'I'm ordered to meet him 12 o'clock at the Bar Météo tomorrow.'

The word 'ordered' was spelled wrong.

12 o'clock? Well, he would surely miss out on the blanquette de veau. Unless . . . he didn't know; would have to see how it went. Meanwhile there was paperwork to be dealt with; none of it of any importance, but the business of dealing with it was at least a distraction. He wondered if Karim would obey orders and keep the appointment, or if he had sufficient faith in him to skip it. Probably not; he would remember Félix's threats and be afraid.

He stamped the last document, appended his signature, and summoned Moncerre from the inspectors' room.

'I'm off to the Bar Météo to meet a chap,' he said. 'We'll leave together – I'll try to make sure of that. And then I want you to put a tail on him. He's an elusive fellow and I don't want to lose track of him.'

*   *   *

As Lannes entered the bar Félix leant forward and slapped Karim hard on the face. Gaspard behind the counter looked as if he was about to move, but Lannes shook his head, and he did nothing. Lannes asked for an Armagnac and crossed over to the table in the corner where they were sitting.

'I've been looking for you,' he said. 'You can be off, Karim. Make yourself scarce.'

The boy opened his mouth as if about to speak, caught Lannes' eye, got to his feet and made for the door. Lannes watched him break into a run as soon as he was in the street, and sat down. Félix fitted a cigarette into his amber holder, lit it, and leant back, blowing smoke in Lannes' face.

'Another of your boyfriends, superintendent? First the Jew boy, now this Arab scum.'

'I'm not the rapist. Nor the procurer.'

'I don't know what you mean.'

'Of course you don't. You know we've arrested Peniel. So don't pretend ignorance. He's been talking too. You didn't think he'd keep silent, did you? A fellow like that.'

'So do you intend to arrest me too? That wouldn't be wise, superintendent.'

'Oh, I don't think we've come to that point yet,' Lannes said. 'After all you're a patriot, aren't you? That's what you told me last summer. Everything you are doing is for France, isn't it? What Gabrielle was doing, that was for France too, wasn't it? Which leaves me speculating as to the reason for her murder. Not – I don't mind telling you – that I have made much progress. I don't think you killed her yourself. That ridiculous theatrical set-up isn't your style, is it? And in any case, Peniel is sure you didn't; his own daughter, he was happy to employ her on your behalf to play dirty games – but no more than that. I may be wrong, but it seems to me unlikely that even a rat like Peniel would happily be an accessory to his daughter's murder. I had the impression that he had some feeling for her, even affection. Still, I think you can tell me some things that would interest me. Can't you? That's why I've come to invite you to have lunch with me. Do you like blanquette de veau? They have it today at a brasserie I know. There are usually German officers there, I should warn you, but that won't embarrass you, will it? Even though you are a patriot.'

*　　*　　*

'It's a difficult concept, isn't it?' Lannes said when he had greeted Fernand and asked to be given a table in the corner of the room, and they had settled themselves at it. 'Patriotism, I mean. Everyone's a patriot these days, aren't they, even if they are on opposite sides. But your game? I don't understand it. Indeed I have to say that I find it childish. First Léon, now Karim – what do you hope to achieve? Or do you just delight in mischief? And then you play games with me too, sending Peniel with these photographs and then sending other copies of them to the Boches. You want to compromise me, that's obvious, but to what purpose and on whose behalf? I'm really interested. Peniel gave me to understand that you were working with the Resistance, and that you were using Gabrielle as a fly trap. He convinced me at first, which isn't surprising since I knew you had used Léon to ensnare poor Schussmann, and then Karim told me you had spoken of a German officer with a taste for brown boys. And then there is Colonel von Feidler. But I've been thinking about it, and I'm not so sure because none of it makes sense. Not good sense anyway. That's why I thought we should have a chat. They have doubts about you in Vichy too, but I suppose you know that, since you were relegated to the office in Marseille. Can't do much harm pushing paper, they told me.'

Félix made no reply. He looked at ease, a smile on his face, one that gave a sense of superiority, security anyway, confidence that there was nothing to alarm or even disquiet him in Lannes' words. He didn't touch the glass of St-Emilion that Jacques had poured him, but dug his fork into the mushrooms à la Grecque. Lannes was content to wait. Silence was always a weapon, but one each was employing now against the other. The blanquette de veau arrived; it was as good as ever. They both ate without speaking, like chess players plotting the next move.

At last: 'Gabrielle was a bitch,' Félix said, 'but useful. Her death was a nuisance, believe me.'

A knight's move, leaping over other pieces on the board?

'It suits me, however, that you don't find her killer. Least said about the case the better. That's why I sent old Peniel to warn you off. I'm sorry you didn't take the message, continued to pursue the case. You've got me wrong, you know.'

'Have I? Tell me how then.'

'You think I'm a bastard, don't you?'

'You're not going to tell me I'm wrong there?'

'I don't give a damn. But you're a fool, Lannes. You pursue cases as if there was no war. It's crazy. Like you said, I'm a patriot. What I do is in the service of France. But you? What are you?'

'I'm a cop,' Lannes said. 'Raping boys – that's in the service of France, is it? Or just your private pleasure?'

'They're not important except for what they can do for me. My job is to compromise German officers – in the interest of France. Then they can be useful to us, sources of information. It's necessary. For France.'

'Oh yes, you found Schussmann useful?'

'I got him wrong. I admit that. I didn't think he'd be such a fool as to top himself. A pity. Your little Jew boy did well, but do you suppose he'd have done the job if I hadn't scared him shitless? As for the Arab rat, he's already selling his arse. For money. All I want is that he sells it for France. So there's this German officer I happen to know fancies brown boys. I supply him with one. Then he's mine. He belongs to me – and to France. As you said, I'm a patriot.'

But what do you mean by that, Lannes thought. He remembered Madame Roland about to die under the blade of the guillotine and saying, 'Liberty! – what crimes are committed in your name!' It was the same with patriotism. He distrusted, was repelled by, the big abstract nouns, justification for so much that was wicked. He had suggested to Bracal that Félix was mad, but perhaps he wasn't. Perhaps he was sane, horribly sane; accommodating himself to the reality of the world they were all condemned to live in. Perhaps he was mad himself to believe that things need not be what they were. Félix's next words seemed to confirm his fear.

'Nobody wants you to find out who killed Gabrielle. Not me, not the Germans, not Vichy, not the Resistance, not your superiors either. Only you, blundering foolishly in a dark wood where you are lost. You're pathetic, Lannes. Who do you think will win the war?'

The second time in two days that question had been put, but he had no wish to commit himself this time.

'I haven't the faintest idea', he said.

'Everything I do is intended to ensure that France is among the victors,' Félix said. 'Remember that.'

'So you say.'

Félix pushed his plate aside, emptied his glass, lit a cigarette, and said, 'It's not only that you don't understand, Lannes, it's that you don't want to. Vichy was necessary, is necessary even now because without it we would be powerless against the Germans. If they win the war, which is still probable, then we need a government here in France, we need Vichy. And meanwhile we need to have whatever influence over Germany and Germans that we can acquire. That's part of my job, information is power, and I collect information. But if Germany loses which, I admit, since the American invasion of North Africa and in view of what looks like stalemate on the Eastern front, is possible, more possible than before, what then?'

'What indeed?'

Lannes wondered how far Félix would go, to what extent he would expose himself. He was conceited enough to be rash.

'What then?' he said again.

'Well, it's more complicated.' Félix smiled. 'More complicated and more dangerous. There's the Resistance, first. How much do you know about it?'

Lannes made no reply.

'You know nothing. Let me tell you then. The heart and brains of the Resistance are to be found in the Communist Party, and the Reds take their orders from Moscow. That's why there was no Resistance, no real Resistance, till Hitler attacked the Soviet Union. You know that much, surely.'

Lannes looked around. The brasserie was empty now, and there was no risk of their being overheard.

'Then Stalin said "jump" and they began shooting Germans who naturally took reprisals. Doesn't worry the Reds of course. Not even if some of their own are shot. They want martyrs and they want a Revolution. So Vichy bears down on them. Fine by me. I need all the information about the Resistance I can get. Gabrielle was useful there too. Whoever killed her did me no service, I assure you. But then there's de Gaulle, Churchill's puppet. And the Americans who want to dismember the French Empire which Vichy defends and which only Vichy can defend. It's a narrow ledge we walk on, but everything – yes everything – indicates that we need Vichy if France is going to emerge from this war an independent State and neither a Russian nor Anglo-American satellite.'

He leant back in his chair. Everything in his words and attitude spoke of his self-belief and self-importance, perhaps also, Lannes thought again, of his derangement. He remembered what his first chief had once said: 'You can make a deal with villainy, but never with vanity. Villains are capable of seeing reason, the vain never.' But what if a man was both vain and villainous? Part of a policeman's craft lay in the ability to put yourself in the other man's shoes, read his mind, guess at his next move. But Félix baffled him. Did he believe the tripe he was talking, or was it all an act? It might be both. He had written himself a part and was speaking the lines he had given the character he was playing and which perhaps, as can happen, he had become. Whatever the truth this interview was futile. He signalled to Jacques to bring the bill.

'All that's beyond me,' he said. 'I'm a cop. My interest is in getting Gabrielle's murderer. I don't dabble in politics. Meanwhile you'll leave the boy Karim alone, and, if you're not out of Bordeaux by this time tomorrow, I'll arrest you on suspicion of involvement in Gabrielle's murder. There would be no limit to the time I could hold you. You were wrong in saying that my superiors don't care who killed her. I assure you they do. Indeed they want an arrest. They don't much mind who it is, but someone more substantial than poor Peniel. You'll do.'

He was taking a risk. He knew that. There were still the compromising photographs. Too bad. He suddenly didn't care. He had thought he might make a deal with Félix, but his old boss was right. It would be pointless to try.

XXIV

All the same he had mishandled things. He didn't know how, but he thought he should have taken a different line with Félix, even a sympathetic one, and shouldn't have let him see he disliked and distrusted him. But there it was. The man's arrogance offended him, did more than offend really; the relish with which he used people as pawns in his game was disgusting. He hoped Moncerre had managed to put a tail on him. It would be a pleasure to fulfil his threat and arrest the blighter if he didn't obey his order to leave Bordeaux.

He was reluctant to return to the office, equally reluctant to go home. There was nothing he wanted to do, nobody he wanted to see. Nobody? He pictured Yvette lazy on her bed, stretched out half naked, her legs open and inviting. Desire gripped him. He turned away towards the river, limping heavily, his hip painful. Mist was rising from the water. It began to rain. He leant on the parapet. Somewhere someone was playing an accordion, a dance tune. But there were no dancers. Gulls shrieked. Darkness closed around him.

When, hours later, he opened the door of their apartment, he was dismayed to hear his brother-in-law Albert's voice. I might have been spared that, he thought. It was months since he had visited them. The last time Albert, who still worked in the Mayor's office and had indeed recently been promoted, had questioned him, searchingly, about Alain. Where was he? Why had he left Bordeaux? What was he doing? Lannes had watched Marguerite refusing to meet her brother's eye. She picked up her knitting and said she had dropped a stitch. When she looked at Lannes, her face seemed etched with anxiety.

Now Lannes steeled himself to greet Albert in friendly fashion, said he was pleased to see him. A lie of course, but appearances have to be kept up within families. He was sure Albert didn't realise how deeply he disliked him.

Albert said, 'Naturally you've heard the news?'

'What news?'

'You haven't? It's terrible. The Admiral has been assassinated.'

Terrible news? Or good news? He didn't know. He had no time for Darlan, but . . .

'Fortunately,' Albert said, 'the assassin has been arrested. A young man, a student. That's all I know about it. The situation's confused. It seems that the Americans had accepted the Admiral as Head of a Provisional Government in Algiers, and that the Marshal had delegated all authority in North Africa to him. But the assassin's motive is unknown as is whoever put him up to it. We're all at a loss, and as for France, well, it's a disaster surely.'

A young man, a student . . .

'It's rumoured that he is a Gaullist,' Albert said. 'Nobody knows for sure, but it wouldn't surprise me. As you know, I've no opinion of de Gaulle; he's a traitor, condemned to death for desertion.'

A young man, a student, a Gaullist. Alain? Léon? Surely not, but . . . he lit a cigarette and found that his hands were trembling. There was that dark side to Alain, and the romantic desire to play a hero's part. The thought was absurd, the likelihood remote; he had no reason to think that the boys were still in North Africa, he hoped that, like Jérôme, they were safe in England – nevertheless . . .

'Others say the young man must be a Red,' Albert said. 'That's possible, certainly. These Communist swine in the Resistance are capable of anything. It might be the best solution, would open people's eyes to what they are really like. Yes, I hope it transpires that he's a Red. Whoever it is, I trust they shoot him, as I'm sure they will.'

They probably would. The situation in Algiers was, it seemed, fluid, as confused as a stage farce, but one that provoked no laughter. Investigation of the crime would embarrass many. Who could tell who might be involved? Better to shoot the boy and batten down the hatches. That's how they would think. Unless of course he was indeed a Communist? In which case they would shout his guilt and the complicity of the Party from the rooftops.

'I expect you're right, Albert,' he said.

When he had shown his brother-in-law out, he found Marguerite in tears.

'It couldn't be Alain, could it?' she said.

'Of course it couldn't. It's a ridiculous thought.'

But it wasn't ridiculous at all.

'Where's Clothilde,' he said.

'She went to her room to write an essay as soon as her uncle arrived. There's something wrong, Jean. She's unhappy. I do hope she and Michel haven't quarrelled. Seeing them together is the one good thing that has happened this year.'

'There's no reason to think they have, is there?' he said.

*   *   *

It was a long time since he had slept well, and he had been up, sitting in the kitchen, drinking the ersatz coffee and smoking, the ashtray already full of stubs, for more than an hour when Clothilde came into the room and kissed the top of his head.

'I love these dark winter mornings,' she said. 'I don't know why because I used to hate them when I was a child. Did you get rid of Uncle Albert easily?'

'Not easily, but eventually.'

'He always upsets Maman. That's why I took refuge in my room and went to bed early. Is it wrong of me to dislike him, seeing he's her brother?'

'Not wrong, darling. It's natural, I'd say. I've never cared for him myself. You're old enough now for me to admit that to you.'

'He always upsets Maman,' she said again.

She had gone to bed early, but there were dark circles under her eyes and her face was pale.

'Your mother thinks you're unhappy. She's afraid you have quarrelled with Michel. You haven't, have you?'

She tore a piece of bread off the loaf and dipped it in his coffee.

'You don't mind, do you? No, Maman's wrong. We haven't quarrelled, not exactly. How could we? We love each other, there's no doubt about that. You do like him, don't you, Papa?'

'Yes, I like him. But there's a but, isn't there? I see it in your face; hear it in your voice.'

She sat down, and breaking off another piece of bread, began to crumble it between her fingers.

'Yes, there's a but. I'm frightened. I'm afraid for him. He's determined to join this legion of French Volunteers against Bolshevism. He says it's his duty, his patriotic duty.'

'That's madness. It's ridiculous. Did you tell him you are afraid?'

'Yes.'

'And?'

She looked up meeting his eyes. Her own brimmed with tears.

'He kissed me, and told me not to be a goose. But I'm not a goose, am I?'

'No, darling, you're not a goose. Would you like me to speak with him?'

'I don't know,' she said. 'I don't know anything, not really, except that I love him.'

XXV

The Alsatian had never been industrious, was content to go through the motions. He kept his desk clear, submitted the necessary reports, which would be written, Lannes guessed, in opaque, non-committal language. However things turned out, he intended to be there in his post when it was all over, acceptable to whoever emerged on top, his copy book spotless. He was the perfect model of a functionary, doing just enough to pass muster, and careful to keep his nose clean. Lannes felt a mild contempt for him, rather liked him all the same, in dark moments wondered if after all he wasn't every bit as futile himself.

Schnyder was smoking one of the Havana cigars which Lannes still managed to get for him by way of Fernand and his black market, tobacco-smuggling connections. He was as ever beautifully dressed, making Lannes conscious of the shabbiness of his own suit which was seven or eight years old, the turn-ups of his trousers beginning to fray. At least Marguerite still ironed his shirts, he thought, irrelevantly, but the one he was wearing couldn't compare with the Alsatian's crisp cream-coloured cotton one. His shoes too were down-at heel; Schnyder's were highly polished – he was separated from his wife – did he brush them himself?

'I understand you saw that actress – what's her name? – Adrienne Jauzion,' he said. 'What was that about, Jean?'

The pretence that he wasn't sure of her name was ridiculous. Did he suppose Lannes didn't know he had been sniffing round her? But how had he learnt of their meeting? Perhaps he paid her maid to keep him informed of La Jauzion's doings?

'She had some information about the Gabrielle Peniel case,' he said.

'That surprises me. Was it useful?'

'Not really. The dead woman used to be her dresser, but what she had to tell me led nowhere.'

There was no need to mention Catherine Haget – Kiki – to Schnyder.

'Meanwhile,' he added, 'Judge Bracal has been questioning the man Peniel. I don't know if anything has come of that.'

'It sounds as if the case is going nowhere,' Schnyder said.

'It's certainly not moving fast, but we've eliminated certain lines of inquiry.'

'Good, good.'

It was clear the Alsatian wasn't interested, but something was worrying him.

'You've a son in Vichy, haven't you, Jean?'

'Yes, he's employed in one of their Youth programmes, seems to enjoy it. Says they are doing good work, and I suppose he's right. We're hoping he'll get leave, be home over Christmas.'

He was tempted to say, 'Why do you ask?' – but refrained. Whatever was worrying Schnyder, let him spell it out.

The Alsatian knocked the ash off his cigar, and drew on it.

'But you've another son,' he said.

'Yes.'

'And he's?'

'Not in Bordeaux.'

'Not in Bordeaux?'

Schnyder frowned.

'I don't want to know more,' he said. 'I value you, Jean, but you are making things difficult for me. People are asking questions about you. I think you'll know what I mean. When I say I don't want to know more, I mean I personally don't, but – you understand my position? I don't know where you stand.'

'As regards what?'

'I don't think I need to spell that out. Let's just say it's uncomfortable if one of my officers becomes an object of suspicion.'

'I'm a cop, that's all, a servant of the Republic, or the French State, whatever you like to call it. A cop investigating a murder, doing my job which, as you know, isn't an easy one. I can't think why I should be – what did you call it? – an object of suspicion. Am I entitled to ask who has been asking questions?'

'You may ask, but you'll understand that I can't give you an answer. All I'll say is this. One son in Vichy and the other . . . not in Bordeaux. You can't be surprised if that provokes questions. There's another thing too. I'd a complaint this morning. It came from one of our Services. You had lunch yesterday, it seems, with one of that Service's men and he has lodged a complaint, says you are harassing him. Now that's specific, he's important seemingly, someone they value. So what do you have to say? What should I reply? You understand my position. It's awkward.'

The sun had come out. Light streamed through the window. Particles of dust danced in the air. The Alsatian shifted in his seat. Lannes took a somewhat crushed packet of Gauloises from his pocket, extracted a cigarette, tapped it on his thumbnail, and lit it. Félix's complaint had come quickly. Probably he had spotted Moncerre's tail; interesting.

'I bought the chap lunch,' he said. 'I don't think that counts as harassment. Not in my book anyway. I had learnt that there was a connection with Gabrielle Peniel, and a closer one with the man who claims to be her father, the chap Judge Bracal has been examining. So I wanted to speak with him, but nothing useful came of it. This Service you speak of – they're spooks, aren't they? Well, we never get anywhere with the spooks, I learnt that a long time ago. I was wasting my time. At least that's what I thought, chasing up a blind alley . . . but now that he's apparently complained, I'm not so sure. Is the complaint formal? If so, I should answer it. In full. Is that what they want? If it is, then I might lodge a counter-complaint. Obstructing a policeman in the investigation of a crime. How would that sound?'

'I doubt if that's what they want.'

'Perhaps I should speak of this to Bracal,' Lannes said. 'He's the investigating judge, after all, who, as I say, has been examining the chap's acquaintance, the man Peniel. Do you think I should do that?'

'I don't think that would be necessary, Jean. I'll do what I can to smooth things over. But please don't embarrass me in this way again. We don't interfere with the Service. You must accept that as an order.'

Not even, Lannes didn't say, when they interfere with us?

All the same, Lannes knew that he would indeed find an opportunity to raise the matter with Bracal. You had to find a way of protecting your back, and it was obvious the Alsatian wasn't going to do that for him. Meanwhile he had other things on his mind, visits to make.

*   *   *

The old professor laid aside his book when the maid ushered Lannes into his study, first placing a ribbon in it to mark his place.

'I don't know why I bother to do this,' he said. 'I've read it so often that I sometimes think I could find my way about it blindfold. Indeed I read it only for – what shall I say? – consolation isn't the right word. But it's a book for all time and more peculiarly for ours, though it was written more than a hundred years ago.'

'What is it?'

'*La Charteuse de Parme*, to my mind the greatest French novel. You've read it of course, superintendent?'

'A long time ago,' Lannes said

'You should read it again. If only because of its sense of politics as a recurrently calculated readjustment of roles. For instance, even as the Prince persecutes the Republicans, he considers how he might be wise to seek to establish a relationship with them, and so effect a new balance of power. Isn't this a true picture of what is happening here in France now? A readjustment, or redistribution, of roles, with actors alert to the new part they will soon be playing. How else to account for the assassination of the Admiral? Very Stendhalian. But you haven't come to hear me chatter about literature. Why are you honouring me with a visit?'

'It's difficult to explain,' Lannes said.

'That wretched woman who was murdered? I can't think you suppose that either Anne-Marie or I can contribute anything to your investigation beyond what you have already learnt from her. So it's Michel?'

'Yes, it's Michel.'

The old man's lips moved. He pulled at his moustache, then, speaking as if his words came from far away, he said: 'One always fails when speaking about those one loves. He's a boy made to be happy and he's condemned to be young in our ruined France. Does that make sense?'

'I know what you mean. The same thought has occurred to me about all our young people, not only my own children.'

'I think, superintendent, you are too sensitive for your profession. Do you drink sherry? It's a taste I acquired when I did some research in England, at Cambridge, many years ago.'

He picked up a little hand-bell and rang it. The maid appeared and he asked her to bring the sherry decanter and two glasses from the dining room.

'There were always sherry parties there,' he said. 'It's a cerebral wine.'

Neither spoke till the maid had supplied them with a glass of the wine which was the colour of pale straw and had an astringent taste.

'Do you want to speak to Michel?'

'I think I may have to, but to you first, in the hope that . . . ' He paused. 'I like the boy. My daughter is in love with him, there's no doubt about that, and she is sure he loves her. It's first love for her, and perhaps for him too. I've nothing to complain of. With regard to that. First love, it's beautiful, but those who experience it are vulnerable. Peculiarly vulnerable it seems to me. I don't want Clothilde to be hurt.'

'And you think Michel will hurt her?'

'What he wants – intends – to do is hurting her.'

'I won't pretend I don't know what you mean. It distresses me too.'

'Can you prevent it? That's what I've come to ask.'

The professor laid his hand on the book which he had placed on the little table by his side.

'Michel's like Fabrice, Stendhal's hero,' he said. 'An ardent boy, an idealist, passionate, in search of adventure, not, I fear, very clever or possessed of good judgement. But . . . he doesn't listen to me. He's fond of me, even grateful to me, but he doesn't listen. I could tell him he's heading for disaster, careering towards the abyss, and he would dismiss my warning as coming from someone who has lived too long to know anything. The certainties of the young are frightening for one of my age. In the novel Fabrice alarms those who love him – it's also part of his attraction.'

As it was of Alain's, Lannes thought, feeling a new sharp stab of anxiety.

'Germany will lose the war,' Lannes said. 'I'm sure that's inevitable now, but there will be horrors before it does, and horrors here in France too. Can't you convince him of that?'

'Could you?'

'I don't know. Probably not. Would you like me to try?'

'Our poor France,' the professor said. 'She's devouring her children.'

XXVI

Léon was cold, but Paris was wonderful; even the pinched impoverished Paris under a low steel-grey sky was wonderful. The trees were bare. He adjusted his scarf and huddled into his thin overcoat. He was waiting, as he had been instructed, on a bench in the Luxembourg Gardens by the statue of the boy called *Le Marchand des Masques*. The boy who was naked except for shorts carved in such a way that they seemed to be moulded close-fitting to his buttocks was holding up a mask, as if inviting Léon to wear it. I don't need it, he thought. I'm nobody here; I don't exist as I was. I should be afraid, well I am afraid often, but I've never been more alive. The boy's so sure of himself and his beauty, no one would refuse him; he's like Alain, that last morning in the dawn when we embraced and he got into the car and I watched it lose itself in the mist. Paris is full of Germans, there's danger everywhere, and I've never been happier. It's absurd.

He picked up his newspaper. It was the collaborationist *Je suis partout* which he had been told to carry. It was disgusting, everything in it was disgusting, except for the literary articles, and even some of them were repulsive too, but it didn't matter; I'm alive, he thought, in Paris, and happy.

The girl approached. She wore an ankle-length black coat and a ridiculous perky fur hat.

'I like your choice of newspaper,' she said.

'It's the voice of our times,' he replied.

The obligatory exchange amused him. It was unnecessary. After all, they'd done this before. But you stuck by the rules. They'd hammered that into him. Into her too of course. And there was another response he had been given to use if he scented danger.

She leant forward and kissed him on the cheek.

'Gosh, your face is cold. Are you all right?'

'But of course.'

'Put your arm round me,' she said. 'There's a policeman over there. Remember we're lovers. I think he's watching us. He followed me into the gardens. Now kiss me. On the lips.'

He held her close, nuzzled her ear. She screwed round and whispered, 'You're shy with girls, aren't you? I can always tell.'

'He's moving away,' he said. 'It's all right. I expect he just fancied you and is disappointed now.'

She disengaged herself.

'It's not just shyness, is it? Never mind. It doesn't matter. Has he really gone? I don't want to turn round.'

'He's gone.'

'Right then.'

She took an envelope from her bag.

'This is urgent,' she said. 'They want it off today. It's coded of course, so it doesn't make sense, but it's important.'

'Isn't it strange,' he said, 'that we do this and we don't know what it is we are doing and we don't know each other, and never will, but yet are colleagues?'

'That's how it is. It's best that's how it is.'

*　　*　　*

Jérôme certainly wasn't lonely – quite the reverse; much in demand, his social life busy, enjoyable too, in this bomb-battered London where everything was provisional. They'd found him a room in Charlotte Street, and every night there were pubs to go to and often a party after closing time. Being French was an advantage because everyone knew the Free French were kept supplied with Algerian wine, and so he always had a bottle to take along, which he did the more willingly since he drank hardly anything himself. The RAF boy Max, who seemed to be Edwin Pringle's lover, was friendly, had even, it seemed, taken a fancy to him, and they laughed about Pringle together. Max had been a dancer before the war – 'Chorus-line, darling,' he said – and took him to theatrical parties. He had an American accent but British passport, which, he said, is 'why I'm a soldier of the King, or rather one of his boys in blue'. He was stationed somewhere out of London but this scarcely seemed to inhibit his social activities. They had gone to bed a couple of times because, as Max said, 'Why not? I'm training to be air crew in bombers, and so who knows what Fate – that big word in inverted commas – has in store for me?' On the other hand there were no emotional complications because Max had always gone for older men though 'Edwin's a joke, the old sweetie, I admit that, and before him I was crazy about a guy in the Foreign Office who decided it was all wrong and he would deny himself sex, not for religious reasons you understand, but because he's a Communist or at least what they call a fellow traveller. It's all right being that now, of course, since Stalin has become everybody's Uncle Joe. Poor lamb – my friend, that is, not Stalin – this self-denial, abstinence, makes him even more miserable, but that's life.' This led Jérôme to tell him about the Fascist boy in Bordeaux, and they sighed and giggled together. Accordingly when Edwin Pringle invited him to his Christmas house party, Jérôme checked first that Max would be there, which meant there was no danger for him, and accepted.

There were days, many of them, when he felt guilty himself, to be happy and having fun in London when Alain and Léon were God knows where in France, and in danger, but that's how it was. He went to the office every morning and wrote the pieces he was told to write, and made his broadcasts once a week, and was assured he was doing good work that was valued. It might be true, he didn't know, and in any case, it was the work he was assigned to and he was serving France, and the idea of a France that would be free again, as best he could. It wasn't what he had dreamt of when they had taken the train out of Bordeaux, and, often waking early, cold and looking out at a London that was still dark and gloomy and often enveloped in dense fog, he felt ashamed and inferior to Léon and Alain, but he accepted that what made him ashamed also brought relief.

The truth is, he said then, that I'm really a coward, a pansy coward who enjoys life and is afraid of danger; and in this mood he began to write a novel.

*   *   *

Alain waited, as instructed, by the statue of Louis XIV in the Place Bellecour, 'under the horse's tail'. To his surprise he recognised the man who approached him: he had known him in the training camp in England as Robert Palisson. He was both a cynic and a fire-eater, a hook-nosed man of the Right who despised Vichy. Now he held out his hand and said, 'So you're Clovis now. I've become Raoul. Welcome to Lyon, welcome to the absurdity of Occupied France. Have you eaten? No? Good. I'm starving.'

He led him to a bistro in the Place Morand. The patron showed them into a back room where none of the dozen tables was occupied.

'You'll be all right here, Raoul,' he said. 'But you'd better give me your ration tickets. I have to account for everything, sod it. There's sausages and lentils. All right? And a flask of Beaujolais.'

When they were alone and eating, Raoul said, 'And so, my little Clovis, here we are in our beautiful France, and tell me, how do you find the Resistance?'

'I'm confused,' Alain said.

'That's a good beginning. That's the best beginning. Let me tell you, there is not a single Resistance. There are many. First of all there are the Communists who distrust those of us who come from London, and would rather do without us, but can't because they need the money we alone can supply. They're devoted to Resistance but you can't, my dear Clovis, trust them an inch because they're all waiting for the happy day when they can launch the Revolution and cut our throats. Apart from that they're splendid chaps. As of course are members of other Resistance groups who started off in Vichy and still revere the Marshal and have convinced themselves – some of them anyway – that he has always seen Vichy as a holding operation, no more than that. And then there are all the part-timers, the "after hours Resisters" I call them. You have to under-stand their position. They're in work, have offices, shops or factories to go to, a home to return to with their wife and children. They live under their own identity unlike you and me, and, though they're sincere – oh, no doubt they're sincere – belonging to the Resistance? Well, it's a snob thing really for some of them, and for others, the optimists, putting down a marker for life after the war when they can show off their good conduct medals. And then – have some more wine, these sausages aren't bad, are they, whatever they're made of, better not ask the patron – there's the politicians. All they want to do is print newspapers, distribute tracts and prepare for their political future. And get money from us, of course, to do all that. Basically they're shits. But sometimes useful shits, even if they have been blown towards Resistance only as the winds of the world have shifted. And then finally there's us, the Gaullists from London, and we've got to control them all, otherwise it's not just us, but France, that is in the shit. Is that clear, or are you still confused?'

'It's very clear and it leaves me more confused than ever,' Alain said.

'Good boy. You're catching on. I should get you a gun. You don't have one yet, do you?'

'No, I don't. But tell me, what's my role? Nobody's really explained anything properly.'

'Now there's a surprise. Let's just say, you're assigned to me as my right-hand man, and don't worry, we're going to have some fun. Some day, if we survive – big if of course – we'll look back on these days as the happiest of our lives.'

*   *   *

'It's so kind of your mother to say she's happy to have me stay with you over Christmas,' Maurice said, 'but are you sure she really means it? Wouldn't she rather have you to herself alone?'

'Not at all,' Dominique said. 'She was delighted when I asked if you might come, and Maman never pretends, she's utterly honest and sincere. Anyway she likes you, and so does Papa.'

'Well, I'm delighted too. I love the work we're doing – well, you know that, you love it yourself – and it's valuable and important, but we both need a break, a holiday even if it's only for a few days. The kids are splendid but they're wearing, you can't deny that.'

'I wouldn't even try to. There's just one thing, Maurice. Alain, you know what I've told you which isn't much, because I don't know much myself, and I've refrained from asking questions – it's better that way – but I think he's not to be mentioned. Papa may speak to me about him, I don't know, but otherwise, well otherwise, there's a veil of silence. You understand? It's awkward and, I think, painful.'

Maurice looked very grave.

'Of course I'll ask no questions. I can see it's difficult. Like so much now, almost everything I sometimes fear. My own father, as you know he's always frightened me rather, but it sometimes seems to me he's frightened himself now, frightened of what the future may bring, I mean. I'm looking forward to seeing your parents again; they were so kind to me when I was in trouble. And your sister of course.'

'Clothilde? Oh yes, I wouldn't mind having you as a brother-in-law. I'm not joking. You're my best friend after all. Almost my only real one actually. So what could be more appropriate?'

The train drew out of the station. Vichy would soon be left behind as the December afternoon darkened and snow fell on the hills.

XXVII

So he would speak to Michel, that was agreed. The boy's grand-father had gone so far as to say that it would be a weight off his mind – 'Even though,' he added, 'I reproach myself for, as it were, failing in what should be my duty myself. But that's how it is. I'm what they call a back number, in the boy's eyes, a relic of a dead civilisation. I don't think I exaggerate. So if you will shoulder the responsibility . . . '

'After all,' Lannes said, 'it's on behalf of my daughter too.'

Suppose the silly boy did indeed join this Legion of French

Volunteers and was killed on the Eastern Front, as was all too probable, would Clothilde in time forget him – as most things, even the worst, are forgotten – or would it blight her life? He hadn't tried to deter Alain from joining de Gaulle's Free French, even though he knew how this would distress Marguerite.

He swung his blackthorn stick as if beheading an imaginary thistle. Damn these politicians who on account of their vanity and with vast carelessness for the lives of others had loosed Hell on the world.

If the boy wasn't killed, could he ever return to France after Germany had been defeated, and, if he did, what would be his fate? Years in prison, at best.

Moncerre and young René were in the inspectors' room next to his office and both got to their feet when they saw him.

'Me first,' Moncerre said, and followed him into his own room.

'That chap you told me to put a tail on,' he said. 'He's a pro, spotted it, and my man lost him. Sorry. I've given him a bollocking of course.'

'It probably doesn't matter,' Lannes said. 'It's interesting, though. He was sufficiently alarmed to call his superiors in Vichy or Marseille and have them get the Alsatian to warn us off. He's a pro, as you say, a spook, as you may have guessed.'

'I can't stand spooks, they always bugger everything up. So, do we?'

'Do we what?'

'Lay off him.'

'Oh, I don't think so. He was using Gabrielle – and others – and this concerns us. He'll turn up again, if, that's to say, he ignores my order to get out of Bordeaux, and when he does, you can have a word with him. He's playing games with us, and I don't care for that.'

Moncerre began filling his pipe. He pushed the tobacco down with his thumb, and struck a match.

'I'm at a loss, chief. I don't know what the hell you are talking about, not really. It might help if you didn't keep your cards close to your chest. Then I wouldn't be feeling my way in the dark.'

He drew on his pipe, and emitted two little puffs of smoke.

Lannes smiled and said he wasn't sure he had any cards. Instead he took the bottle of Armagnac from his cupboard and poured them both a glass. He handed one to Moncerre who downed it straightaway, and told him to fetch young René in.

The boy was excited, a little pink in the cheeks, and looked, as he sometimes did, like a schoolboy about to present what he knew, or at least hoped, was good work to his master. It pleased Lannes to think that there was still something fresh and puppyish about him, and that he hadn't yet been worn down by the demands and disappointments of their job.

'I think I've got somewhere,' he said. 'At last.'

Moncerre glanced at Lannes, raised an eye, picked up the bottle and refilled his glass.

'I don't know of course,' René said, 'but it's like this. I did a round of all her pupils again, as you asked me to. Most were still unwilling to say anything, and perhaps had nothing to say, and I don't mind admitting I was losing hope and on the point of agreeing with Moncerre here that it was all pointless and that we weren't going to get anywhere. Then – you remember Madame Duvallier, chief, and her daughter Charlotte who told you of the suggestion Gabrielle had made to her – well, I got nowhere with the mother once again, indeed she was like a brick wall, insisting she had nothing to say, and I was just about to leave, thinking it was all futile, when her husband came in. He's a doctor, quite a well-respected, even distinguished physician indeed, I've checked up on that. To my surprise when we had been introduced and his wife insisted again she had nothing to add and I was to tell my chief to stop bothering her or she would lodge a complaint, he said he would see me out because he had to go to the tabac having forgotten to get tobacco for his pipe. Well, I suspected this was an excuse to speak to me alone, and so it proved, because he said he had something to tell us – 'Oh, not a confession, nothing like that,' he laughed, – but I don't know, he was decidedly edgy, I thought. Anyway we made an appointment for him to come here this afternoon, at four o'clock. What do you think, chief, is that all right.'

*   *   *

Dr Duvallier was on time, which made Lannes wonder if he was eager or anxious. He allowed René to take his Homburg hat and dark velvet-collared overcoat, settled himself in the chair opposite Lannes' desk, and began to fill his pipe from a leather tobacco pouch. His hands were steady but a few wisps of tobacco fell on to his waistcoat. He smiled, and said, 'I feel I should apologise for my delay in speaking to you, superintendent, and indeed I would reproach myself if I had realised sooner how things stood. But you must understand I knew nothing of the circumstances of Madame Peniel's death till very recently. You may find that hard to believe, or indeed understand, but the fact is that I gave up reading the newspapers the day the Armistice was signed, and my wife did not tell me of your own visit, superintendent. You may find that also difficult to believe, but the truth is that Madame Duvallier prefers not to speak of what she finds distressing or unpleasant. She suffers from anxiety, you understand. Consequently it was only a few days ago that I learnt of what Charlotte had told you and of the allegations relating to Madame Peniel. Perhaps I should say that Charlotte is my stepdaughter, the child of my wife's first marriage. Her father was one of my closest friends, we were like brothers indeed as well as being colleagues, and when he knew he was dying he told me it was his dearest wish that I should care for his widow and daughter. But Charlotte and I are not easy together. She's a difficult girl, withdrawn, and one who resents me as an interloper. You understand?'

'Are you suggesting that she wasn't speaking the truth when she told me of Madame Peniel's improper suggestions?'

Duvallier applied a match to his pipe and puffed vigorously.

'Not at all, not at all. I wouldn't accuse the girl of lying, perhaps not even embroidering. Exaggerating perhaps, because I have to say that the story she told you surprises me. I had known Gabrielle, Madame Peniel, for a long time; she is one of my patients – was one of them, I suppose I should say – and she always seemed a lady of the utmost respectability. However, that's irrelevant. My reason for coming here is quite different. She consulted me a few days, perhaps a week, before her unfortunate death, complaining of insomnia, anxiety, loss of appetite. I diagnosed a condition of hypertension – not remarkable, certainly not uncommon, in these terrible times. I prescribed a simple sedative, a placebo really, such as I have often found effective, and, to be honest with you, super-intendent, thought no more of it. You must understand that I have many patients and quite a few of them in a comparable state of distress or anxiety. Indeed I would go so far as to say that there is an epidemic of anxiety, the causes of which are not identifiably personal. You understand?'

Lannes lit a cigarette. An epidemic of anxiety? Who was free of that? Marguerite might be said to be one of the sufferers, but . . .

'And you identified no objective reason for her state of mind?' he said.

'None at all, and now I reproach myself. I'm a conscientious doctor, as I'm sure my patients would confirm, but, like so many in my profession, I'm overworked, all the more so because, as you will know, so many doctors here in Bordeaux were Jews who are now forbidden to practise. Consequently one may give in to the temptation to seize hold of the simplest explanation, as, in this case, I confess I did. It is only now that I have concluded that the poor woman may have been afraid, and evidently had reason for her fear. This distresses me. You understand?'

'Perfectly,' Lannes said. 'Your distress is indeed understandable. However, I notice that you referred to her as Gabrielle. Does this mean that you knew her socially as well as professionally? Were you friends, or perhaps more than friends? Please don't be offended by the question.'

The doctor smiled.

'I am not someone who takes offence easily. Your question is natural, eminently reasonable, superintendent. But the answer is "no". If I spoke of her as Gabrielle, that is because it is how I first knew of her when she was dresser to Madame Jauzion, who is also one of my patients, one of my most distinguished patients, as I'm proud to say.'

'And then Madame Jauzion dismissed her,' Lannes said. 'Do you know why?'

'That was no concern of mine, and I have to say that Gabrielle never spoke of it. Indeed it was only subsequently that she became my patient, and, if she said anything, which she may not have, for naturally it was none of my business, it was only to imply that she preferred to pursue her career as a music teacher. In which, as you will have gathered, I'm sure, she was very successful. That was why I recommended her to my wife when Charlotte expressed a desire to learn the piano. Which now, regrettably, seems to have been a mistake on my part, as I'm ready to admit. How rarely, superintendent, do even the most insightful of us know other people as well as we suppose we do! No doubt this is a conclusion that you will have reached as a policeman. Which brings me to my other reason for presenting myself here. I fear that you and your young inspector here may have formed a poor opinion of my wife, may indeed have thought her obstructive. I wish to apologise on her behalf. Madame Duvallier is a very private person who resents what she perceives as intrusion in her life. But I ask you not to judge her by her manner. She too is a prey to anxiety. I think that is all I need say.'

Lannes thanked him for coming. Then, as René rose to hold out the doctor's hat and coat, said, 'One other thing. I wonder if Madame Jauzion's uncle, the advocate Labiche, is another of your patients?'

Duvallier, one arm in his coat, turned to look Lannes in the face.

'I fail to understand the relevance of your question which, however, I am happy to answer. Certainly he is and a most distinguished personage, as you will know. However, we have few dealings. His health is excellent.'

'Not another who suffers from anxiety then?'

'Certainly not.'

He allowed René to help him into his coat.

'If I am permitted to ask,' he said, 'are you making progress? Are you close to discovering who killed the unfortunate woman in what was, I gather, such an appalling way?'

'You may ask, of course,' Lannes said, 'but we too have our professional secrets.'

'Of course. I understand perfectly.'

When he left, Moncerre said, 'That question wasn't an afterthought.'

'No, I don't think it was. I really don't think it was. And I find it improbable that he didn't learn the circumstances of Gabrielle's death – as he put it – till recently. Which makes his real reason for coming here a matter of some interest to us.'

XXVIII

Bracal's long fingers tapped a little tune on his desk, a habit, Lannes had observed, when he was thinking. At last he said, 'I got nothing from the man Peniel, I'm sorry, even ashamed, to say. He's a wretched type, obviously, and you usually find that there comes a time when fellows of that sort crack under questioning. You'll know that yourself of course. Anyway I've handed him over to the Vice Squad, and they've banged him up. So he's available whenever you think you may want him again. He can't do a disappearing act.'

'I've a notion,' Lannes said, 'that he may feel safer where he is.'

'Perhaps, perhaps. You probably understand the type better than I do.'

This was doubtless true. Like all investigating magistrates, Bracal would have little experience of getting his hands dirty. They dealt with crime as if it was an abstract proposition. In common with most policemen Lannes had been accustomed to feel a mild contempt for these gentlemen in well-cut suits who never had to descend into the gutter, but supposed they could solve cases from their desks – and this without any of the understanding, which comes from practical experience, of the dark impulses that may bring a man to the point of murder. Nevertheless, Bracal was one of the better ones. Lannes had come to find him sympathetic, even to respect him.

'Things are going to get worse,' Bracal said, 'before they get better. Which I'm sure they will, even though better times for France may prove difficult for those of us who've stuck to our posts and done our duty as we perceive it in these dark years. I don't deceive myself about that. Collaboration has been imposed upon us. We're compromised. Which is why I would advise you to turn a blind eye to anything, in this case or another, which seems to involve the Resistance. I'm speaking as a friend, Jean, if you will allow me to call myself that, not as your superior.'

He got up and poured them each a glass of cognac, as before drowning his own in soda water.

'It's going to be a strange Christmas,' he said, 'a miserable one for many. What are your plans?'

'My son Dominique came home yesterday for the holiday, bringing a friend with whom he works in Vichy. The boy's father's a minister there. Edmond de Grimaud. You probably know of him.'

'Indeed, yes, I used to subscribe to the review he edited. On account of the literary pages, which were of high quality, rather than its politics. Your son's happy in his work?'

'I believe so.'

Bracal's fingers resumed their little tune.

'It's a mess, isn't it?' he said. 'So much idealism, so much folly. I trust your son is not too committed. It's going to be so difficult to come out of this well.'

For a little neither spoke. There were such silences, unavoidable silences, Lannes thought, all over France. You were tempted to say just what you thought, and then put the temptation aside. Bracal was probably worried that he had already gone too far in what he had said about the Resistance and about his lack of enthusiasm for the political line taken by Edmond de Grimaud's review. He had spoken 'as a friend', but nobody could be sure of how far friendship might stretch. What could any of them take on trust?

'Vichy has lost North Africa,' Bracal said, picking up his glass and sipping the brandy-and-soda. 'That seems clear. The assassination of the Admiral was convenient for all sorts of people. For everybody really. Nevertheless, the Germans are still here. There's going to be no early end to the Occupation. We have a difficult year ahead, perhaps more than a year. Some day the Americans, and I suppose the British too, will try to form what I believe they are calling the Second Front against Germany here in France, but that day is a long way off, I fear. I don't think I need say any more. I may already have said too much. You understand? Meanwhile what are your immediate plans?'

'I think I'll have another chat with our friend Peniel.'

'I wish you luck with that one. You think the case is still worth pursuing? You intend to get to the bottom of it?'

'But naturally. What else should I do?'

He didn't say what he had often thought: that it was only by continuing his investigation as if there was neither war nor Occupation that he could maintain his self-respect, even perhaps – the thought came to him – his sanity.

'It's taken a turn,' he said, and recounted the conversation with Dr Duvallier. 'The more I think of it, the more it puzzles me, and I even begin to wonder if I have been approaching the case from the wrong angle, and that the involvement of the spook who calls himself Félix may have been a red herring. One of my inspectors, Moncerre, has insisted from the first that it was what he calls an old-fashioned pre-war crime, by which he means that it is a private domestic affair, nothing to do with the war or the Resistance. I should say I've no evidence to support this view. Yet it's tempting to incline towards it.'

This wasn't true, or not quite true. He really had no opinion on the matter, but he had been afraid that he would be ordered to set it aside; and Bracal's disordered manner had sharpened this fear.

'Duvallier?' Bracal said. 'The name means nothing to me. But if this is your line, well, it seems harmless to pursue it.'

There was a knock on the door. Bracal's clerk came in and said that the German officer charged with liaison, Lieutenant Schuerle, would like to see the judge. Bracal sighed and assented.

'Carry on, then, Jean,' he said.

As Lannes rose to leave the office, Schuerle extended his hand and smiled.

'Superintendent Lannes,' he said, 'I trust I haven't importunately interrupted your meeting? In any case it's a pleasure to see you. I would be interested to have another conversation. Perhaps we can arrange that very soon? After Christmas perhaps? Meanwhile I offer you the compliments of the season.'

'And to you,' Lannes said.

He looked at his watch as he descended the wide marble staircase. He had made an appointment to meet Michel for lunch at the Café Régent. He was late already. He hoped the boy would not have gone away.

XXIX

Michel was alone on the terrace, his head bent over a newspaper. It was a bright day, bitterly cold, a keen wind blowing from the east, but he was wearing only a dark-coloured jerkin over an open-necked blue shirt. Lannes paused and watched him for a moment. It was going to be a difficult conversation and he wished it wasn't necessary. The old waiter, Georges, approached. They shook hands and Lannes said they would eat inside. Hearing his voice, Michel looked up and got to his feet. Lannes was again conscious of his beauty. No wonder Clothilde was in love with the boy. But it was disturbing, this Aryan poster-boy perfection.

'I hope I haven't kept you waiting.'

'It's no matter, sir. I was content reading.'

The newspaper was *Je suis partout*, which Lannes despised and detested.

'There's a wonderful article by Robert Brasillach.'

'Ah yes, he used to write well about the cinema and Clothilde's mother has enjoyed his novels.'

No point in saying he loathed the violent language and anti-Semitism of this devoted advocate of ever-closer Collaboration, or even that he suspected Brasillach was one of those intellectuals for whom words are a drug so powerful that they become so completely divorced from reality that he didn't consider that what he wrote might have consequences in the real world of action, not opinion.

The plat du jour was a cassoulet which would undoubtedly be mostly beans. Lannes handed over his ration tickets, a required formality that Fernand usually dispensed with at his brasserie, in his case anyway. He ordered a half-litre of the house Médoc which he knew to be much better than many expensive bottled wines.

'Clothilde's brother Dominique has arrived from Vichy. He's very eager to meet you.'

'Me likewise.'

It was difficult to know how to begin. He would be saying things which Michel would not want to hear and which it was probable the boy would resent, thinking he was not entitled to speak to him in this way. And yet if he was really serious with regard to Clothilde, Lannes was entitled to have his say. Nevertheless, while they ate he spoke of Dominique's work.

Then, 'We don't know each other well,' he said, 'but Clothilde's mother has become very fond of you, and as for Clothilde.'

'She's wonderful, and Madame Lannes' – his face brightened in a dazzling smile – 'Madame Lannes has been so kind and welcoming to me.'

'But,' Lannes said, 'Clothilde has told me of your ambition, of what you want to do, and it frightens her. It alarms your grandfather too, and I have a great respect for him. You know what I'm talking about, don't you?'

'Naturally. But what can I say? I adore Clothilde – my intentions towards her are entirely honourable, I assure you of that – but she's a girl, a young woman, and women don't understand these things. As for my grandfather, I have of course a deep affection for him – he has been so kind to my sister Anne-Marie and me, and I respect him – but he's old and, again with all due respect, he's out-of-date, he doesn't understand the world as it is today or the plight that France finds itself in. So for me it's a matter of duty. You will surely understand that, sir.'

Lannes stretched out his hand to pick up the boy's newspaper.

'This thing, it's all wrong, you know. No matter how well it is written, it's wrong.'

'You don't believe that France and Germany should work together and that only an alliance between our two great countries can guard us against the Red menace?'

'I'm a policeman,' Lannes said, 'not a politician, and as a policeman, a servant of the Republic, I have no political opinions, but as a private man, a citizen, I can say that, yes, I agree that France and Germany should work together, and indeed, as an officer of the French State, I am required to collaborate with the Occupying forces. But I do this from duty, not from choice. It's difficult to explain.'

He laid down the newspaper and took hold of his wine glass but didn't lift it to his lips.

'A long time ago,' he said, 'well before the war, Monsieur Laval remarked that France would always have a border with Germany, that they were a nation of seventy million people to our forty million, and that we must either come to an agreement with them or fight them every generation. He was a pacifist in those days, Monsieur Laval. Perhaps in his heart he still is. No matter: he was right. 1870, 1914, 1939 – it shouldn't go on. But what did he mean by Germany? Hitler wasn't then yet in power. There's another Germany, a different Germany, that we might be friends with. But with Hitler there's no equality of friendship – the relation is that of master and servant.'

Michel frowned but said nothing. Lannes thought, at least he's listening.

'I'm going to say something, Michel, that you won't agree with, something indeed that would get me in trouble if you reported it. But you won't do that, not only because you love Clothilde – I'm sure of that – but also because I believe you have a sense of honour. It's this: Germany is going to lose the war. It's become inevitable. The Wehrmacht is fighting hard on the Eastern Front, but its advance has evidently been checked, and, now that the Americans have entered the war, Hitler is doomed. It may take some time, years even, but it's certain. If you do as you intend, and enlist in this Legion of French Volunteers against Bolshevism, you are joining the losing side. You might be killed – well, that can happen to anyone in wartime – and it would distress Clothilde. It might break her heart. I don't know, but I'm sure it would leave a wound which would never be wholly healed. I ask you to think of that. But if you are not killed, if you survive, what then? I know the French. We don't forgive easily; we've a lust for revenge. It's always been like that. Think of the Revolution and of the Commune. There are many who will be ashamed of how they have behaved during the Occupation and they will seek to expunge their shame by turning on those who have collaborated more conspicuously with the enemy. And this is to say nothing of the Resistance.'

He paused to light a cigarette and found that his hands were shaking. He pushed the packet of Gauloises towards the boy who took one and held out his face for a light. Lannes knew he had to speak of Sigi de Grimaud. He hesitated, unsure of how to do so. He had seen Michel look at him and read hero-worship, even infatuation, in his gaze.

'It's not true,' he said, 'that men are divided into two classes, masters and slaves, as I've heard your friend Sigi assert. Most are neither, merely men – and women – who seek to make the best of things, even when they've been dealt a poor hand. You're an idealist, I think. Perhaps your friend Sigi is an idealist too, among other things' – murderer and crook, he thought, but didn't say. 'It's natural to be an idealist when you're young, natural and even right. But idealists can do great harm, because idealism clashes with the reality of things. That's why most of us grow out of it. Ideals rarely accord with reality. And as for the Communists – the Red menace you spoke of – I don't like them either; they're idealists themselves also. They believe in absolute truth, as perhaps in his way your friend Sigi does too. But there's no absolute truth. I've learnt that as a policeman.'

He drew on his cigarette. Smoke swirled between them. He almost said 'love, friendship and family – these are the things that really matter' and then he thought of how his relations with Marguerite were strained because he had betrayed her by doing nothing to stop Alain – that other idealist – from joining de Gaulle; and he wondered if he was a hypocrite.

So instead he said, 'I'm asking you only to think of what I've been saying, also to remember how you will hurt Clothilde and your grandfather and sister too if you persist in your intentions. Meanwhile we look forward to seeing you over Christmas. Dominique is eager to meet you.'

He gestured to Georges who brought him the bill.

'I have to get back to work,' he said. 'One more thing: I was talking recently with a German officer who also believes that Germany has already lost the war and that Hitler is leading his country to ruin. It was rash of him to say so of course. Courageous too. It always takes courage to look reality in the face because it's much easier to believe that reality will accommodate itself to our wishes.'

He got up. They shook hands. Then Lannes laid his hand on the boy's shoulder.

'Please,' he said.

He turned at the door. Michel's head was bent over his newspaper again. Was it too much to hope that he might be reading it more sceptically? Probably yes; nobody changes his fixed opinion because of one conversation, and nobody likes to be told that he is walking blindfolded towards disaster. He was afraid, horribly afraid, that he was going to have to speak to Sigi, to urge him to free Michel from his influence. And what could he offer in exchange?

XXX

He had spoken of getting back to work, but he had three visits to make that afternoon, and only one of them could, strictly speaking, be characterised as work.

He went first to the rue des Remparts because it was the nearest to the Place Gambetta. He felt guilty because he hadn't been there for some time, but then, he thought, what wasn't an occasion for guilt these days?

When Miriam joined them and took her place in what was evidently her accustomed chair, it occurred to Lannes that after these months together, since she took refuge there, she and Henri were coming to look like a long-married couple. Perhaps, if they survived, they would indeed marry. It would be like coming into harbour after a stormy voyage. Henri indeed looked better, despite wartime privations, than he had since his young wife Pilar – another damned idealist! – had left him to engage in the Spanish war from which she had never returned. Did Henri, he wondered, suspect that she had betrayed him, as indeed she had by becoming the mistress of Edmond de Grimaud, though, to complicate matters further, she had done so for political reasons, at the command, he believed, of her party chiefs, in order to betray him too? De Grimaud who was, absurdly, Miriam's stepson, though a man of her own age and one who, by her account, had tried to get her too into his bed.

Thinking of these things, wheels within wheels, as Henri opened a bottle of white wine, he said, 'Dominique is home for Christmas. Since you're his godfather, he will want to come to see you.'

'But of course, it would be a pleasure. You know how fond I am of the boy.'

'Young Maurice is with him. They're good friends, as you know. However . . . '

The same thought, he was sure, rippled through the silence. Miriam was in hiding. Maurice was a nice boy. A sweet boy, she had called him, and he had spoken gratefully of how she had behaved to him when the old count was alive, but could he be trusted to say nothing of her presence? Could anyone be trusted, these days, with anything?

'He's been more than a year in Vichy,' he said. 'He's sure to ask about you.'

Miriam covered her face with her hands, rubbed them up and down.

'I'm not in real danger,' she said. 'They're not deporting French Jews, are they?'

'Not yet.'

'Well then . . . if we can't trust those we are fond of, everything's finished.'

'Gaston liked him, didn't he?' Henri said. 'They talked literature together, didn't they? Wasn't the boy one of his pupils – his real pupils, I mean? The boy brought him his poems for criticism as I recall. Gaston thought highly of him, said he would be a real poet.'

Toto, the little French bulldog snuffled, shook himself, got to his feet, and looked up at Henri inviting him to scratch the back of his head.

'Miriam's right,' Henri said, responding to Toto's demand. 'Everything makes me nervous these days, but she's right. If we can't trust people we're fond of, then nothing is any good.'

If only it was that simple, Lannes thought. The truth is, we are all too tired to think straight, and no decision is safe.

'You look bruised, Jean, exhausted,' Henri said. 'Have you discovered who killed that unfortunate woman? Or can't you say?'

Lannes picked up his wine glass and sighed.

'I'm lost in a maze. Do you happen to know of a Dr Duvallier? He was her doctor. I'm told he is a fashionable physician. He came to see me, ostensibly to tell me she had been suffering from anxiety. But it wasn't anxiety that killed her.'

Miriam looked up.

'Duvallier? He was – may still be – Jean-Christophe's doctor. He used to give him injections – for anxiety again, he said. I don't know what the injections were, but he came to the house once when I was ill and examined me. I didn't care for him. He had wandering hands. My husband, the old count, threw him out that day, said he was a scoundrel. But then he said that of so many, it probably didn't mean anything. Still, he's not someone I would trust.'

*   *   *

'Yes, you'll find her in,' the concierge said. 'To tell you the truth, superintendent, I'd rather she was no longer one of my tenants. She's brought a German officer home more than once, and I've told her we can't have that here. This is a respectable house, I said. To tell you the truth, I would have told her to pack her bags and be gone; only she broke down in tears when I reproached her, and, well, I've a soft heart, whatever you may think, and she's an unhappy girl. The number of empty wine bottles, I needn't say more. If you can talk some sense into her, I'd be grateful.'

She was a long time in opening the door and when she did so she looked at Lannes as if she had never seen him before. Then she nodded, vaguely, and stood aside to let him enter. She was wearing a thin blouse which revealed her breasts and her skirt hung squint. There were dark circles under her eyes and when she went to pull the cork from a bottle of wine which was already half empty her hands shook.

'Have you come to tell me who killed the bitch?' she said.

'I'm afraid not.'

'Then you've come to wish me a happy Christmas? That's a joke, superintendent. Happy Christmas – I've been thinking of making an end of things. Give me one good reason why I shouldn't? No? Then give me a cigarette and have a glass of wine.'

'Your concierge is worried about you.'

He lit her cigarette and she drew deeply on it.

'That's great,' she said, 'that's lovely. My concierge is worried.'

'She's not pleased that you brought your German boyfriend here.'

'Great,' she said again. 'But she needn't worry. That's over. He couldn't take it any more. So there's nothing left for me, is there, if I can't even satisfy a Boche, not even one who was a nice boy, a really nice boy who called out to his mother when he was asleep. Do you wonder I hate myself?'

Again, as on his previous visit, she burst into tears and threw herself down on a couch, burying her face in the cushions. Lannes took the cigarette from her hand and placed it in an ashtray which was already near overflowing. He waited, smoking, till her sobs died away, and said, 'Dr Duvallier. Tell me about Dr Duvallier.'

She twisted round, looked up and her face opened in a smile.

'That bastard,' she said.

'Tell.'

'Give me another cigarette,' she said, 'I'm out.'

'Keep the packet,' he said. 'I've another. Dr Duvallier? He was Giselle's doctor, yes?'

She rolled the cigarette between her fingers.

'You called him a bastard.'

'Did I? So I did. And he was one. She relied on him, he's a handy man with the needle, you see. I told you she had tempers – didn't I? – terrible sudden tempers? Maybe I didn't, I don't remember what I say to anyone now, and that's perhaps because I talk mostly to myself. But she had. She was what they call volatile. Now up, now down, one moment sweet as a sucking dove and the next screaming in fury. It took me a long time to realise. Indeed, it was only after I had left her and resolved never to see her again, that I realised what it was. He would come running when she was in a state, ready with his needle to calm her down. She was an addict, morphine I'm sure now, having seen others like her when I was in Paris. Do you see?'

'And yet,' Lannes said, 'she seems to have been a success as a piano teacher. Several parents of her pupils speak well of her. It doesn't fit with your picture of her.'

'Maybe she'd taken a cure, I don't know. Or reached a state of – what is it? – equilibrium – that's the word. Some addicts manage that, you know. You do know, don't you?'

'Yes, I know it's possible.'

The room was airless and also cold. Kiki rose, slowly, and crossed to a table by the shuttered window. She wound up the gramophone that sat there, and put a record on: American jazz and a singer sobbing her heart out. He didn't understand the words but the message was clear: there's no place to go, no place to go. He saw a chain gang and a woman nursing a dead baby.

He said, 'Tell me, Kiki, was Duvallier one of the clients for her entertainments, one of the men she supplied with young girls?'

'I don't know,' she said, her voice scarcely more than a whisper, 'I really don't know.'

She threw her glass into the empty grate.

'It wouldn't surprise me.'

He found a hearth brush and dustpan and swept up the broken glass, aware that she was crying again. He wondered if it was safe to leave her alone.

'Will you be all right?' he said, and heard the feebleness of his words.

'All right?' she said. 'Sure, I'll be all right. What is there not to be all right about?'

'And you won't do anything foolish?'

'Like keeping going?' she said.

'That's not what I meant. You know that's not what I meant.'

'Yes, I know. No, I won't.'

'Promise?'

'You are old-fashioned, superintendent, out-of-date. The way things are, you think promises mean anything? That's sweet, that's really sweet.'

*   *   *

He was reluctant to make the third visit, but he had neither seen nor heard anything of Karim since he had fled from the Bar Météo, and he felt a responsibility for the boy who had turned to him for help when Félix had assaulted him, and, then, made to use him as bait. Karim had been afraid, reasonably afraid, and yet he had shown a certain jaunty courage which Lannes responded to. And the boy's care for his wreck of a mother was also appealing. Thinking of her, Lannes bought a bottle of rum from the Alimentation; on his previous visit the old woman had been incapable of speech till he had fetched her one. The old woman! – she was certainly younger than Lannes himself, younger perhaps than Marguerite. Then he went into the tabac next door and bought two packets of Gauloises. Recognising him as a cop, the man shrugged his shoulders and didn't require him to obey the regulation which would have had him hand over an empty packet in order to be supplied with a new one. It was intended, Lannes knew, as a means to discourage the black market in cigarettes, and was as futile as most such regulations were.

The smell on the staircase was appalling, a mixture of boiled cabbage, urine, dust and stale alcohol. It would be no better in the apartment. He knocked and had to do so three times, with long intervals between them, before the door was opened. She was wearing a filthy housecoat, which hung open to the waist, and carpet slippers. A cigarette was stuck to her lower lip and her breath stank of rum. He held out the bottle which was immediately seized, then, without a word, she turned away, and he followed her into the room which, like Kiki's, was cold and stuffy at the same time. She picked up a dirty glass and poured herself a stiff drink from his bottle. She knocked it back, shuddered, and jerked her thumb indicating that he should go through to the bedroom.

'He's in,' she said, and sat down, one hand on her glass and the other on the bottle, in case he should wrest it away from her. Last time she had immediately recognised that he was a policeman; perhaps she was now beyond caring. Or perhaps she saw no reason why a cop shouldn't also be one of her son's clients.

He must have heard the knocking for he had roused himself and was sitting on the edge of the bed. A towel that had once been white was wrapped round his middle. Otherwise he was naked, and it was strange how fresh his skin looked in that filthy apartment.

'You weren't expecting someone else?' Lannes said.

'Not particularly.'

He gave a half-smile. It was a hesitant smile as if he didn't know how he stood and was wondering whether he was in trouble or whether, perhaps, Lannes had come there for the same reason so many other men had. He scratched his thigh under the towel.

'Have you got a cigarette?'

'Certainly.'

'Thanks.'

He held out his face for a light and Lannes had the image of Michel doing just that, in the same attitude, and with the same doubtful questioning look in his eyes, just a couple of hours previously.

'Are things all right?'

'What do you mean?'

'Félix,' Lannes said. 'He hasn't troubled you again?'

The boy drew on the cigarette, held the smoke in his lungs before emitting it. He swung round to lie on the bed, pulling his knees up.

'No,' he said. 'I reckon you frightened the bastard off. Thanks for that.'

'You'll let me know if he does, won't you?'

'Sure.'

Lannes was uncomfortable standing by the bed on which Karim lay apparently at ease now. He looked for somewhere to sit, but there was nowhere except the end of the bed by the boy's feet.

He said, 'The man who introduced you to Félix – I forget what you knew him as . . . '

'The old Jew bastard, you mean? What about him?'

'His daughter was murdered. Not a nice woman, she procured young girls for men who like that sort of thing. He arranged what they called shows for her clients. I wondered if it was only girls.'

Karim smiled.

'The old bastard,' he said. 'No, there was nothing like that. Not till Félix. He had other things on his mind when he came to call. I don't need to tell you what they were.'

'Pity. It was just an idea. Does the name Duvallier – Dr Duvallier – mean anything to you?'

'You're joking, aren't you? Look, you know what I do and I'm not pretending with you to be other than I am, but you don't suppose the men I go with give me their names, not their real names anyway. I didn't know the old Jew's name till you told me.'

He put his cigarette between his lips and left it there, screwing up his eyes against the smoke.

'All the same,' he said, 'I'll come clean because you've been decent with me and I reckon that as cops go you're all right. I have heard the name. There are those who have what they call a habit. There are some who are disgusted with themselves and can only do it with what you might call a bit of help. You can guess what from, and I've heard it said that if you're in need and can pay his prices, Duvallier is the doc you want. But that's all I know. Myself, I don't need the sort of help he can offer, and, to tell the truth, I wouldn't recognise him if he was standing where you are now.'

'But you could find someone who has needed that help?'

'Perhaps, I don't know. It's all rumours, and in any case, I'm not a snitch. In my milieu, it's not the thing to grass to the police. No offence meant, superintendent. Like I say, you've been good to me and I appreciate it.'

'In your milieu,' Lannes said, 'it's not a bad thing to have a friend in the police. Think of that, and ask around about Duvallier, will you? That's not an order, Karim. Just think of it as a request and remember that you're in my debt.'

'As you say.'

The boy stubbed out his cigarette, smiled broadly, and slipped his hand under the towel.

'There's more ways than one of paying a debt. So, what do you say?'

'Thank you but no. Boys aren't my thing. You know that.'

'Sure I do. Leave me another couple of cigarettes, will you?'

'Have the packet.'

'It's not your last?'

'If it was, do you think I'd be offering it?'

XXXI

Truth to tell, he thought as he climbed the stairs, he would have liked to go straight to bed, just to lie down and think of nothing. But of course he couldn't, it was Christmas Eve, and in any case he knew that sleep wouldn't have come to him.

Maurice and Clothilde were playing cards, but the boy got up as soon as Lannes entered, to shake his hand. Lannes had thought when they arrived last evening that he looked harder than when he saw him in Vichy more than a year ago, at the time indeed when news came of the German invasion of Russia. Perhaps it was just that his hair was cut shorter. All the same he had gained assurance. When he had stayed with them for a few weeks in the summer of 1940 he had been shy and nervous as an unbroken colt.

Lannes kissed Clothilde, said he didn't want to interrupt their game, offered a drink which was politely refused, and went to the cupboard to give himself a nip of marc.

'That's capote,' Clothilde said, laying her cards on the table. 'You look as if you've had a hard day, Papa. Dom's helping Maman make supper. It was made clear I wasn't needed.'

He knew she was dying to ask if he had managed to see Michel. He smiled.

'It could have been worse,' he said. 'Go on with your game.'

In the kitchen Marguerite was standing behind Dominique and stroking his cheek.

'I was just saying,' she said, 'that they should lift the curfew on Christmas Eve to let us go to Midnight Mass. It's wicked not to. It was so lovely when we could all go together.'

It had been the one church service in the year which Lannes used to attend.

'Don't worry, Maman, I'll come to the first Mass in the morning with you,' Dominique said. 'That's a promise. You'll have to wake me of course.'

'You're a lamb,' she said. 'You've always been that.'

Lannes thought of the mother and son he had just left in their stinking apartment, the boy caressing himself as he lay all but naked on the bed, the woman bent over the table with one hand on her glass and the other on the bottle.

He said, 'It's good to have you home.'

'Your grandmother's dying to see you too,' Marguerite said. 'Fortunately she is well enough to come for Christmas dinner tomorrow, along with your Uncle Albert.'

Lannes was sure she would have told Dominique this already and that the words were intended as a reminder to him. Not that this was necessary. He had after all supplied the gigot of lamb they would eat, thanks to Fernand's connections in the black market.

'That's good,' he said.

'If only Alain . . . ' Marguerite said.

'Don't cry, Maman. Some day it will be over and we'll all be together again.'

*   *   *

Lannes had always disliked his mother-in-law and found her tiresome, but when he opened the door for her on Christmas Day, he felt an unaccustomed surge of pity. She seemed to have shrunk. The privations of the war had aged her. She might even be as ill as she claimed to be. Surprisingly too she appeared ready to be amiable. Doubtless that was on account of Dominique, always her favourite grandchild. But she even refrained from nagging Clothilde, at least for the first half-hour of the visit. Now she sat upright in her chair, dabbed at her eyes with a lavender-scented handkerchief, and accepted a glass of Dubonnet. 'For my heart,' she said. When Maurice came into the room to be introduced, she asked if he was 'Clothilde's young man'; he blushed, and Lannes wondered if he might indeed have hopes in that direction; he remembered they had got on well when Maurice stayed with them in the summer of 1940 – but that was before Clothilde met Michel. Maurice might be more suitable. Meanwhile Dominique tactfully eased his embarrassment by introducing him as his friend and 'also my colleague in Vichy'.

As they settled themselves at table, his brother-in-law Albert began to question the boys about the mood in Vichy and to inveigh against the iniquities of the Resistance. Lannes saw the distress on Marguerite's face and said, 'It's Christmas, Albert, let's have no politics. Let us try to forget the war if only for a day.'

'I find that hard to do, Jean, when France is so bitterly divided. How, for instance, can we not be conscious of Alain's absence and be wondering where he is and with what scoundrels he is associating?'

'Please,' Marguerite said.

She was close to tears.

'Wherever he is and whatever he's doing,' Dominique said, 'he will be acting in accordance with his conscience. I'm sure of that.'

'Can't we just be happy for once?' Clothilde said, rising to collect the soup plates. 'Have you finished, Granny?'

'It was a little too highly spiced for me.'

'All I say is,' Albert said, 'we can't hide our heads in the sand just because it's Christmas.'

He turned to Dominique.

'We'll talk about it after the meal.'

Lannes, relieved, got up to carve the lamb.

'Where did you get this, Jean?'

He pretended not to have heard.

'We have a terrible job,' Albert said, 'trying to clamp down on the black market.'

The lamb was beautifully tender. Madame Parage bent her head over her plate. She was persuaded to take a second helping, even though she protested that she never had an appetite these days.

'There's your favourite flan for dessert, Granny,' Clothilde said.

'I can never eat a thing these days, but I'll maybe just have a tiny taste.'

Clothilde exchanged a look with Lannes and bit her lower lip to prevent herself from laughing. They both knew the old woman would eat as much as was put on her plate.

So the meal passed without too much acrimony. It hadn't been as bad as Lannes feared. He went through to the kitchen to make coffee and smoke a cigarette. Clothilde joined him there.

'Did you see him? What did he say?'

'He's thinking about it.'

I hope he is anyway, he thought.

'He said he loves you. There's no doubt about that.'

'But . . . ' she said.

'Speak to him about it again yourself. I hope you may find him more receptive.'

'He's going to visit tomorrow. I'm dying for Dominique to meet him. But I'm nervous too.'

He should speak to Dominique himself first. He might have more influence on the boy.

Later they played whist, Dominique and Madame Parage against Maurice and Clothilde, while Marguerite and Albert talked – about what, he wondered? – and he read a Maigret novel and wished it was as easy to solve crimes in real life as it seemed to be in fiction.

When at last Albert and his mother left, Clothilde said, 'It's terrible the way Granny always cheats. She was peering at your hand all the time, Maurice.'

'That's why I like to partner her,' Dominique said. 'We always win.'

'I know,' she said. 'Remember how Alain used to fume and sulk.'

In bed, Marguerite said, 'Thank you for stopping Albert. I hate it when he speaks like that. He feels things too deeply. He's so full of anger.'

And apprehension now? he thought.

He leant over to kiss her on the cheek.

'It went well enough, didn't it?'

'What sort of Christmas can Alain have had?'

There was no possible answer to that. For a long time they lay there without speaking, both hoping for sleep. He wondered how others had spent the day: Alain and Léon wherever they were, Jérôme in London, safe unless a bomb fell on him. Henri and Miriam in their anxious domesticity, that poor girl Kiki, alone with her bottle, Karim and his wreck of a mother; and then there was Michel who might break Clothilde's heart. Yes, he must speak to Dominique about him.

XXXII

It might have been worse. There had been few tears, no open quarrels. But Clothilde wasn't happy; she suspected he hadn't convinced Michel. Dominique didn't care for him. Before he and Maurice made off to the station to return to Vichy, he said, 'You must stop it, Papa. He's not right for her.'

'Why do you say that? Your mother approves of him.'

'Maman always looks for the best in people, she's too kind. But I was shocked when I heard about this Legion against Bolshevism idea. So was Maurice. Just because we work in Vichy for the National Revolution doesn't mean we are pro-German. You know that, don't you? Some of the boys we work with and train, well, we're keeping them from doing that sort of thing. And they don't have Michel's advantages. Of course, I'm prejudiced, I admit that. I had been hoping that she and Maurice would . . . he hasn't said anything, but I'm sure he's at least half in love with her.'

'Sadly,' Lannes said, 'she's more than that with Michel, much more than that.'

'You must stop it, Papa.'

If only he could. He would have to plead with Sigi to break his hold on the boy, but he was sure he would fail. Try, fail, fail again, fail better, he told himself. Meanwhile there was work to be done and in these dead days between Christmas, the New Year and the Epiphany, it was at least a distraction.

* * *

Old Mangeot was at the desk in the Pension Bernadotte, a half-smoked cigarette attached to his lower lip. It had gone out and he struck a wax match to relight it, and said, 'A Happy Christmas to you, superintendent, and there's not much anyone can wish anyone for the New Year, is there? When is it all going to end? And how? That's what I ask myself. I take it you've come to see Yvette, since I've been keeping my nose clean as I usually do, and I can't think of anything else that would bring you here. The slut will still be in her bed, but that won't worry you, will it?'

'Since it's Christmas,' Lannes said, 'I'll pretend you don't mean what you're saying.'

'Just my little joke, superintendent, just my joke. What I say is, we haven't yet been forbidden to laugh, have we now?'

Yvette rubbed sleep from her eyes.

'Well, this is a treat.'

She got out of bed, naked, with an abrupt sinuous movement, put her arms round Lannes' neck and kissed him on the mouth.

'It is good to see you,' she said. 'A real treat like I say. Going to join me?'

'Don't be silly, Yvette,' he said, disengaging her arms. 'Either get back into bed or put some clothes on. I don't mind which. You'll catch cold otherwise.'

And indeed there was a damp chill in the room. He looked away from her, out of the window over the roofs at the slate-grey sky. Instead of doing as he asked, she lit the little paraffin stove and put a coffee-pot on it. She leant over the stove, with her buttocks towards him in an attitude that Degas might have delighted in painting. When the coffee bubbled, she filled two little cups, gave him one and took the other back to the bed where she sat upright with the sheet pulled up to her breasts. Her right leg was free of the duvet and she smiled in a manner that was more friendly than inviting when she saw that he couldn't take his eyes off it.

'So if you won't take what I'd be happy to give you,' she said.

He thought of Karim making the same offer, which in his case he hadn't felt any temptation to accept. She sipped her coffee and looked at him over the cup held just below her lips.

'You do want me really. You know that,' she said. 'Free for you, it wouldn't cost you anything.'

Except my self-respect, he thought.

'You can't blame a girl for trying.'

'I don't, Yvette, but I wish you wouldn't.'

'That's encouraging. Give me a cigarette, please, and sit down. It's unnerving seeing you standing over me.'

'I don't believe that for a minute,' he said, but did as she asked.

'Duvallier,' he said, 'Dr Duvallier. Does that mean anything to you?'

'Should it?'

'I don't know. I hoped it might.'

'Sorry. Can't say it does.'

'Peniel didn't mention the name when he made that proposition to you?'

'He didn't mention any names. I didn't give him time to before I sent him off with a flea in his ear.'

'A pity. It was just an idea.'

'This doctor. Do you think he killed that woman?'

'I've no reason to think so. And yet . . . '

'What do you mean?'

'It's curious,' he said. 'I'd never heard of him either, but he forced himself on my notice. I'm always suspicious when somebody does that. And what I've learnt of him since makes him more interesting still.'

'I do like it,' she said, 'when you take me into your confidence, like you did when we had lunch that day. It makes me feel good. So I'm sorry to disappoint you.'

'You're a nice girl, Yvette.'

'I can be better than nice if only you'd let me.'

He hadn't really hoped that she would know anything about Duvallier, and when he was back in the street, he admitted that he had gone there less to pursue his investigation than for the pleasure of being with the girl and to assure himself that all was well with her. If he had been a different man, he would be in bed with her now instead of standing there unwilling to return to the office and uncertain of what he should do next. And would that different man have been better or worse than the man he was? Better perhaps if half an hour of sex freed him from loneliness and his pervasive sense of futility; worse more likely because he would have been ashamed of having betrayed Marguerite. But would that make him bad? Wasn't a sense of shame creditable? Were Gabrielle Peniel's clients ashamed? Was she ashamed of having procured young girls for them? He remembered the advocate Labiche looking at that photograph of himself with the naked child of ten or eleven years, and dismissing it, tearing the photograph up and saying 'this is of no significance'. Were the men who paid for sex with Yvette – or indeed with Karim – ashamed? Or did they experience a sense of relief and feel good?

There were so many people he should speak to. He ran over the list in his mind: and the truth was he wanted to see none of them. He wanted to be alone, thinking of nothing. But when he was alone, there were too many thoughts he couldn't avoid. Like the Resistance. They had killed two German soldiers in Paris. In revenge twenty hostages had been taken and shot. Over Christmas. And then there were the rumours of torture chambers. More than rumours – he couldn't doubt their existence. The screams of the victims might be audible only in the imagination, but they were real enough. He imagined Alain suffering what they called interrogation and was seized with nausea.

Did it matter who had killed Gabrielle Peniel when all France was a prison, a torture chamber opening on to the morgue?

And that foolish boy, Michel, eager to join in the madness!

His steps had brought him to the Place Gambetta. The terrace of the Café Régent was full of German soldiers. Some of them would be victims too, homesick boys, caught up in the Hell their Führer had unleashed on the world. He found he couldn't enter the café. His hands were trembling as he lit a cigarette, the flame dancing in the cold still air. There was nothing he wanted to do, nobody he could bear to speak to – except Alain, and that was impossible. All his life he had tried to do his duty, and now it seemed futile. Why not go back to Yvette, and say he was wrong, had returned for the comfort she offered, also – though it would have been unkind to say this – for the illusion of life which she would provide.

But he didn't. Of course he didn't.

And yet there was nothing he could bring himself to do. He had never felt so low, so empty, so worthless.

A hand fell on his shoulder.

'Superintendent, well met.'

He turned to see Sigi, a broad smile on his face. He was wearing a double-breasted camel-coloured overcoat and highly polished tan shoes. His head was bare and he looked disagreeably prosperous and at ease with the world.

'You've been naughty, superintendent,' he said, 'but since you're one of the family, I forgive you.'

'Stop this nonsense.' Lannes said. 'The old count wasn't my father.'

'Oh but he was, I assure you.'

Lannes had been briefly disturbed the previous year when Sigi, who might himself have been one of the old count's bastards – and the product of incest at that – rather than only his illegitimate grandson as he was supposed to be, had tried to persuade him that the count had seduced his mother when she was a maid in his household. But he had rejected the idea. His father was his father and his mother had been virtuous. In any case he had no reason to believe that she had ever been a servant in the rue d'Aviau.

'Come,' Sigi said, 'we'll have lunch,' and turned into the Café Régent, waving to a couple of German officers sitting on the terrace. Lannes was interested to note that they acknowledged the greeting, and followed him. Why not? He had known he was going to have to speak to the man, though he had never felt less like doing so.

Sigi ordered champagne.

'Not for me,' Lannes said. 'Please bring me a demi, Georges.'

'You do make me laugh, superintendent,' Sigi said. 'It's pathetic. And I find you have been bothering poor Jean-Christophe again. You must know that the poor sot can tell you nothing about anything. What will you eat?'

'A sandwich,' Lannes said. 'A cheese sandwich. And I'll pay for it myself, and for the beer.'

'I do believe you're angry with me, superintendent.'

It was all Lannes could do to refrain from answering his mockery by saying that he loathed and despised him. He remembered seeing an English film, *Rebecca*, the year before the war. The sneering actor who had played the cousin of the dead woman – he couldn't recall his name – had looked very like Sigi: self-satisfied, malicious and, ultimately, stupid. He would have liked to punch him in the face, but like Daladier and the English Prime Minister with the umbrella at Munich, he was – for the moment anyway – committed to appeasement.

'Angry?' he said. 'No, I wouldn't say that. There's a lot between us, as you know, too much, and I've no reason to like you. Or you me of course. We're on different sides of the fence. You have your beliefs and I have mine. If I was angry with everyone who thought differently from me, it would be absurd, wouldn't it? Far from being angry, I'm going to appeal to your better nature.'

'You think I have one? That's a surprise, especially as I know you still believe old Marthe when she tells you I killed the old count, our father.'

'Your father, perhaps,' Lannes said. 'Not mine. And even if you did, it's not something I could ever prove. He fell downstairs, hit his head and died. Nobody saw anyone push him. An accident. That's how it was, isn't it?'

'Old Marthe suffers from delusions, as I've told you before. She used to adore me when I ran about her kitchen as a child, and now she hates me. You can't believe a word she says.'

'In any case,' Lannes said, 'it's a different matter I want to talk to you about.'

'I'm flattered.'

'No, you're not. But you might be curious.'

Old Georges brought them their order.

'It's usually only the Boches who call for champagne these days,' he said. 'You're lucky we're not out of it.'

Lannes pushed his sandwich aside. He had no appetite.

'I'm going to appeal to your better nature,' he said again.

And again Sigi smiled, showing his teeth, as he said, 'Do I have one?'

'It's possible.' He lit a cigarette. 'Almost everyone has. Buried somewhere. Even Hitler perhaps. I'm told he loves his dog.'

Lannes hesitated. The café was all but empty. Perhaps people were put off by the sight of all these Germans braving the cold on the terrace.

'I spoke to young Michel the other day,' he said. 'Perhaps he told you what I said.'

Sigi lifted his glass.

'Your health, superintendent. Your very good health. Of course he recounted your nonsense. The boy tells me everything.'

'And?'

'And . . . nothing.'

'My daughter loves him. She's afraid for him.'

'It's the way things are, superintendent. Men are warriors and the women weep when we march off to battle.'

The man's calm was infuriating. He's enjoying this, Lannes thought.

'This plan,' he said. 'This intention to join this French legion, I know you've put it up to him, that it's your idea. It's crazy. You've backed the wrong side, Sigi. Germany will lose the war, it's losing it already. The boy will be killed, or, if he survives, disgraced and punished after the war. Is that what you want?'

Sigi continued to smile.

'Look outside, superintendent. The Germans are still here, and they're going to be here for a long time to come. There's a war against Bolshevism – a crusade, if you like, and young Michel is eager to be part of it. True, I admit, Germany has suffered setbacks in the East. All the more reason for idealistic young Frenchmen to join the struggle.'

'And will you do so yourself?'

'I have other duties.'

The man's complacency was exasperating. Lannes wondered if he was indeed entirely detached from reality.

'And what are these duties?'

'I can't tell you that. They're confidential.'

Lannes had a dossier on him. It detailed his criminal past. He knew he had protectors, chief among them Edmond de Grimaud who was perhaps his half-brother, certainly his uncle. He had himself reason to be grateful to Edmond who had saved his career by putting pressure on the advocate Labiche when he threatened to destroy it, and in return he had compromised himself by closing down the investigation into poor Gaston's murder for which he had no doubt Sigi was responsible. He still felt soiled when he thought of it. And now came this boast of protection. He didn't question it. Sigi moved in the shadows where ordinary criminality rubbed shoulders with the secret world which itself was inextricably woven into the world of politics.

'That's irrelevant,' he said. 'We're talking about a boy – what is he, nineteen or twenty? – whose head you have filled with foolish ideas which one way or another will destroy him. I'm asking you – begging you – to cut him loose.'

'And if I don't . . . ?'

'If you don't . . . '

'Are you threatening me, superintendent, brother? As you threatened a friend of mine whom you ordered to leave Bordeaux, but who is nevertheless still here? Yes, that surprises you, doesn't it? It shouldn't. I told you I have protection. You don't understand, do you? It's you, not me, who is in a precarious position. If I were to repeat what you have said about the outcome of the war, where would you be? The tables have turned, brother. Now it's I who could have you locked up. But of course I won't. I have family feelings for you, as does our brother Edmond. But leave young Michel alone, or there will be nasty questions asked about your son Alain who is no longer in Bordeaux. But where is he? And who arranged his departure from the city and perhaps from France? Think of that.'

Sigi leant back in his chair, swinging it on to its hind legs, and smiling.

'You're in check, brother. It may even be checkmate. As for Michel, he is mine. I have trained him, moulded him, prepared him for the heroic role he must play.'

It was ridiculous. The man was mad, intoxicated with the part he had written for himself, and that brave foolish boy, with his charming smile and the good manners which delighted Marguerite, was to be his first victim; his beloved Clothilde the second one. Lannes had humiliated himself in vain. He had failed his daughter.

He got up, put some money on the table and walked away. Laughter from a table of German officers followed him into the square.

XXXIII

There was no restaurant car on the train, and when they had to change at Brive, Dominique and Maurice went to the buffet in search of food. They had talked very little on the first part of the journey, and not only because the compartment was crowded as was always the case now. They got a sandwich and a lemonade each and settled themselves at a table in the corner of the café.

'You look unhappy,' Maurice said.

'Yes, I think I am. At any rate, if not unhappy, I'm worried and anxious. And I didn't sleep at all well last night.'

'I know what you mean. Going to see your godfather and Miriam, well it disturbed me. It made me wonder if . . . '

'If what?'

'I don't need to spell it out, do I, Dom? She's my grandmother, well, my step-grandmother really, the Comtesse de Grimaud, who has always been understanding and kind to me, and there she is living in hiding.'

'Because she's a Jew,' Maurice said.

'I was ashamed when, just before we left – I haven't told you this, have I? – she took me aside and said, "You won't tell your father that you've seen me, where I am." It's not right, I thought.'

'No, it's not right. But you won't say anything to your father, will you?'

'No, I won't. And that's not right either. This sandwich is horrible.'

'Mine's not so bad. I told you you should have gone for a cheese one.'

'It doesn't matter. I'm not hungry anyway. I really like your father, Dom, but all the time we were there, he seemed so unhappy. As unhappy indeed as you look now. I got the impression he thinks we shouldn't be in Vichy. Perhaps we shouldn't, I don't know, and yet the work we are doing there is good. Surely it's good?'

'You know it is. We both know it is. As for Father, poor man, he's chained to a duty he no longer believes in. At least that's how it seems to me. There's our train coming in.'

They hadn't spoken of Clothilde, though she was on the minds of both.

*   *   *

They were shooting pheasants. Jérôme was surprised. It seemed strange to be doing this in wartime. Sir Edwin had apologised.

'It's not a real shoot, you know. Just a rough one, walking up on the birds. You can't get beaters now, you see.'

Jérôme had refused the offer of a gun, saying he wouldn't know how, and been surprised to see that Max had one.

'I love playing the English gentleman, ducky,' Max said. 'And actually I'm not bad with a gun. I once shot a coyote in Mexico.'

So Jérôme walked beside him, smelling the wet leaves and thinking how remote the war was. There was no wind and a mist rose from the river and hung over the edges of the stubble fields they crossed. There were very few birds.

'Damned poachers,' Sir Edwin said.

Jérôme wrote letters in his head. Darling Maman, you would be delighted if you knew where I am, safe in England and spending a few days in the sort of house that features in the novels you like to read. My host is a Member of Parliament. Henry James used to stay here sometimes and Turgenev once paid a visit. In the salon there's a lovely Corot of cattle standing in a stream under willow trees. The war seems very far away . . . Léon darling, how I wish I knew where you are and how I wish you were with me now. I have been in no danger from Sir Pringle, as you call him – it should really be Sir Edwin, you know – because the American boy Max is here. It's silly to speak to you of such matters when you are in danger every day. But of course you'll never get this letter, it won't even be written. It's terrible to be here in comfort and even more terrible that I am so relieved that my courage hasn't been tested and I've not been proved a coward. Unless it's cowardly to be happy that I am not in danger, not even in much danger, I suppose, even if the Germans start bombing London again, which Sir Edwin says they're no longer capable of doing in any force . . . Dear Alain, but here he could find no words. He was inferior to Alain and Alain knew it. Of course he was inferior to Léon too, even more inferior perhaps, because Léon being a Jew was in even greater danger than Alain, but Léon never made him feel inferior because he had chosen him to confide in and he knew all the worst that Léon had undergone . . . Dear Michel, I know you have no time for me, but I can't stop thinking about you. There was a moment once when our bare arms brushed against each other, and another on the beach when you asked me to oil your back and even as I did so I knew that the pleasure we both derived was different, yet for both of us perverse. Of course I know I'll never do more than that and most probably never touch you again, perhaps never see you, except in my dreams or the minutes before I go to sleep.

There was a shot.

'That's my baby,' Max said, and a large white spaniel lumbered off to retrieve the bird.

*   *   *

Alain rolled over in bed, stretched his hand out and felt no one there.

He sat up, wary, listening. The morning light was grey-yellow, fog hanging heavy over Lyon. There was silence in the apartment. The girl might have gone out. To do what? Silence was frightening. You imagine things in the silence – the boots on the staircase, the breaking open of the door, the gun in your face. He reached out for his trousers, and began to dress. Of course the girl wouldn't have gone out – he hadn't paid her anything last night, had he? – and she wouldn't leave him alone in the apartment in case he scarpered, unless of course she had set off to betray him. But what reason might she have to think there was anything to betray? Where was his wallet? He searched his pockets, no sign of it, remembered he had put it under the pillow. Yes, still there, thank God, and no, he couldn't have paid her. Had they agreed on a figure?

She came back. She was wearing only a slip which revealed most of her fat thighs, and was carrying a tray with two bowls of milky coffee.

'That's quick,' she said, seeing him already half-dressed in shirt and trousers, though his feet were still bare. 'You were sound asleep when I got up.'

She put her arm round him and kissed him on the cheek.

'I've got an appointment,' he said. 'What's the time?'

'No idea. I never know the time. Drink your coffee, such as it is. It's still early, must be, look at the light.'

'It was dark all day yesterday, never light at all.'

'So it was. Where are you from? You're not Lyonnais, I can tell.'

'Toulouse,' he said. 'The rose-pink city. I'm Toulousain.'

'Are you now?'

The coffee was very weak.

'Sorry I'm out of sugar,' she said.

She lay down on the bed, her head propped against the pillows.

'You were all right, last night. For a novice.'

'What makes you think I'm that?'

'A girl can tell. It was your first time, wasn't it?'

He felt himself blushing, remembering Miriam and how she had spoken these same words to him.

'Certainly not.'

'Liar. Not that I care.'

He straightened his tie.

'How much do I owe you?'

'Nothing. You don't owe me nothing. I'm not a tart, though I could tell from the first you thought I was. I picked you up because I liked the look of you. I sometimes do that, with boys. You here long?'

'Just passing through,' he said.

'After your appointment?'

'Yes, after it.'

'Then back to Toulouse?'

'Yes. Back to Toulouse.'

'Pity, we could have had some fun. That's how it goes. Give me a kiss.'

When he leant over the bed she held him tight and pressed her lips hard against his.

'I don't know your name,' she said.

'I don't know yours.'

'That's how it goes,' she said again. 'Watch out for the Boches. They're everywhere now. It's not like it was when this was still the

165

Free Zone. Take care, beautiful. You're up to something, I can tell. I don't know what it is and I don't want to know, but take care. If you run into trouble, remember this address. It's quite safe since we don't have concierges here in Lyon, in case you haven't noticed. My name's Anne, by the way. What's yours?'

'You can call me Richard,' Alain said.

'Richard? Nice name. Why not?'

*　　*　　*

The girl was late. Léon's instructions were clear: wait for no more than fifteen minutes after the appointed time, then leave and walk to the second meeting place, which was a brasserie on the corner of the rue St-André-des-Arts and the rue Dauphine. Get there exactly an hour later than the time fixed for the first meeting. He looked at his watch. The fifteen minutes were up, but he would give her another five. He lit a cigarette, folded his newspaper and thrust it into his coat pocket. He would have liked to dispose of it in a bin. He felt contaminated – there was an article denouncing 'the Jewish plague' which was altogether vile.

He was shivering and told himself it was only the cold. But he felt a tremor of fear. Of course there were innocent explanations. Anything might have detained her. The metro might have broken down for example. That sometimes happened these days on account of a power failure. But he feared for the worst. You always feared for the worst. He would finish his cigarette and then leave. Two policemen were approaching. He forced himself to sit still and not look at them. If the girl had been arrested and had talked, then it wouldn't be just two cops – surely. But you couldn't tell. That was the frightening thing, you never could tell. A middle-aged man on a bench on the other side of the statue pulled the brim of his Trilby hat down as the policemen passed. Then he got up and turned his back on them.

Léon dropped the stub of his cigarette and put his foot on it. He made himself walk slowly, as if he hadn't a care in the world, and out of the gardens to cross the road and turn into the rue de Tournon. He had more than forty minutes to kill before he should be at the brasserie. Of course he might go there early and order something to eat. But instructions were instructions and anyway the idea of food made him feel sick. He turned into a bookshop. The woman at the desk paid no attention to him. He took a book from the shelves, but the print was a blur, and his hands were shaking.

'I couldn't help noticing you in the gardens.'

It was the man in the Trilby hat.

'You looked anxious,' he said, 'when these policemen passed. Are you in trouble?'

'Trouble?' Léon said. 'No trouble. Not that kind anyway.'

'What kind then? I can't believe somebody stood you up. Not a boy like you. If that's the case, you must allow me to buy you a drink.'

Léon relaxed. Nothing to worry about, just an attempt at a pick-up.

The man took the book from him.

'Gide,' he said. 'You have good taste. I used to know him well when I was young. He's got away, you know. I believe he's in North Africa, Tunis, they say. What about that drink? What do you say?'

Léon smiled, 'I can't I'm afraid. I have an appointment.'

'Shame. Some other time perhaps. Here's my card. Do please give me a ring. I find you quite charming. What do you say to lunch tomorrow?'

Léon looked at the card. Joachim Chardy. He recognised the name, had read one of his novels. About delinquent schoolboys. He'd enjoyed it when he was – what? Fifteen? So why not?

'I'd like that,' he said.

'I'm delighted. Shall we say Lipp at 12.30, best to be early these days. You know Lipp, I take it.'

'I've never eaten there.'

'Then it will give me great pleasure to introduce it to you.'

He stretched out his hand and touched Léon lightly on the cheek.

'Charming,' he said again, 'I look forward to it. Now I mustn't keep you from your appointment. But first, allow me to buy you this book.'

'I've already read it actually.'

'No matter. Let me inscribe it for you. But I don't know your name?'

Léon glanced at the book Chardy was holding.

'Olivier,' he said.

It's all right, nothing to be afraid of, he thought as he left the shop and descended the hill, just an old queen, normal life, and why not? Lipp, something to look forward to. But what if the girl didn't come to the brasserie? If he was cut off? The ridiculous idea came to him that he could drop out, and, thinking this, he was ashamed. Then he remembered how Chardy had pulled the brim of his hat down over his eyes and got up and turned away as the policemen passed. What did he have to hide? Not, surely, just his interest in him? After all, he no longer looked like a minor, he was sure of that.

XXXIV

'There is never,' Lannes said, 'well, only rarely, a single reason for a crime, not for murder anyway. Something like theft, that's different, easily explicable. But murder, it's the culmination of a series of other acts, of a variety of emotions, hopes, fears. Of course there may at the end appear to be a single motive, but the crime itself, the act of killing, is the product of a whole series of different and often conflicting motives which swirl around like a gusty wind and eventually impel the man or woman who is not yet a murderer to become that. This crime of which we spoke at our last meeting is a tangle of different motives. The dead woman, the victim, some would say she was asking for it – that's been made clear to me. She did things which were not only illegal but wrong – you'll admit there is a difference – the law's one thing, morality another, I'm sure you understand that.'

He broke off, uncertain where his words were leading him, and traced a circle in the dusty earth with the point of his stick. It was extraordinary to be speaking like this to a German, but Schuerle made no immediate reply, merely smiled, encouragingly perhaps.

They were sitting again in the public garden, on the same bench actually, in sight of the fountain, and it was a beautiful clear winter morning, dew still sparkling, the sky cloudless, blue as the French rugby jersey which, in moments that now seemed fantasy, he had dreamt of seeing Alain wear. He lit a cigarette and drew the smoke, comfortingly, into his lungs.

'You know,' he said, 'something of what the dead woman, Gabrielle, was engaged in, procuring girls, some of them minors, little girls, for the perverted pleasure of those whom she would have called her clients, a number of them, I've no doubt, men of position, perhaps in the general view utterly respectable, some of them anyway. There's the possibility – I put it no more strongly than that – that some may have been members, officers even, of your army. That's what you were afraid of, isn't it?'

'What my superiors were afraid of,' Schuerle said.

'Quite so, but which are the more guilty? The woman or her clients? And what brought her to it? Greed, resentment, innate viciousness? I don't know. She didn't like men herself, I'm sure of that. Was she abused herself as a child? It's possible, even probable, I think. And the men themselves, her clients. What brings a man to seek that sort of pleasure? I know a couple of them, one her client some time back. A miserable feeble fellow, a drunkard too, terrified of his domineering father. Repulsive certainly – the sort who might inspire a man who thinks of himself as normal and decent with the desire to kick him, punch him in the face, beat him up. But pitiful too, pitiable even. Am I making sense?'

'I was on the eastern front,' Schuerle said, 'from the first day of Barbarossa. I've seen Jews rounded up and shot and thrown into a pit. You may have heard of the Einsatzgruppen responsible for what, between ourselves, I don't hesitate to call atrocities. Some of them were, as you say, normal and decent, not themselves monsters, good husbands and loving fathers. You don't need to tell me that the nature of man is intricate, baffling. Do you know why I sought you out, superintendent, why I suggested we should meet and talk again? It's because I felt a sympathy between us, and hoped that we might talk, as we are indeed talking, of these matters that I cannot keep to myself, and dare not speak of to my comrades. So I put myself in your power.'

'As I am in yours,' Lannes said. 'Your predecessor, Kordlinger, nearly broke me, you know. If I hadn't been supplied with information that would have damaged him . . . '

'I don't want to know about that,' Schuerle said, 'but this case of yours, does it in fact, as far as you have discovered, compromise any officers of the Wehrmacht?'

'Not to my knowledge.'

'And what we are learning to call the Resistance, that would interest my superiors too.'

'It is easy to be led astray. The circumstances of the murder pointed in one direction, and yet they weren't convincing. That was its first interesting feature to my mind.'

'And the second, if I may ask you.'

'The murdered woman herself, getting to know her, and all the more so because much of what I have learnt is contradictory. That's why I say that the roots of crime go deep, and are twisted, like the roots of many plants. You know the weed which we call nettles – I've no idea what the German name for them is. If you tear up a nettle you encourage other ones to grow. You don't eradicate the weed. On the contrary it spreads and proliferates.'

'Brennnesseln,' Schuerle said. 'They sting nastily, but my grand-mother used to make excellent soup from them. So what pains may also nourish. Strange, isn't it? If I had not lost an eye, I wonder if I would see things as clearly as I do now. I speak metaphorically of course.'

Lannes made no immediate reply. It was strange how they seemed to be drifting into intimacy, strange too how deserted the Garden was on such a morning. It felt, briefly, as if they had somehow detached themselves from the war and the Occupation. And yet that question of Schuerle's about the Resistance which would – how had he put it? also interest his superiors, wasn't it? – did this mean that he wasn't off-duty as he appeared to be?

There might indeed seem to be a flow of sympathy between them, and Schuerle might have spoken at their first meeting too in a way which suggested that he not only believed that Germany was going to lose the war, but was anti-Nazi himself. But could he be trusted? Might he be trying to lure Lannes into indiscreet talk? Whom or what could you take at face value now?

'I spoke to you of my grandfather,' Schuerle said, 'an upright man, but also narrow and harsh. A devout Lutheran who nevertheless fathered more than one child on village girls, to my grandmother's distress. Yet he was regarded as a man of honour, and indeed prided himself on his honour. You're a policeman. You don't need me to tell you that, as I have already said, the nature of man is intricate. Do you know who killed that woman or do you at least have suspicions?'

'You always suspect people who tell you lies, or less than the truth, and yet the innocent do that too. But, yes, I have someone in mind.'

'And this would not concern my superiors?'

'Not to my knowledge.'

'Good. That is satisfactory.'

'In any case,' Lannes said, 'the man may be innocent.'

'Which of us is truly that? Don't we all commit crimes in our imagination?' "Der Mensch ist doch wie ein Nachtgänger; er steigt die gefährlichsten Kanten im Schlafe."'

'You forget that I don't speak German.'

'A thousand pardons: Man is like a sleepwalker; he climbs dangerous ledges in his sleep. Goethe. But he also said "Die Menschen sind im ganzen Leben blind." Men are blind throughout their entire lives. I often wonder what our Führer pictures in the night. Does he have bad dreams? He has made ours a nation of sleepwalkers, and the ledges we climb are perilous. Do you have Jewish friends, superintendent?'

Lannes lit a cigarette, surprised to find his hands steady.

'Why do you ask?'

'Because they should know that the ledge on which they are perched is about to give way. Even if they are French Jews. And there is no shortage of men in your administration ready and willing to co-operate.'

'Thank you,' Lannes said. 'Strange too, isn't it, how one feels obliged to thank the bearer of bad news.'

'In some cities of Ancient Greece they put such messengers to death.'

XXXV

Lannes was sitting, smoking, in Gabrielle Peniel's apartment. The concierge hadn't been pleased to see him.

'I thought you'd have finished here,' she said, 'and I hope you will soon have done with us. My employers are anxious to let the apartment again. You can't blame them. And my other tenants don't like to see you people coming and going. There can't be anything more for you to do here, surely.'

Lannes said, 'That's none of your business. We'll decide when the place can be let again. You may assure your employers that we are as eager as they are to be done with this investigation.'

Everything in the apartment spoke of the high regard Gabrielle had had for herself, and yet at the same time it was curiously impersonal. How had she worked? The encounters she arranged had surely taken place elsewhere; he couldn't imagine her permitting such activity in this place which bore no resemblance to a brothel. He went through to the bedroom where she had been killed. It didn't make sense. Assuming her murderer was a man, why had she allowed him in there, and why was she in a state of undress, given what he had learnt of her inclinations? Perhaps he had proposed taking her out to dinner, and she had gone through to change, and he had surprised her when she was attending to her maquillage? That made sense of a sort. So it was surely someone she knew well and trusted, for there had been no evidence that she was alarmed, no evidence certainly that she had put up any resistance. He thought of what he had said to Schuerle about the roots of crime and of his belief that to solve a case you must first solve the mystery of the victim. Was he any closer to doing that? Dr Duvallier had said she suffered from anxiety, but he had found no evidence of that; Adrienne Jauzion that she had a terrible temper and was given to fits of rage, yet everything here, so cold and impersonal, spoke to him of restraint and composure. The style of the killing too; that, as he had concluded some time before, simply didn't fit either the Boches or the Resistance. So Moncerre was right; it was a pre-war crime, even if he was wrong also and it wasn't, despite appearances, a crime of passion, not what was normally meant by the phrase anyway. Hatred, yes, quite probably, but cold hatred, and calculation.

So: who hated her? Kiki certainly, and she had reason to wish her dead, might even have been capable in her misery of killing her. It was possible to construct a scenario. They had been lovers once. Suppose Gabrielle, in her complacent narcissism, had suggested they resume their old relationship. How would Kiki have reacted? The question dismayed him because the answer wasn't impossible. There would perhaps have been contempt in any suggestion Gabrielle made, and Kiki snapped.

No, that wasn't convincing; but was this not perhaps because he didn't want to be convinced? Perhaps not, surely not: he could envisage Kiki killing her in the circumstances he had imagined, but not subsequently staging that set-up, smoking a good cigar and drinking champagne. Not even pouring most of the champagne down the sink.

What was it Schuerle had said? The nature of man is intricate, baffling. True enough; Gabrielle baffled him. What he had learnt of her didn't come together to form a coherent picture. What was the key to her character? These photographs of herself over which he could imagine her lingering? What else? She liked money, was greedy for money, he was sure of that. And she had a taste for corruption.

Did any of it matter really? (He lit a cigarette from the stub of the one he was smoking.) Set aside everything else – Marguerite's unhappiness, Alain in danger wherever he was and whatever he was doing, his fear that Dominique's work in Vichy would be held against him when the wheel completed its revolution, Clothilde's love for that brave foolish boy who was running hard to disaster – set against all that, why should he care that a greedy and nasty woman had been murdered?

Because you're a cop, was the answer. Because a murderer shouldn't escape the consequences of his crime? Certainly, though on both sides murderers were doing that all over France – in the name of course of some Higher Good!

And then there were the Jews. Why had Schuerle given him that warning? Was it a test? Or a kindly warning, expression of genuine sympathy?

He liked him; felt indeed a surprising affinity with him. And yet he had asked that question about his knowledge of the Resistance, asked it tentatively, certainly, hadn't probed further but had that question been the reason for seeking out the meeting? He didn't want to believe this was the case. Yet the suspicion was there. Whatever the answer, he couldn't doubt that what Schuerle said was true. He must warn Miriam, and the old tailor, Léopold also, who would probably give him a sour smile and reply: 'So you think, superintendent, it is now time I reach for the brandy?'

He got up and realised he was tired. There was nothing for him here, and yet this visit hadn't been in vain. Sitting in the dead woman's apartment had helped him think things through. He knew who had told him a lie.

Leaving the apartment, he didn't trouble to replace the seals. There was nothing more for them there.

'You can look for a new tenant,' he told the concierge. 'We're through here. However, I would like another word with the little maid, Marie. Do you know where I can find her?'

'That poor child, she's suffered enough without being plagued further by you people.'

'Nevertheless,' Lannes said, 'I've a question I must put to her.'

'If you insist. Well, as it happens she's cleaning for Madame Farage on the third floor. But she's not in today. That lady's as mean as a Jew and won't pay for a maid to come every day. She'll be here the day after tomorrow.'

'What time will she finish work then?

'Between twelve and one usually.'

'Keep her in your lodge when she finishes. I promise you I'll try not to distress her. Please assure her she's not in any trouble.'

XXXVI

Lannes sent a note by messenger to Adrienne Jauzion asking if he might call on her that afternoon, around four; he had a couple of further questions about Gabrielle Peniel. Then he arranged for the dead woman's father to be brought to his office at two o'clock and sighed to see the pile of paperwork on his desk. He lit a cigarette, leafed through the letters and documents, scribbling his name here and there, taking nothing in. It was a relief when the telephone rang and it was his old journalist friend Jacques Maso asking if he could come to the Rugby Bar for a drink and a sandwich.

'Why not? It'll be a pleasure.'

Jacques was already there, sitting in his usual corner, under the old photograph of the last Stade Bordelais team to have won the French championship, back in 1911.

'Time we won it again,' Jacques said. 'We've a good side this year, though, despite everything. You should come with me to a match.'

'To tell you the truth I'd almost forgotten the game was still being played.'

'We have to keep something of normality going,' Jacques said. 'I was at the club last week and they were asking about Alain. They think well of him, you know, have high hopes for him. Hope he will be back playing again soon, next season perhaps.'

'If only! Kind of them, however,' Lannes said. 'What did you reply?'

'I was cagey, evasive. What are you drinking?'

'Same as you, beer.'

'And to eat?'

'I don't know. A cheese sandwich perhaps.'

Jacques called to the waiter, then said, 'So, Jean, how goes it?'

'How do you think?'

'Yes, stupid question. How's Marguerite?'

'So-so. Hating the war.'

'Which isn't a war.'

'Isn't it? You should pay us a visit. She'd like to see you. She remembers the dancing.'

'Ah yes, the dancing. Long time ago. Another world.'

The waiter brought them two demis and a couple of baguettes, with cheese for Lannes, ham for Jacques.

'So?' Lannes said. 'Are we just catching up?'

'What else should we be doing?'

'I don't know. You called me.'

'So I did.'

Jacques bit into his sandwich.

'I think this pig died of old age,' he said.

'As an old Jewish friend of mine might say, it should be so lucky.'

'You still have Jewish friends, Jean?'

'Don't you?'

'I don't speak about them.'

'Wise man. Prudent.'

Jacques spread his hands.

'Careful anyway, which is more than you seem to be, which is why I called you. I'd a visit yesterday from a chap asking questions about you. I think he was a spook.'

'Brilliantined hair and smoking Celtiques through a holder?'

'You know him then?'

'For my sins. Yes, he's a spook but also a bit of what they call a loose cannon. What did he want?'

Jacques pushed his sandwich aside, pulled out his pipe and began to fill it.

'If I knew anything to your discredit.'

'And what did you reply?'

'I said, of course I do, he's one of my oldest friends.'

'Good answer.'

Jacques drew on his pipe and puffed out smoke.

'Seriously though,' he said, 'I got the impression he doesn't like you.'

'I interfered in a couple of his little games,' Lannes said. 'He's an idiot in my opinion. Go on, please.'

'First, he asked me if you were queer. That seemed a bit odd.'

'These games I spoke of, he was trying to use a couple of boys to compromise German officers. You can't be surprised I think he's an idiot. A nasty one, certainly, because he didn't care a damn about what might happen to the boys. What did you say?'

'Resisting the temptation to say you used to go to parties in drag, I told him to fuck off. Then he asked me about Alain.'

'And?'

'I repeated my suggestion. But I'm worried. He's out to get you, Jean, and now that you've told me how you interfered with what he would call his work, I'm more worried still. I think you should watch your back.'

'Never easy to do that,' Lannes said. 'But thanks for the warning.'

XXXVII

Peniel looked shabbier than ever and in only a few weeks his face had acquired the grey look that prisoners have as a result of poor food, poor air, idleness and boredom. He shifted on the wooden chair as if there was no flesh on his buttocks.

'I don't know why I'm here,' he said. 'I've told you anything I know, not that it was much, and I've done nothing wrong. It's persecution.'

'You may be right,' Lannes said, 'but it doesn't matter. There are lots worse off than you and with less cause.'

He lit a cigarette and went to the cupboard to pour out an Armagnac.

'You don't drink alcohol, do you? Would you like a glass of water?'

'I don't want anything, except to be out of here.'

'Well, it's possible we might arrange that, depends on your answers to my questions. First, the chap who told you to telephone me, Félix I know him as, and gave you that envelope to hand over. How did he come to know of what your daughter was ready to supply?'

'How should I know? He just did.'

'That's not very helpful, Ephraim.'

'Édouard. My name's Édouard.'

'As you like. It's no concern of mine that you're Jewish. Others of course think differently. The advocate Labiche, for example. You know he's a member of that absurd commission set up to deal with – eradicate? – the Jewish Question. And yet he was an old client of your daughter's. I find that interesting, don't you? Did he know she was Jewish?'

'I don't know what you're getting at.'

'Don't you? Pity.'

He got up and crossed over to the window. The light was already beginning to fade and the square was deserted. The room was cold. Shortage of coal made it impossible to keep his stove going for more than a couple of hours in the day. He turned round to look at Peniel.

'Vice aren't much interested in you,' he said, 'Gabrielle being dead. On the other hand they're happy to hold you as long as I want them to. So it's up to you. You can either answer my questions or go back to your cell. Understand?'

'Why should I trust you?'

'You'll be no worse off if you do. Did the advocate know Gabrielle was Jewish?'

'He didn't care. She supplied what he wanted. That was all he cared about. Before the war, anyway. Little girls.'

'Can you supply me with a list? Of the girls and the clients?'

'What has this to do with Gabrielle's murder?'

'That's my business. The list?'

'I could. I suppose I could.'

'Do that.'

'I'd have to think about it. Names, I mean. It couldn't be complete. I knew only some of them and then not always by their real name or family name. It was better that way, you understand?'

'And Félix. How did you meet him?'

Peniel passed his tongue over his lips which were dry and cracked.

'He approached me, said I'd been recommended. I don't know who by. I didn't ask. It was no business of mine. Said he would pay well, and he did. I needed the money. You don't know, super-intendent, what it's like, being poor, without an income. So, there it was. Besides he'd learnt I was Jewish. And he said it was for

France. He'd look after me, he said, if there was any trouble. Fine job he's made of that.'

'I see. Tell me about Dr Duvallier.'

'That bastard.'

'Was he one of your daughter's clients too?'

'Duvallier? I don't know. He may have been. Once. But I don't know. That would have been when we weren't speaking. Before the war, well before it.'

'Why do you call him a bastard then?'

'Because, because, if you must know, I have reason to resent him. You remember when I was in trouble before, when I was a doctor, doing well, and then struck off the medical register – you remember that, superintendent? Nothing was proved, was it, there was only suspicion, which was why you had to let me go that time too. Well, I've always believed it was Duvallier who reported me, shopped me as they say, cast suspicion on me, and suspicion was all it was, but enough to ruin me, and what's more he was at that game himself – that was the word anyway – and other games too, and you wonder I call him a bastard.'

The words spewed out of the little man's mouth and he spoke so rapidly and with such venom that for the first time some colour came into his cheeks and his hands were trembling.

'A handy man with the needle,' Lannes said. 'Or so I've heard. Gabrielle was a morphine addict, wasn't she?'

Peniel surprised him.

'I cured her of that,' he said. 'She was in trouble, and she came to me, calling me Father, which she had never done before, and I cured her, or saw to her cure. It cleaned me out – these cures aren't cheap. But I did it. Because I felt it was my duty to help her.'

'Touching,' Lannes said. 'And it was Duvallier who supplied her with the stuff, and yet he remained her doctor. That puzzles me.'

'I told her to get rid of him, but she was obstinate, said he suited her. There was nothing more I could do. Do you think he killed her?'

'Why should he have done that?' Lannes said.

For a moment Peniel made no reply. Then he spread his hands. It was an oddly coy gesture.

'Because he hated her,' he said, 'and was afraid of her. Isn't that enough?'

'What do you mean?'

'I've no evidence. It's just what I think. I've had time to think, sitting where you put me, and I reckon it was the doctor. But it's just a hunch. Don't ask me how I come by it because I don't know. There are a lot of things I don't know, I've come to realise that. But if I was you I would look at his financial position. It's often money, isn't it, that leads a man to kill. Have I told you enough to let me go?'

'When I have that list.'

'Oh yes, the list. Do you promise?'

'Would you believe me if I did? It's the chance you have to take. It's the only chance you have. One other thing: why did you hand the boy Karim to Félix?'

'Because he asked for him. Said he needed a brown boy, that is, said he had to be a young one, and he was the only one I knew.'

'You didn't care what use Félix might make of him?'

'Why should I? It's what he's for. Rent. And not only to keep that stinking cow his mother in rum, whatever he may have told you. He sells his arse, shamelessly, because that's what he likes, what he does.'

'To you also.'

'And so? I've had him, certainly, there's no point in denying it, but I've had better. There was never more to it, and when I told him there would be money in it, his eyes lit up and I couldn't have held him back even if I'd wanted to. Which I didn't. Why should I?'

'But there was no money. Just a beating and a rape'

'And that's my affair?'

Lannes turned away and opened the window to let cold winter air into the room. He was going to be late for his appointment with Adrienne Jauzion.

'You're disgusting, Ephraim,' he said.

For the first time in their acquaintance the little man smiled.

'Édouard,' he said. 'Édouard, it's not good to be an Ephraim now. Superintendent, I'll make a confession. There are days when

I disgust myself. But a man's got to live, and I am what I am. I don't hide from myself like some people I could mention do. So, yes, I'll prepare that list for you. And then?'

'I'm a man of my word,' Lannes said. 'Usually.'

XXXVIII

'She's expecting you,' the elderly maid said. 'Indeed you're late, she's been expecting you the last half-hour, and she's not accustomed to being kept waiting. So don't look for a warm reception.'

'That's all right,' Lannes said. 'I'm not often received as a friend.'

The reception might not be warm, but the apartment overlooking the Place de l'Ancienne Comédie was, and it struck Lannes that it was probably one of the few in the city to be kept at a pre-war temperature. When the maid showed him into the salon, the scent of flowers – mingled lilies and roses – was almost overwhelming. Adrienne Jauzion was stretched out on the First Empire chaise-longue, as she had been when he had called more than a year previously to ask her if the man found dead in the public garden was indeed her father, and again the orange Pekingese lay on her lap, and she was stroking it with her right hand. She wore dark glasses, though the light was dim, and Lannes wondered if she had a headache, or was perhaps suffering from a hangover. He apologised for troubling her.

'You're late,' she said, but there was indifference in her tone rather than the reproach he had been warned to expect. 'Bring us some tea, Berthe. Please sit down and smoke if you wish. I suppose it's still the matter of Gabrielle's death that brings you here, superintendent, but I can't think I have anything to add to what I have already told you. Nevertheless, I agreed to see you because I recognise that I have reason to be grateful, and, as for being late, that is not the sort of thing that irritates me now as it used to. My days are empty as it is, since I decided I would no longer appear on the stage while the Germans are here. That surprises you perhaps? You hadn't thought me a patriot, I suppose? Well, it surprised me too when I discovered that being applauded by German officers in the stalls made me feel sick. Just a little sick, but sick enough to lead me to this decision. Perhaps it amuses you, superintendent.'

'Not at all,' Lannes said. 'We all – many of us anyway – find ourselves acting these days in ways which we hadn't expected. Perhaps it's because we are weary of it all.'

'Weary and ashamed,' she said. 'I think you understand me, superintendent. I had never felt ashamed before. In a curious fashion, it's a strangely liberating feeling.'

Was the choice of adjective unconscious? There was the ring of sincerity in her voice, and yet, Lannes thought, she was an actress after all, accustomed to make even the most banal lines she was required to speak sound sincere, from the heart. It was quite possible her decision was calculated rather than spontaneous, that she judged, as he did, that the war had turned against Germany, and thought that being known to have withdrawn from the stage during the Occupation would put her in credit when the day of Liberation arrived. He wondered if the Comte de St-Hilaire had offered her such advice.

The maid wheeled in a trolley and poured tea into fine Sèvres china cups. The tea was pale, straw-coloured, aromatic and – he was sure – expensive. He wondered where she found such a luxury. St-Hilaire again, perhaps. Then Berthe handed him a plate with a couple of little almond biscuits on it, and withdrew. The Pekingese woke up, and Adrienne Jauzion popped a biscuit into the dog's mouth. It chewed it solemnly and flicked out a long pink tongue.

'Did it ever occur to you that Gabrielle was a morphine addict?'

'What a strange question, or rather what a strange way of putting it.'

'Strange?'

'Unexpected perhaps. Is it relevant to her murder?'

'Not immediately,' Lannes said. 'I have reason to believe she was cured of her addiction, and certainly the post-mortem offered no evidence of needle marks. Yet there is a relevance, or seems to be. Dr Duvallier.'

'Ah,' she said, taking a fat Turkish cigarette from the silver box that stood on the little table by the chaise-longue, and fitting it into a long amber holder. She waited for Lannes to rise and light it, and said, 'He used to be my doctor. Then I found reason to dismiss him.'

'And that reason? I've been told he is "a handy man with the needle".'

'Precisely, though I have to say it was only in retrospect that I associated Gabrielle's violent changes of mood with drug addiction. Perhaps I was naïve, but I had no previous acquaintance with such things.'

'Kiki knew.'

'You have seen her? How is the poor child?'

'Miserable, unstable, drinking. I wonder if you might be able to help her?'

'As I've explained, I have withdrawn from the stage for the time being, and so have no need of a dresser. Is this why you've come here?'

'No, I came to ask you about Dr Duvallier. But the girl needs help.'

'As I told you, I saw her with a German officer. Let him help her.'

'There's no help there,' Lannes said. 'In any case the relationship is at an end. Over. Finished. I think she's suicidal.'

He got up, partly because his hip was aching, and crossed the room to the window. He parted the thick velvet curtains and looked out on the square. It had begun to rain and the café tables were deserted.

'I am sorry to disappoint you,' she said, 'but I am scarcely in a position to help anyone. Indeed there are days when I fear I can't even help myself. I rarely sleep more than couple of hours a night, and then I lie awake thinking and feeling nothing. Nevertheless, since I'm under an obligation to you, superintendent, you may ask her to visit me. Perhaps we can at least share our emptiness.'

'Thank you.'

'For nothing,' she said.

He turned round and said, 'Duvallier. I may tell you that he interests me because he forced himself on my attention. Then he told me a lie, saying that he became Gabrielle's doctor only after she was no longer in your service. It's always interesting when someone lies, unprompted. Why did you dismiss him?'

'Because I saw him lunching with my uncle, the advocate, and because of the way they looked at each other and laughed together. You know of my . . . ' she paused, swallowed, and continued, 'my experience with my uncle . . . '

'Duvallier told me the advocate was one of his patients. He seemed rather proud of it.'

'More than a patient, I'm sure of that. Do you think the doctor killed Gabrielle?'

'It's possible. There's no motive I know of, but it's possible. I am suspicious of anyone who without good reason brings himself to my notice. Gabrielle tried to recruit his step-daughter for the purposes you know of, but there's no motive there. Nothing happened, and in any case I don't believe Duvallier feels any affection for the girl, may even regard her as a nuisance. Nevertheless . . . you understand that I'm thinking aloud.'

Adrienne lifted her little dog up and kissed it on its upturned nose, then let it lick her cheek.

'It's all too horrible,' she said. 'Gabrielle was greedy. You've probably learnt that. Greedy not only for money, though that, certainly. For admiration too, which is what she got from Kiki for a long time.'

'The only photographs in her apartment were of herself,' Lannes said.

'That doesn't surprise me. And Duvallier.'

'Yes? Duvallier. Another lady told me he was creepy, "had wandering hands" was how she put it.'

'I wouldn't know,' she said. 'But after I saw him with my uncle, the thought of his hands on my body revolted me. He liked to boast of his connections and his aristocratic patients. I suppose he was – is – greedy too. He was always very pleased with himself. A vain man. Vain and conceited, there's a difference, isn't there?'

'Yes, there's a difference, but it often comes to the same thing, an excessive self-regard and an inability to feel for others. Thank you,' Lannes said, 'you've helped clarify my mind. Perhaps Gabrielle and Duvallier were alike, each having to be the centre of their world. You can't use children as she arranged for them to be abused and as I rather think he may have abused them himself unless you are devoid of the sensibility that allows you to see others as individuals in their own right. All such abuse is egotism carried to a pathological point.'

'It's all horrible,' she said. 'A mess. I can manage emotions only on the stage, and I've cut myself off from that. But yes, tell that poor girl, Kiki, to come to see me. If you like. Not that I can promise anything.'

'I don't look for promises,' Lannes said. 'But, again, thank you.'

'St-Hilaire respects you. Did you know that? When you sent a message asking for this appointment, I immediately called him and he said I should trust you. I can't tell you how unusual it is for me to trust anyone.'

'I'm grateful.'

He remembered how he had called her a copper-plated bitch and how Kiki had spoken of her as 'the Ice Queen'. We're wrong about most people most of the time, he thought.

XXXIX

There was a moment when Michel almost drew back. It was when he saw tears start in Clothilde's eyes and he was tempted to take her in his arms and kiss them away. But of course he didn't, not then, not at first anyway. He really loved her, he was sure of that, and it was terrible to be going to war without having done with her what he most wanted to do. He had kissed lots of girls, but Clothilde wasn't just another girl, and when her lips quivered and he thought he might be killed and she wouldn't even know he was dead, he found he was trembling himself. What was almost worse was that she found nothing to say. There would have been no difficulty if she had argued with him, or even screamed at him; he would have fought back, asserted his male superiority. 'We men are hunter warriors,' Sigi had told him, and this was true, obviously it was true. Men were crusaders, and the Crusade today was against Bolshevism. But this abject misery made him feel guilty.

His sister Anne-Marie had wept too, but that hadn't mattered. It was the sort of thing sisters do, are indeed supposed to do, when their brother goes to war. 'You would prefer me to be a coward?' he had said; and her tears and his words merely served to confirm that he was right. As for his grandfather, the old man was simply out-of-date, beyond it. He had told him that to his mind there was no difference between Bolshevism and Fascism, which was evidently absurd. He was going to fight for France, not for Fascism; for France and the New Europe that would arrive from the ashes of War. 'And will there be a place for Jews in this New Europe?' the old man had asked; 'a place for liberals and democrats, even a place for the Church? Democracy?' In Sigi's words, that was an old bitch gone in the teeth, liberalism was a creed for cowards and sentimentalists, and Christianity a slaves' religion. But he hadn't wanted to tell his grandfather, whom he respected and to whom he owed so much, that he belonged to a dead world; so he had merely said, 'Grandfather, it's a matter of honour,' and been rewarded with a deep sigh and a tear-stained embrace.

There had been tears too from Count Paul, and this surprised him. 'But you yourself have spoken of the Crusade against Bolshevism,' he had said. 'That was then,' the old Russian said. 'I've done wrong, been foolish, to put these ideas in your head. You will be killed and killed in a lost cause. A waste of everything you are. Stalin is stronger than Hitler, believe me, my son. Hitler is as foolish as Napoleon. To invade Russia is the act of a madman. He is losing the Battle of Stalingrad. Holy Russia has recovered its soul, and Hitler will never reach Moscow or Petersburg. My dear boy, there are lessons to be learnt from History, and one is that the Germans always lose. When Prince Andrei extolled Napoleon and called him a Great Man and a genius in war, his father, the old Prince Bolkonsky, laughed at him and said, "Who has he defeated? Only Germans. Everybody has always beaten the Germans." Believe me; the old Prince was wiser than his son. Stalin has adopted the same strategy as Kutuzov in 1812. That wise old man said that Patience and Time would save Russia. So it did and History is repeating itself.' And then the old Russian, the veteran of the Foreign Legion, had sobbed and put his arms round Michel and kissed him passionately, so that Michel for the moment wondered if perhaps Philippe hadn't been right when he called Count Paul an old aunt who had indecent designs on him. This must be nonsense. It was only that the drama of the war had in some way reawakened the old man's mystical faith in Russia and he saw the Bolshevik Stalin as the Tsar, even though he was a Red one.

None of this mattered, not really, not as Clothilde's abject misery did. For a moment he was tempted to yield, to take the easy course and say, 'Very well, I won't go. I love you and I won't go.' It would not only be easier. It would make her happy. Her tears and sobs would turn to cries of joy, and he would fold her in his arms. There was all at once nothing he wanted more to do. But was it love or cowardice that prompted him, for he knew, deep down, that he was indeed afraid of this venture into the unknown? So, instead of yielding, he admitted his fear and then spoke of her brother, Alain.

'I know what he's doing, even though so little has been said to me, and we don't think alike, we're in a sense enemies, even though we are both, in our own minds, patriotic Frenchmen. So I respect him. But he's your twin, and I know that he hurt you, especially as he went without speaking a word to you as you've told me. And I've seen your mother's face when his name is mentioned, which it isn't often, I think, because it's too painful. For your father too, I suppose, though of course he's said nothing to me. The truth is that Alain and I are alike. You know that ass Philippe – all right, he's been a friend of mine and a friend of Alain too, sort of anyway, but I despise him because he thinks of nothing but being comfortable and having a safe career that will make him rich. You wouldn't want me to be like Philippe, darling, would you? Why, even that little pansy, Jérôme, who used to waggle his backside at me like a bitch on heat, has had the courage to join de Gaulle with Alain, because I know that's what they've done even if no one has said so outright. So you see. It's a matter of honour. I love you, of course I do, when the war's over I want to marry you, but I couldn't love you if I despised myself, and you couldn't love me if I was a weakling. I'm sure you couldn't.'

He said all this, and much more, in different ways, time and again, repeating himself, and at last he held her in his arms and kissed her tears, then kissed her on the lips and stroked her cheek.

He pushed back her hair and kissed her again, and said, 'It's because I love you,' which wasn't quite true, or only partly true, but was what at that moment he felt to be true.

All the same it was a relief when the next day, after a night when he had been too much on edge to sleep, he boarded the train for Paris where he was going to enlist. Sigi was with him, and Sigi was certain he was doing the right thing. In Sigi's company all doubts dissolved, and when Sigi laughed and said, 'I presume you left your girl in tears. That's the proper send-off for a warrior,' he didn't feel guilty but smiled, a touch shyly as if he was being paid a compliment. Which in a sense he was, because it meant that Sigi was proud of him.

XL

It was a relief to close the apartment door behind him, but one that made him feel ashamed. Clothilde had said little. She didn't need to. Her face was a picture of misery. There was no response when he hugged her. It wasn't that she was refusing comfort, rather that nothing he might say or do could soften the blow or ease the pain. Her heart was like a cracked plate. Would it ever be repaired? As for Marguerite, her response was to sigh and murmur that she only wished Dominique was at home. He knew what she meant, and he couldn't even take it as a reproach; Dominique was gentle, sympathetic, understanding as he wasn't. He resisted the temptation to say that Dominique had spoken of his dislike and disapproval of Michel whom Marguerite had found so acceptable.

'Oh yes, go to work,' she said. 'You always run away to work when one of us is in distress.'

Pointless to say he had no choice. All the more pointless because he knew that she was right. Work was a way of escaping from all this. And wasn't he perhaps at fault? Shouldn't he have played the heavy father, knowing what he did of Michel's devotion to Sigi? From the start that had worried him, made him afraid. And then there was Michel's perfect Aryan poster-boy beauty! Had he been a coward, simply hoping that tomorrow would never come? His own attempt to deter Michel had been miserably feeble; he couldn't hide that truth from himself.

Well, from the day of the Marshal's first broadcast when he had announced that he was asking for an armistice, he had known that things would get worse before they could get better. He'd used the line often enough in the dark months since. So had Bracal, others too. It was the dark truth with which they lived.

And work itself wasn't safe. He had tried not to think of what Jacques Maso had said about the questions Félix had asked him; they were disturbing, yet what was the point of dwelling on them?

There was a cold wind blowing from the East, all the way from the Urals perhaps. He turned up the collar of his coat and leant heavily on his stick. Things must be as they must be.

Young René Martin was waiting for him in the office.

'Have you anything for me, chief? I feel like a spare wheel on a car.'

'Who doesn't? No matter. I'll be glad of your company this morning. I'm going to speak with Gabrielle's maid again. We'll go and have a coffee first.'

It wasn't just to give the boy something to do. The girl might well respond better to him. Or was it just that he didn't want to be alone with his thoughts going round and round in a circle and arriving nowhere?

They stopped off in the Bar Jack as they had done on the first morning of the case, and again Lannes asked for an Armagnac which on this occasion he poured into his coffee.

'Are we really getting anywhere, chief?'

'You did well alerting us to Duvallier. If there's any progress it's in that direction.'

'Do you think he did it?'

'I don't think anything, but he puzzles me. Why did he force himself on our attention?'

The girl was in the concierge's lodge, sitting on the edge of a hard chair and twisting her fingers round each other.

'I'm sorry to bother you again, Marie,' Lannes said, 'but we've a couple of questions more, I'm afraid.'

'There's nothing to be frightened of, you've done nothing wrong and nobody thinks you have,' René said, and gave her a smile which brought a blush to her cheeks.

'You know Dr Duvallier, don't you?' Lannes said. 'I suppose you met him quite often when he visited Madame Peniel?'

The girl smiled for the first time, showing her rabbit teeth.

'You like the doctor, do you?' René said.

'Oh yes, he was always so kind and genial. Once when I did something to irritate Madame, he said, leave the poor child alone, she's doing her best, and, if you snap at her, it'll only make her more nervous. Which of course it did – she had a sharp tongue. I told you that already, didn't I?'

'Yes, that's right, you did,' René said. 'It doesn't sound as if she was a nice woman.'

'She had high standards. That's what she said, but I didn't always know what she meant. I was often confused and she would tell me I was a stupid girl.'

'I don't think you're stupid, Marie,' René said, smiling at her. 'I think you notice rather a lot.'

'Would you say Madame Peniel and the doctor were on good terms?' Lannes said.

'Well, she was nearly always pleased to see him when he called, but I don't know that he really liked her. I once heard him tell her she was a hard woman.'

'And what did she say to that?'

'She just smiled, and said she could be a good deal harder when she wasn't satisfied as he would soon find out if he didn't keep to their agreement, something like that, and then she noticed that I was still in the room, and told me to get out. Dr Duvallier spoke to me as he left, and said I mustn't take everything Madame said seriously. She doesn't always means what she says, he said, it's because she suffered from an epi-something, I can't remember the word, an epi-something of anxiety. He smiled as he said that and patted me on the cheek, but I don't know, he was worried about something, I think.'

'When was this?'

'I can't remember exactly, maybe ten days or fifteen before . . . before . . . '

'Before she was murdered?'

'I suppose so.'

'Thank you, Marie. You've been very helpful.

'But I haven't said anything, have I?'

* * *

'You do think he did it, then, chief.'

'I told you, I don't think anything, but it's a possibility. I want you to call on him again, and make an appointment for him to come to the office again. Just a few points to be cleared up. I can trust you not to say anything that might alarm him.'

XLI

Bracal looked as unruffled as ever. His manner seemed to say, 'I'm a functionary of the French State. Nothing I do is my personal responsibility.' He sat behind his desk as if it was a barricade protecting him from the disorder and violence of the world.

'But it's nothing to do with us, Jean,' he said. 'I'm an examining magistrate; you're a superintendent in the PJ. So, yes, it's deplorable, disgusting, shameful too as you say, a round-up of Jews – French ones this time, French citizens – is indeed imminent, another train requisitioned to ferry the next consignment to the East. But there's nothing you or I can do about it. Should we resign because we disapprove? What would be the point? Would it make anything better? Of course it wouldn't. I don't ask you if you have Jewish friends. That's no concern of mine. As it happens I have, or had, friends who were Jews myself though none in Bordeaux, which isn't surprising since I am an incomer here myself. But one of my uncles, in Paris, was married to a Jewess, a German one as it happens, and she was arrested in the *Vel' d'Hiv* roundup. She's probably dead now, poor woman. I say poor woman, though in truth I rather disliked her the only time we met, not because she was Jewish but because . . . oh, never mind why. As for my uncle, my mother tells me he's desolate. But there was nothing he could do. That's the world we live in. I think we should have a spot of brandy.'

Lannes sighed. It was all wrong, but Bracal was also right. What was happening was shameful, but many French people were indifferent to the shame. Some even said 'the Jews have nosed their way in everywhere'. Others, like his brother-in-law Albert, were openly anti-Semitic; he spoke of 'cleansing France'. When Lannes told him he had fought alongside Jews at Verdun, he waved him aside irritably. 'That has nothing to do with it,' he said.

So now Lannes accepted the brandy Bracal offered him and lit a cigarette.

'But there's something more, isn't there, Jean?' Bracal said.

'Yes, there is.'

'Which you are nevertheless reluctant to bring up.'

Reluctant? That wasn't the right word. More accurately he was afraid – and ashamed of his fear too.

'Do you believe there are people who are untouchable?' he said.

'In the present circumstances, undoubtedly. I don't like to admit that. Justice shouldn't be subject to expediency. Nevertheless, I can't deny that it's the case, now more than ever.'

Bracal crossed the room to poke his stove. Vicious jabbing with his poker encouraged only a brief spurt of flame.

'We're short of coal,' he said, 'and the quality of such coal as we get is poor. It hadn't occurred to me that war and occupation meant one would be cold from October to March. So, what is it, Jean? What's troubling you?'

'I had Peniel brought to me again the other day. I made a deal with him, promising we'd release him if he supplied me with certain information: a list of Gabrielle Peniel's clients. He wasn't happy, but he's come up with the list. Now I'm not sure that my promise was wise. As a Jew he may be safer where he is, under lock and key.'

'But that's not what's brought you here today?'

'No. It's the names on the list. One name especially. I've under-lined it.'

Bracal put on his reading glasses, then tapped a little tune with his fingers.

'Labiche,' he said. 'The advocate. I see what you mean.'

'Of the Service des Questions Juives.'

'And so, untouchable. Untouchable indeed. There's nothing you can do with this, Jean.'

'You think I should forget it?'

'Things won't always be as they are. Besides this isn't evidence. It's one man's word. And who is the man? A disreputable criminal type – as you must agree – who is also a Jew. Furthermore, even if this wasn't so, it would surely be a matter for the Vice Squad, not the PJ – unless you have the advocate lined up as a suspect in your murder investigation. And even if you have . . . '

'Even if I have. He's untouchable. Is that what you mean?'

'Is he in fact a suspect?'

'I've no reason to think so. I'm sorry to have wasted your time.'

'Don't apologise. Time with you is never time wasted, even when you make me uncomfortable. I don't like this any better than you, Jean. You haven't spoken of this list to Commissaire Schnyder, I suppose.'

'I didn't think it would interest him.'

'He's an efficient policeman all the same.'

'An efficient bureaucrat, and a careful one. So there's nothing to be done about the advocate's name appearing on Peniel's list. Is that what you recommend?'

Bracal smiled and squirted some more soda into his brandy.

'You know that as well as I do,' he said. 'File it away. Bury it deep. One day. You never know. And are you any closer to having a suspect for me – a suspect for the murder, I mean.'

'You're still interested?' Lannes said.

'Don't think so badly of me. A pre-war crime, you said, didn't you? That would be nice.'

'Yes, I'm closer. I've no proof, but I'm closer. But only if my candidate makes a mistake.'

'And you think he will?'

'I think he may. He's a respected figure, and that always imposes a strain on people who've been living a lie. They feel a burden of guilt from which professional criminals are free. It's a matter of ripping off the mask they wear.'

XLII

The sky was steel-grey, there was no wind and the streets of Mériadeck were silent. It wasn't only the cold that kept people inside. There was no light in the old tailor's shop, and when Lannes banged on the door, there was no response. He tried the handle without success. He peered through the window. The pane was smeared with dirt and it was difficult to make out anything in the dark interior. He tapped on it, and there was still no answer. An old woman approached. She had the yellow star sewn on to her coat, and, when she saw Lannes, she stepped into the gutter to pass him by. But he stopped her and said he was looking for old Léopold.

'I know nothing,' she said.

'I'm a friend,' he said. 'I'm here as a friend.'

'We no longer have friends. None of us have friends. So I can't help you. I must be on my way.'

'I think something may have happened to him.'

'And what's new about that?'

He remembered how Yvette had said 'we look after each other in Mériadeck'. No longer, it seemed. You couldn't blame them. You couldn't blame them for anything, not now.

There was a locksmith across the road. That too was closed and shuttered. He banged on the door, and again was met with silence. He banged a second time, more loudly, and this time was answered.

'Go away. We're closed.'

Lannes hesitated a moment.

'Police,' he shouted. 'Open up.'

He heard movement. A bolt was removed and a man's head poked round the door.

'I'm sorry to disturb you,' Lannes said.

'You're police and you're sorry to disturb me? That's good, that's rich.'

'I need your help.'

'You're police and you need my help. Pull the other one.'

Nevertheless, the door was now opened and a stocky middle-aged man wearing a dirty polo-neck jersey and baggy corduroy trousers stood before him.

'It's old Léopold, the tailor,' Lannes said. 'He's not answering his door.'

'Why would he?'

'I'm a friend. I'm not here on duty. I think something may have happened to him.'

'You think something may have happened to him? He should be so lucky. And you're not here on duty? A policeman and a friend of the old Jew. Who'd have thought it? By the waters of Babylon we sat down and wept . . . '

'When we remembered thee, O Jerusalem,' Lannes said. 'That's enough. Cut the jokes. Be a good chap and get your tools and see if you can get me in.'

The man looked at him full in the face for the first time.

'All right,' he said. 'Anything for an easy life. That's another joke. Sorry. You can't blame me for being suspicious.'

'I don't.'

Opening the door was the work of a minute.

'That's that,' the man said. 'Over to you. I don't want anything more to do with anything. You'll be able to lock up after yourself now.'

The light inside was dim, and there was a smell of dust, blood and brandy. The old tailor was in his chair, but he wasn't going to get out of it ever again, not of his own accord. His left wrist was cut, two diagonal strokes, criss-cross, and the knife had fallen to the floor. Lannes picked it up and laid it on the table beside the bottle which had only an inch or so left in it. He hadn't bothered with a glass. He had told Lannes he drank brandy only when he was afraid, but Lannes didn't believe that this had been the case. He had just decided it was time to go. There was a note on the table, two words only: *Why not?* Lannes had liked him and respected him. He would do him the justice of seeing that there was no fuss about the death. Rigor mortis had worn off. A stoic's death, he thought. Better than what had most likely been in store for him. Miriam had been his niece. He would have to tell her, but of course only because she was entitled to know, not because she should take the responsibility of making funeral arrangements. She was out of sight, safe or as safe as might be, in Henri's attic. No need either for a police investigation or autopsy; the old man wouldn't have wanted that. He would call an undertaker himself, get him to do what was necessary, and pay his bill. He felt he owed Léopold that. He would tell Yvette who had been fond of him – 'we look after each other in Mériadeck'. The pair of them might be his only mourners. There was no sign of the orange cat that had no name but Cat. He remembered Léopold's sour joke: all his previous cats had had names, but this one didn't, to remind himself that he was no longer Léopold Kurz the tailor, but only an old Jew. It would have been like him to have seen to the cat before . . .

He used the key the locksmith had left him and crossed the road to the bar below the Pension Bernadotte. The proprietor nodded in recognition and came out from behind the bar to shake his hand. Lannes asked him if he had known the old tailor. Of course he had; this was Mériadeck. Was there something wrong?

'He's killed himself. If you call that something wrong.'

'I don't know as I do. I'm not a Jew myself, but what they are doing to them is wicked. And I don't care who hears me say so. So if he's given them the slip . . . '

'That's one way of putting it.'

'It's my way anyway.'

He went behind the bar and poured two glasses of marc. He gave one to Lannes and raised the other to his lips.

'Old Léopold,' he said.

'Old Léopold.'

Perhaps there would be three at the funeral.

Lannes asked if he knew of an undertaker, and if he might use the telephone to call him.

'It's a public phone. Here's the number.'

When he had made the necessary arrangements and assured the undertaker that, no, though he was a policeman, there was no police interest and he was calling as a friend, he downed his marc, said thanks for the drink, and mounted the stairs to the Pension.

Old Mangeot was behind the desk as usual, digging into his mouth with a toothpick. He smirked when he saw Lannes.

'You're out of luck, superintendent. She's got company.'

'I'll wait.'

He sat down, leaning his head against the wall and closing his eyes. Reason said, what was one old man's death among so many? Reason was wrong as it often was.

He heard Yvette's door open and her voice saying, 'So long, sweetie.'

A young man passed, walking hurriedly, averting his eyes. Little more than a boy. Alain's age, Léon's too. He wondered if it was his first time. He knocked on Yvette's door and waited till she called, 'Who's there?'

'Lannes.'

She was naked and counting banknotes.

'Been waiting long? That was a nice boy. I was tempted to let him have it for free, but a girl's got to pay the rent. What's up? You're looking very serious. You're not jealous, are you?'

'Don't be silly. Put a dressing-gown on, or something.'

'So?' she said.

'It's old Léopold.'

'He's done it then?'

She sat down on the bed, her mouth open.

'You knew what he planned.'

'Not exactly, but . . . it was when he brought me the cat.'

She began to cry. He sat down beside her and held her in his arms, holding her tight and kissing her cheek.

'He said she would need a home . . . she's in the basket over there. Old Mangeot made a fuss about me keeping a cat, it's against his rules, he said, but I told him to fuck off. He's really done it?'

'I'm afraid so.'

'Poor old bugger. I really liked him, you know.'

'So did I, but it was his choice. For the best perhaps.'

'I know . . . but . . . all the same . . . kiss me again. Please.'

Later, he said, 'Are you sure you'll be all right?'

'Expect so. But thank you. For coming to tell me and for, well, everything.'

'That's all right. And you're happy to have the cat?'

'Course I am. Poor no-name cat. I won't ever give it a name. I owe the old boy that.'

XLIII

The telephone call was from Jules, the proprietor of the queer bar that used to have an English name, 'The Wet Flag'. He had already called twice, Lannes was told, but refused to speak to anyone but him.

'He sounded agitated,' young René said, which surprised Lannes who on his meetings with the man had been impressed, against his inclination, by Jules' self-possession – which was remarkable considering the dubious reputation of his establishment and its louche clientele.

'A shit of the first order,' Moncerre said.

'He said it was a personal matter,' René said.

'Personal with him means trouble, deep trouble.'

'Probably,' Lannes said, 'but I'll take the call nevertheless.'

All the same he hesitated, and when Jules said, 'It's urgent. I need to see you at once, alone, I can't tell you on the phone,' replied, 'All right, don't say anything, I'll be with you in half an hour.'

'I'll have to go,' he said. 'Did you manage to make an appointment with Duvallier, René?'

'Yes. Three o'clock tomorrow.'

'How did he sound?'

'Difficult to say. Not nervous. Quite calm really, almost pleased. Even – I know this sounds strange – amused.'

'Do you want us to come with you, chief?' Moncerre said.

Lannes lit a cigarette, shook his head.

'I think not. Whatever it is, he said "alone" and he's not likely to speak honestly if I have company. I'll call you if I need you.'

Whatever it is . . .

That was the problem. Why was he so sure it concerned Karim? He remembered how Jules had asked him to go easy on the boy the first time he had interviewed him, after Schussmann had shot himself. And, he had to admit, Karim aroused his own protective instinct. Why else would he have gone to the trouble of getting him safely out of Bordeaux then, and of helping him when Félix tried to use him so callously? What sort of mess had the boy got himself into now?

It was bitterly cold, freezing fog hiding the sky, the streets almost empty of people. What was there to bring the Bordelais out on such an afternoon when there was so little to buy in the shops and where at any moment you might see German soldiers to remind you of the humiliations to which you were subjected? Most had of course become accustomed to the realities of Occupation in the more than two and a half years since the Armistice, and everyone knew that the end wasn't in sight. Indeed the German grip had become tighter, partly on account of the increasing Resistance activity which also provoked more repression from the French state too.

Lannes leant heavily on his stick. The old tailor had looked curiously serene in death. There had even been a wry smile on his face, as if he had cheated them. Or was that his imagination? He couldn't be sure. But at least Léopold had chosen his own way out, though any sense of triumph must be tempered by the reflection that he had nevertheless given the bastards what they wanted – one Jew fewer. As for Yvette, poor girl, he had so nearly done what he had resolved not to do, what they both wanted, and he was ashamed to know how close he had come.

Jules was leaning with his elbows on the bar counter, and plucking at the wart on his cheek. It was a gesture which irritated Lannes. Was it unconscious, or did he deliberately draw attention to the disfiguring growth?

The bar was empty but for a couple of middle-aged men who, seeing him enter, quickly finished their drinks and left.

'Sorry to frighten your custom away,' he said.

'Tell you the truth, I'm happy to see the back of that pair.'

'So?'

Jules picked up the bottle of Armagnac which stood on the counter beside him, refilled his own glass and gave one to Lannes.

'You're going to need it,' he said.

'Bad as that?'

'Worse.'

'It's Karim?'

'How did you guess? It's Karim. Of course it's Karim. Thanks for coming so quickly by the way. He insisted I call you, which surprised me I have to say. You've certainly made an impression on him.'

'Oh yes? Where is he then?'

'He's in a bad way, trembling like a leaf and barely able to speak. I put him up in my own bedroom.'

'Been there before, has he?'

'None of your business.'

'As you like.'

'I'm fond of the kid, I'll admit that. Otherwise . . . in my line I can do without shit, and this is deep shit. Tell the truth, I wouldn't have known what to do if he hadn't said I must call you. I just hope he's right to rely on you. I hope to all the gods I've ever blasphemed that he's right.'

'Well, I can't know about that till I've heard what he has to say – if he's capable of saying anything.'

'He'd better be,' Jules said, and pulled at his wart again. 'Not that I want to know, whatever it is. My curiosity's strictly limited. That's how I keep going. Here's the key. It's the first door on the right. You'll be gentle with the kid, won't you?'

*   *   *

Karim was lying on the bed, in the foetal position. He wore only a singlet despite the freezing weather and a pair of blue cotton trousers. His leg twitched as Lannes closed the door and he turned his head towards him. His mouth was swollen and had been bleeding, and there were streaks of dried blood on his chin and on the dirty singlet. His left eye was bruised and already beginning to turn black. He gave a little moan or whimper, and screwed round to pull himself up with his back against the headrest. His mouth hung open and his lips moved as if he was making to speak, but instead he swallowed and no words came.

Lannes poured him a drink from the bottle he had brought up from the bar.

'I know you don't,' he said, 'but get this down. You need it.'

The boy stretched out his hand which was shaking and with difficulty got the glass to his lips. He did as he was told, knocking it back in one. Then he shuddered as if his stomach was heaving, and coughed. He lay back on the bed holding himself together and sweat started on his face.

'There's no hurry,' Lannes said. 'Take your time. Take all the time you need.'

He laid his hand on the boy's shoulder.

'It can't be that bad,' he said, though he knew it could. It could always be that bad.

He lit a Gauloise and gave himself another shot of the brandy; and waited, maybe five minutes, maybe longer. The room was very silent and cold, and the boy had stopped shaking. A dog barked somewhere in the street below. Its bark turned to a howl as if it had been shut out from its home and didn't understand why the world had turned against it.

'He's dead,' Karim said. 'It wasn't me but he's dead. You have to believe me. I didn't even know she had a gun.'

'So he's dead and you didn't know she had a gun. Who was he? Do you know that?'

For the first time the boy looked him in the face and when he spoke his voice was firmer.

'Of course I do. It was that bastard, the spook you called Félix.'

'Félix?' Lannes said. 'You're sure? Sorry, silly question. You couldn't not be sure.'

He put a cigarette between the boy's lips and lit it, another for himself.

'We'll take it slowly,' he said. 'The whole story, from start to finish.'

'Will you help me?'

'The story. Just what happened.'

He sat down on the bed by the boy's feet.

'We've got as long as you need,' he said.

It took time. The boy spoke in spurts, breaking down and crying more than once. He mostly kept his eyes averted, only once or twice looking up to see how Lannes was taking it. He was trembling again. He had been brought into the world of his worst dreams.

The old woman, his mother, had let Félix in. No problem: from her point of view he was a client and they needed the money.

Lannes imagined her turning away and back to her chair by the table which would have been littered with dirty dishes, plates of half-eaten and rejected food, overflowing ashtrays and of course her bottle of rum. Karim was asleep or near asleep, stretched out on his bed. He sprang up when he recognised Félix, who said, 'You little bastard, you filthy cunt,' and hit him, swinging his fist into his face so violently that Karim who had been getting to his feet was knocked down. Félix took hold of his hair and hauled him up, and then he hit him in the belly, so hard that Karim would have fallen down again, if Félix hadn't kept hold of his hair. Then, with his free hand, he swiped him twice across the face.

'I'd kill you,' he said, 'happily, if I didn't need you.'

'No,' Karim said. 'No, please . . .'

He couldn't meet Lannes' eyes when he said this; he was ashamed of his fear. Ashamed to have pleaded with the man.

Félix smiled.

'You fucking Arab whore,' he said, 'I see I'm going to have to remind you who you belong to.'

He threw Karim back on the bed. Karim screamed. Then, he didn't know exactly, there was a loud bang, then another, and Félix was thrown across him. The first shot had hit the wall, the second the back of Félix's head.

Or perhaps it was the other way round. He struggled out from under him and saw his mother standing there.

'She didn't even look surprised. She just let the gun fall from her hand and turned away.'

When Karim had pulled himself together and dabbed at his bleeding face with a towel, she was back sitting at the table with her glass in one hand and the other on the bottle of rum.

That at least was the course of events as Lannes reconstructed them from the boy's halting and disjointed story. It might be true. It might not. But there it was. Karim, exhausted by the telling, was weeping again.

Lannes said nothing while he smoked two cigarettes. Whatever the truth, Félix had asked for it. And – he thought of his conversation with Jacques Maso – he himself had been done a service.

'Are you going to arrest me?'

'For what?'

'And Maman?'

He had never called her that in speaking to Lannes; the old woman, the old bitch, the old sow, never Maman.

'A boy's best friend is his mother,' Lannes said.

He was in no man's land. He knew that. Whichever way he moved would determine which danger he was running towards.

'I'll take you home,' he said. 'But first wash your face.'

He pointed to a jug and basin which stood on a little marble-topped table.

'I'll have a word with Jules meanwhile.'

*   *   *

He knocked on the door that let in to the bar. Jules responded at once, as if he had been waiting for a summons.

'Did anyone see him arrive?'

'There were a few of my regulars in the bar when he turned up. But they wouldn't think anything of it, and in any case they're not the sort to blab. How is he?'

'Not good. But trouble's over. Nothing for you to worry about.'

'Thank Christ. I like a simple life.'

'You do? That surprises me. All the same we might be better to leave by a back door if you have one.'

'You're not taking the kid in?'

'No reason why I should. Like I said, trouble's over.'

Which of course it wasn't. It was only the First Act curtain. Nevertheless . . .

'Nevertheless,' he said, 'I don't want to bring the boy through the bar. That's certainly the conclusion your customers would jump to. The boy's had a bad scare. That's all you need know, Jules.'

'And you'll be gentle with him.'

'Your concern touches me. But there's no reason why I shouldn't be.'

*   *   *

The stench on the staircase was worse than ever, and there was no response when Lannes banged on the door. Karim bent down and called out 'it's me', and they heard shuffling footsteps and the sound of a bolt being withdrawn. The old woman with a half-smoked cigarette stuck to her lower lip took one look at Lannes, and turned away, back to her bottle.

Karim put his hand on her shoulder and asked her if she was all right.

She shook it off and looked at him with what might have been contempt. She picked up her glass and said nothing.

Lannes led the way through to the bedroom. He hadn't doubted the boy's story, only perhaps the details. The dead man was lying face down, the back of his head shattered. Lannes rolled him over, and some of the brains fell out. If he hadn't been told it was Félix, there wasn't enough left of the face to recognise him, but he didn't doubt the boy's identification. His belt had been unbuckled and his fly-buttons undone.

'I wonder if anyone saw him arrive,' he said.

Karim shook his head. He looked as if he might be about to faint. Lannes told him to sit down. He obeyed of course; for the moment he had no will of his own. He was as feeble as a pawn on the chessboard, but in real life you shouldn't sacrifice a pawn.

Lannes took out a handkerchief, picked up the gun, checked that it was now empty and slipped it into his pocket. He wondered how long the old woman had had it and where it had come from, but the answer wasn't important, and in any case he wasn't going to inquire. Probably she wouldn't be able to give an answer anyway. Others, their neighbours, must have heard the shots, some of them anyway, but in these times, this place, they would be happy to know nothing about anything.

It would be dark in half an hour. He already knew what he was going to do, and he knew that in coming to this decision, he had crossed his own rubicon. He went through the dead man's pockets, removing his notecase and any papers, then on second thoughts replaced them.

There was a trunk under the bed, a huge canvas trunk, the kind people take on a sea voyage. He leant down and pulled it out. It was covered in labels of shipping lines serving North Africa and the Levant.

'What's in this?'

Karim stirred.

'It's the old woman's costumes,' he said. 'You wouldn't think it to look at her now, but she used to be in a dance troupe. They toured all over the Mediterranean. It was in Algeria she met my father, or so she says. Sometimes even now when she's having a good day and has had only a couple of drinks she likes to get them out and run her hands over them. When I was a boy of ten or twelve, we would both dress up in them and dance together to the gramophone. She wasn't like she is now then, you understand. It was, well, lovely. You wouldn't think it but she was quite a looker even five or six years ago.'

It was extraordinary to think of, to picture that raddled hag as an attractive woman and Karim as a pretty boy wearing one of her suggestive costumes and dancing with her. But people could always surprise you when they gave you a glimpse of the hidden parts of their life.

'Empty it,' he said. 'We're going to need the trunk. So take the things out and lay them aside.'

When the boy didn't move, he said, 'I'm going to help you, Karim. But I can't do it all by myself. So, do as I say, there's a good boy.'

He sat and smoked while Karim took out the costumes one by one, stroking some of them as if the sight brought back memories of happier days.

He thought they could get away with it, and if they didn't, well, there would be no defence he could offer.

When the trunk was empty, he took off his overcoat, told Karim to take hold of Félix's legs while he got hold of him under the arms, and together they lowered him into the trunk. It was a tight fit, and they had to fold his legs up, but they got him in, and Lannes sat on its lid to hold it shut while he fastened the clasps. And, astonishingly, the boy still asked no questions, not even when Lannes said they would have to wait till it was dark.

At last the light failed, he put his overcoat on again and they carried the trunk into the other room. The old woman looked up, and said, 'Why are you letting him steal my trunk, you little bastard?'

'Don't be silly, Maman, he's helping us clear up the mess you made.'

'The mess I made! What do you mean, mess?'

'It's all right,' Lannes said, 'you'll get your trunk back.'

He told Karim to go and check that there was no one on the stairs. He wondered if the woman remembered what had happened, what she had done, or if she had blotted it out with rum.

The trunk was heavy, and one of the handles was frayed and in danger of snapping. But they got it down the stairs, meeting nobody, and out into the night. There was an alley, a cul-de-sac, fifty yards down the street, Lannes remembered. They turned in there and, when they were behind some rubbish bins, laid the trunk down and tipped the body out. Lannes had been tempted to leave it in the trunk, but the labels might invite dangerous questions. Probably they wouldn't. Who would have thought the old woman had once been what it seemed she had? But it was a risk better not taken.

When they were back in the apartment with the trunk, Lannes said, 'I'm keeping your gun. You're not safe with it.'

'What gun?' she said. 'I don't know nothing about a gun.'

'Good,' he said. 'Best you don't.'

He picked up his stick. At the door Karim said, 'Will it be all right?'

Nothing is ever all right, he thought.

'I can't see why it shouldn't be,' he said. 'He's nothing to do with you, remember that. But if you need to get in touch with me, which I'd prefer you didn't, do it by way of Jules, not young Jacques. There's no cause for him to be involved.'

'I don't know what to say.'

'That's all right. Best to say nothing. You don't know anything, so you've nothing to thank me for.'

He walked towards the river. He had broken the law, dishonoured his trade, and yet he wasn't ashamed. Indeed he felt freer of shame than he had for a long time. Which was absurd. And he was touched that the boy had turned to him for help, turned to a cop whom he hoped he could trust. Who would have thought the old woman could have hit her mark? A bullet in the back of the head. A stroke of luck, really, it surely signified an execution. He leant on the parapet over the rushing black of the water, took the gun from his pocket and hurled it in. There was scarcely even the sound of a splash. So much for Félix, for the moment anyway.

He stopped off in the Café des Arts for an Armagnac. The place was just about to close. He hoped Marguerite and Clothilde would have retired early to bed. He would have to sponge the jacket of his suit and it was better to invite no questions. 'What sort of day have you had?' 'Ordinary enough. I've dealt with a suicide, arranged a funeral, come within a whisker of betraying you with a tart –' not that he liked to think of Yvette as that – 'and covered up a homicide. Just routine. It's the way of the world we're condemned to live in.'

He lit a Gauloise, turned up the collar of his coat and stepped out, back into the night.

XLIV

The sponging hadn't got rid of the bloodstains. He would have liked to dispose of the suit. Let it follow the gun into the Garonne. But Marguerite would be sure to notice its disappearance. She might not ask questions, being afraid of the answers she might get, but she would be worried. So he had hung it in the back of the wardrobe, postponing explanations of its condition, the marks of blood on the jacket, till another day, and left home before either Marguerite or Clothilde was awake. He went to the little bar in the rue Vieil du Temple for coffee. He would have to tell Miriam of her uncle's suicide, but it was too early to call on them. And in truth he was reluctant to have to speak to anyone this morning. Someone, but he couldn't remember who, had once written that whoever forms a tie to another is doomed; the germ of corruption has entered his soul. The line had always rung false, the more so when he applied it to his feeling for Marguerite and the children. These were natural ties. How could they doom you? No doubt it depended on what you meant by the word. Family – that was where happiness was to be found, but also fear. And was Clothilde doomed by her feeling for Michel? Alain by his attachment to his Idea of France, Dominique by the very gentleness of his character, and Marguerite . . . he preferred not to think of his wife whom he had come so close to betraying with Yvette. Another tie there, and one that disturbed him.

And now Karim . . . why had he assumed responsibility for the boy whose activities he found repulsive? If his complicity in Félix's death was ever discovered, his career would be at an end; worse still, he would himself be an object of contempt since nobody would believe that he wasn't one of Karim's clients, his lover indeed. But how could he not have acted as he did? The sight of the bruised boy curled up in misery on Jules' bed had aroused his sense of pity, just as Léon had done. And that dreadful old woman who had once been beautiful and danced with her son as if they were on a stage and life too was beautiful, he was in debt to her, for that bullet in the back of Félix's head had done him a service too. Nevertheless, the germ of corruption, it couldn't be denied.

He took his second cup of coffee, laced with a glass of marc, into the street and sat at the little table the barman had just put there. The sky had cleared. Starlings wheeled above him and there was no wind. He remembered how he had sat there one morning and Léon had come round the corner leading Henri's little dog, Toto. Was that the day when Léon had said that at last he could forget he was talking to a policeman?

Henri was still in his dressing-gown, with carpet slippers on his feet, when he opened the door to him.

'Is something wrong?'

'No more than usual. I apologise for the early hour. It's just that I've a busy day ahead. How are you? How's Miriam?'

'Tired and anxious. Both of us. You look terrible yourself, Jean.'

'No worse than I feel. Sadly. And I'm afraid I've bad news for her.'

'Léon?'

'No, not Léon. I've no news of him. Nor of Alain.'

'It must be hard for you, Jean. Don't suppose I don't know how hard it must be, not knowing where Alain is. I'll tell her you're here. I don't know how much more bad news she can endure.'

They sat, scarcely speaking, while they waited for her to come down from the attic. To tell the truth Lannes welcomed the silence; it was companionable in its way. They'd known each other so long that there was no need to fill it; just being there with Henri was comfort of a sort. Then Henri opened a drawer in his desk and took out a postcard which he gave to Lannes. It was an old card dating from the Belle Époque, a picture of a Theatre Bill, the kind of thing you come upon in a box at one of the stalls beside the Seine.

Lannes turned it over. The message read: *I have so much to thank you for.*

'Léon?'

'I'm sure of it. It's postmarked Paris, as you see. That's why I was afraid you had news of him. Any news is likely to be bad, isn't it, if he's in Paris? Doing whatever he might be doing.'

'I've had no news,' Lannes said again. 'But you're right, except that if something were to happen to him, it's unlikely we would hear of it.'

Nevertheless, he thought, if Léon can send Henri a card, why can't Alain do the same for us? There was one answer which he shrank from and another with which he consoled himself: if he's in France, he has probably been forbidden to communicate with us, and perhaps Léon has written to Henri – without signing the card – only because he is lonely and afraid.

'I've been thinking,' Henri said, 'if he survives this war – if we both survive it – I'm going to adopt Léon as my son and heir. I've no one else, you know, and besides, now that his mother is dead, he has only Miriam and me.'

When Miriam joined them, descending the stairs cautiously as if she couldn't trust her legs, Lannes was again dismayed by how she seemed to be wasting away. What would Henri do if she was seriously ill? Was there a doctor he could trust?

She held out her cheek to Lannes for a kiss and hugged him hard.

'So you have more bad news,' she said.

'I'm afraid so. Is there any other kind these days? It's your uncle, old Léopold.'

She sat down.

'There are only two kinds of news, I suppose. Either he's been arrested in this round-up I've read about in the newspaper Henri buys, or he's dead. Which is it?'

'He's dead.'

'How?'

'He killed himself. I'm sorry to be the bearer of bad news.'

'I don't know,' she said. 'Is it bad news? He's escaped them, hasn't he?'

'Yes, he's escaped them. He chose his own way. You can't blame him.'

'Oh I don't. Perhaps I envy him.'

'Don't speak like that, Miriam,' Henri said. 'Please.'

Lannes explained that he had arranged for his burial, said it was impossible that Miriam should attend; it was more than ever imperative that she remained in hiding here, not only for her own sake, but for Henri's.

'And Léon's,' he added.

'Léon's? Do you really believe we'll ever see him again?'

He held up the postcard.

'We must believe we will. We must believe we'll see all of them again.'

Michel too, even Michel, he thought, for Clothilde's sake.

'What about his cat? He always had a cat. What has happened to it? Can you bring it here? I'm sure Toto wouldn't mind, Henri, would he?'

'Léopold gave it to a girl he knew and trusted. She's very pleased to have it.'

'A girl he knew and trusted? I suppose she's a tart. The old sinner always had a fancy for tarts.'

'Yes,' Lannes said. 'You could call her a tart. But she's a nice girl who was fond of the old man.'

'That's that then. I don't really want it. It was just an idea came into my head.'

XLV

Waiting for Dr Duvallier, it was strangely reassuring to feel like a policeman again. Then: it's just that I'm back on the tightrope, he thought, and you can fall off any minute, either side, and I'm not sure that there is a net to catch me if I do.

'Do you want me with you, chief?' Moncerre said.

'Have you something else urgent?'

'Nothing at all.'

'Well, you said from the start it was a pre-war crime. You may have been right.'

'I've read your notes. I don't see how we can prove anything,' Moncerre said. 'Not unless he's a fool.'

They were all three on edge; young René because he was responsible for bringing Duvallier to his notice; Moncerre because he was always in a sour mood these days, and not only on account of his wife, no matter what he said – Lannes knew he should broach the subject, but was afraid of the answer he might get; and Lannes himself because he was wondering when they would hear of the discovery of Félix's body. There was nothing to connect him with it, he was sure of that; nevertheless . . . he took the bottle of Armagnac from his cupboard and poured them all a drink.

Old Joseph, the office messenger, stuck his head round the door, and said, 'Your man's here.'

'Put him in the ante-room, will you, and bring him in in ten minutes. No harm in keeping him waiting,' he said. 'Moncerre, I want you to take the chair in the corner, behind him. Sit where he's aware of your presence, but can't see you without turning round. You sit here, René, and take notes. I'll make sure he realises you're recording everything he says.'

'Do you really think he's our man, chief?'

'No,' Moncerre said, 'it's just a game he's playing. We've nothing on him.'

'Happily, he doesn't know that.'

Lannes got to his feet when Joseph showed Duvallier in. The

doctor approached, holding out his hand, which Lannes affected not to notice. He told René to take Duvallier's coat and hat and hang them up.

'It's good of you to come, doctor,' he said.

'Oh I hope I'm a good citizen, ready to help the police, and in any case I'm interested to know if you have made any progress.'

'Progress? No, I wouldn't say that. These are two of my inspectors. Inspector Martin you already know of course, and Inspector Moncerre. We call him the bull-terrier because when he gets his teeth into a case, he never lets go. If you don't object, Inspector Martin will make notes of our conversation. He has excellent shorthand, and of course we'll have his notes typed up for you to read before we take any further action, assuming, that is, there is any to be taken. Are you agreeable?'

'Perfectly. And you don't object in turn if I smoke?'

'Not at all.'

The doctor took out a tobacco pouch in soft maroon leather and began to fill his pipe. He pressed it down with his thumb, and put a match to it. A couple of little puffs and it was going.

'I'm at your disposal, superintendent, but I should perhaps say that my time is not unlimited. I have a consultation at five and it is now' – he pulled a watch from his fob pocket, clicked it open – 'a quarter past three.'

'You told me, as I remember, that the advocate Labiche was one of your patients?'

'But one in excellent health. And a very distinguished citizen of Bordeaux, as you must be aware.'

'Distinguished, certainly. Did he know Madame Peniel – Gabrielle?'

'I should think it most unlikely. They moved in very different circles, as, again, you must be aware.'

'Very different circles? You have a note of that, René? And Gabrielle's father?'

'Her father? I know nothing of any father.'

'Perhaps you know him as her uncle. Édouard, or perhaps, Ephraim, Peniel.'

'Should I?'

'That's not for me to say.' Lannes lit a cigarette. 'So if he claimed to know you, he would be lying. Is that right?'

'I wouldn't say that. No, I wouldn't go so far as to say that. I'm a well-known figure, superintendent. I would suppose that there are many in Bordeaux who know me by sight or reputation, but of whom I am ignorant. Forgive me, but I am rather puzzled by these questions.'

'I appreciate that you are well known, doctor. One person I've spoken to told me you are known to have – how did he put it? – a handy way with a needle.'

'Who told you that?'

'Rather a disreputable young man, I confess. Not a reliable witness. Nevertheless, when he said that was your reputation – in his milieu, as he put it – I was naturally interested. Of course I had no reason to believe him. Nevertheless.'

'I should hope not. The suggestion is slanderous. Naturally, as a doctor, I occasionally have been required to give some of my patients an injection. Of a sedative, you understand. For anxiety.'

'For anxiety? I understand. But Gabrielle was a morphine addict, wasn't she?'

'Who told you that?'

Lannes smiled.

'Keep calm, doctor. An informed source, shall we say? I'm sure that, as a doctor, you respect the principle of confidentiality. We in the police respect it too.'

'If you are suggesting that I supplied her with morphine, that too is slanderous.'

'I've made no such suggestion,' Lannes said. 'Quite the contrary. The same source actually told me that she had been cured of her addiction, and certainly there is no evidence that she was taking drugs at the time of her death.'

Duvallier swallowed twice, then put a match to his pipe. His hand was quite steady.

'The poor woman did indeed have such an addiction, and indeed I administered a cure. She put herself in my hands because she trusted me. Trusted and respected. I've certainly nothing to be ashamed of. Quite the contrary.'

Moncerre got up, and crossed the room to stand behind the doctor. He put his hands on his shoulders and pressed down hard.

'Quite the angel of mercy, aren't you, doc? All the same, why don't you admit it? Like the superintendent said, you're a handy man with the needle, aren't you?'

'Superintendent, I came here of my own accord, to help you with your enquiries, not to be slandered.'

'Inspector Moncerre asked you a question. That's all. Putting a question isn't slanderous. Besides, you came today because I asked you to come and I did so because you interest me and I have some other questions to put to you. You interest me because you forced yourself on my notice, and I tend to find that suspicious. Why did he do that? I asked myself. And then you told me two lies. First, you gave me to understand that Gabrielle became your patient only after she left Madame Jauzion's employment, and then you said that Madame Jauzion was herself still your patient. But she dismissed you, didn't she? Then I learnt why she did so: because of your association, your peculiar association perhaps, with her uncle, the advocate Labiche, whom she detests. Detests with good reason, I should add. It was a stupid lie, an unnecessary one, and I am always curious when I am told needless lies. The result is that I find myself questioning anything the liar says to me. And now this afternoon you have told me another: saying you have no knowledge of Édouard, or Ephraim, Peniel, who is, or believes himself to be, Gabrielle's father, and who certainly acted as her accomplice in procuring underage girls to satisfy the perverted demands of her clients. What do you say to that?'

Duvallier made no immediate reply. He looked Lannes in the eye, as if challenging him to hold his gaze, and raised his chin, in the manner of press photographs of Mussolini. Then he put another match to his pipe, and said, 'I've already told you I know nothing of the man you speak of.'

'Interesting,' Lannes said. 'We'll come back to him later. Were you on good terms with Gabrielle?'

'She was my patient. Our relationship was purely professional.'

'You visited her frequently, didn't you?'

'No more than other patients who require my attention. I'm a conscientious physician, superintendent, as anyone will tell you. Moreover she was, as you know, my stepdaughter's piano teacher.'

'Quite so. And suffered, as you have told me, from attacks of anxiety.'

'Precisely.'

'You never quarrelled with her?'

'I had no reason to do so.'

'And yet, there was an occasion when she seemed to threaten you with some unpleasant consequences, admittedly unspecified, if you failed to keep to an agreement you had made with her.'

'I have no memory of such an occasion.'

'And yet we have a witness to it.'

Duvallier drew on his pipe. Lannes opened the drawer of his desk and took out a notebook, which he pretended to consult.

'It's clear enough,' he said. 'I have it in writing. You explained to our witness that Gabrielle was a hard woman who didn't always mean what she said. On account of her anxiety perhaps?'

The doctor smiled.

'Of course,' he said. 'That poor little girl, Marie. She was alarmed. Unnecessarily alarmed, for it meant nothing. But I put her mind at ease.'

'I see. It meant nothing, and you put her mind at ease. And this agreement?'

'It was of no importance, of so little importance that I forget what she was talking about. She spoke wildly sometimes, poor woman. Superintendent, as I said, I have a consultation this afternoon. I came here – at your request, as you say, to try to help you. But, to speak frankly, you are wasting my time, which is valuable, and your own, which is doubtless valuable also. So I think that's enough.'

He got to his feet and looked round for his coat.

'As you say, doctor, time is valuable and I am grateful to you for giving me so much of yours. There is just one other thing. The man, Peniel, Gabrielle's father, whom you say you don't know, gave me a list of Gabrielle's clients, that's to say, of the men for whom she procured under-age girls. Your name is on that list, along with the advocate Labiche's. What do you have to say to that?'

Duvallier picked up his coat.

'What do I have to say? That the suggestion is monstrous, slanderous, utterly untrue, without foundation, and if it's repeated, I shall have to consult my lawyer. Besides, this Peniel is well known to be a disreputable character. I believe he was once a doctor, struck off for performing abortions. His word is worthless, everyone knows that. Nobody would hang a cat on his word.'

'I'm sure you're right,' Lannes said. 'You seem well informed, considering that you don't know the man. That will be all, for this afternoon. Thank you for your time. Perhaps you will be kind enough to call here tomorrow morning, and sign the record of our conversation which Inspector Martin will have typed out for you.'

When Duvallier had gone, Moncerre, without saying anything, filled their glasses.

'Why the hell, chief,' he said, 'have you let him go?'

'Did he do it?' young René said.

'Oh yes, I think so, don't you? Moncerre, I want you to put a tail on him. Someone reliable this time. As to your question, sometimes you have to play out the line to land your fish. René, you'll pick up the girl, Marie. Take her to the Pension Bernadotte, and get old Mangeot to give her a room. Then tell the girl Yvette she's to keep an eye on her. She's not to leave her room. And tell old Mangeot that I'll have his guts for garters if he lets anyone know she's there. Speak to Madame Mangeot too, she's a decent enough old thing. As for your tail, Moncerre, tell him Duvallier will go looking for the girl. And, René, when you've seen to Marie and explained the position to her mother, you'll type up the record, make two copies, and take one through to Judge Bracal. It'll be his case from now on. Oh, and say to the Mangeots and Yvette that I'll be round there in the morning. I think that's everything.'

XLVI

As usual these days he had slept badly. There was no joy at home, Marguerite's eyes filling with tears several times in the evening, and Clothilde looking like the tragic heroine of a romantic novel, which, poor girl, in a sense she was. The evening meal was passed in silence, and when Lannes picked up a book to read, he found himself unable to concentrate even on the adventures of his beloved musketeers. In any case he couldn't now read of the young d'Artagnan without Alain's face coming between him and the page. When he took Marguerite a cup of lime tea in the morning, she turned away from him. He told himself it was in reality the world from which she was withdrawing, but, though he pitied her, he also resented her misery. Clothilde's was different. He could sympathise more easily with it, but had no words of comfort for her. He feared after all that she would never see Michel again – and if she did, wouldn't he be changed, damaged, by whatever he was going to experience?

There was a pile of paperwork on his desk, and for once he almost welcomed it. No matter how tedious and futile, it would at least serve as distraction. But he had done no more than run his eye over the first couple of documents, in which, needless to say, there was nothing of interest or importance, when old Joseph poked his head round the door to say that the Alsatian, as even he now called Commissaire Schnyder, wanted to see him.

'Urgent, he says, I've not seen him in such a tizzy.'

'Ah well, I've got something to cheer him up,' Lannes said, taking the box of smuggled Havanas which Fernand had handed him the previous week, and which he had forgotten till now to pass on to the Alsatian. He wondered if Duvallier had lodged a complaint. No matter if so; the case would be with Bracal that afternoon, and so out of his hands.

Schnyder's room was the only warm one in the building. How did he manage it?

The Alsatian had company, a lean tawny-skinned man in a dark suit. Lannes felt foolish to be carrying the cigars.

'I believe you left these in my office, sir,' he said, laying the box on the desk.

'What? Oh, my cigars?' Schnyder said. 'I wondered where I had left them. A present from a friend at the Spanish consulate.'

'You're a lucky man to have such a friend. So this is Super-intendent Lannes? I've heard much about you,' the visitor said, extending his hand.

'Nothing bad, I hope,' Lannes said.

'This gentleman has come from Vichy – he belongs to an organisation he would rather not name, but which . . . '

The Alsatian broke off, uncertain how to proceed.

'And I myself,' the man said, 'generally prefer to pass incognito. The name Fabian will serve well enough. Superintendent, I arrived in Bordeaux because we have a problem, only to find that it has taken what I may call an even more unfortunate turn. I believe you may be able to help us.'

'I'm at your disposal.'

'Perhaps we should all sit down. What I have to say is embarrassing, and may take some time.'

The Alsatian shifted in his seat, and ran his hand through his hair.

'May I offer you a cigar?' he said. 'They're genuine Havanas, as you see, Romeo y Juliettas, not, I have to say, my favourite brand, but these days one must be grateful for what one can get, or is given.'

The man who called himself Fabian said, 'Thank you, but I prefer cigarettes.'

'As you like,' the Alsatian said. 'It occurs to me that it might be most suitable if you were to discuss your problem with Super-intendent Lannes alone, and in any case, I must apologise. I have an important meeting with the Prefect, for which I am in danger of being late. So perhaps, Jean, you will be good enough to take our visitor to your own office. It's been a pleasure to meet you, sir.'

* * *

'A careful man, your commissaire,' Fabian said, settling himself in the chair in which Duvallier had sat the previous afternoon. 'And of course he is wise to be careful. Do you suppose he really has an appointment with the Prefect?'

'I've no idea,' Lannes said. 'There's no reason why he shouldn't have.'

'And every reason why he should prefer to know nothing of my little problem. We live in days when it is often wise to be ignorant.'

'If you say so.'

'Would it be possible to get coffee, no matter how bad it may be?'

'I'll ask Joseph, our office messenger, to have it brought to us.'

When he came back into the office, Fabian had placed a packet of the Italian cigars called Toscani on the desk, and was cutting one in half with a pocket-knife.

'I'm a terrible liar, you see,' he said. 'I really prefer these to cigarettes and also to Havanas. It's a habit I learnt in Indo-China where I spent several years – which accounts for my complexion, malaria, you know – and developed a taste for the cheroots they make in Burma which used to be available everywhere in the East. These are the nearest equivalent I have found in Europe, and fortunately a friend in the Italian embassy in Vichy keeps me supplied with them. Like your commissaire with his friend – in the Spanish consulate, didn't he say? May I offer you one?'

'Thank you, no, I actually do prefer cigarettes.'

He tapped out a Gauloise and lit it.

'The coffee will be terrible,' he said. 'May I offer you a glass of Armagnac?'

'Alas no. I suffer from liver trouble, another legacy of the East I'm afraid. But don't let me stop you.'

Lannes crossed to the cupboard, took out the bottle and a glass, brought them back to his desk and poured himself a drink. He wouldn't touch it till Joseph arrived with the coffee, at which point, he assumed, his visitor would explain why he was there.

'The Italians still have an embassy in Vichy?'

'It lingers on. To little purpose. Like so much these days, wouldn't you say?'

'Perhaps.'

'You've been recommended to me,' Fabian said. 'As an honest man.'

He smiled, as if, Lannes thought, the idea of there being an honest man amused him because it was improbable.

'By a mutual friend, Edmond de Grimaud. He speaks well of you.'

'Kind of him.'

'We spoke of you the other night, after I had had dinner with him, and his son and your son too – Dominique, isn't it? A charming boy, de Grimaud's also, two charming boys indeed. I imagine you are proud of the work they are doing.'

'I'm told it's useful.'

'Another careful man. I like that. But perhaps you are not careful in quite the same way as your commissaire? Would I be correct in supposing that his chief care is to avoid responsibility and, as the vulgar expression has it, keep his nose clean?'

Fortunately, at that moment, Joseph came in with the coffee, and Lannes had no need to answer the question.

'You are right,' Fabian said. 'Terrible. If there was no other reason for looking forward to the end of the war, it would be enough to hope one might again have drinkable coffee. You've had some dealings with a man calling himself Félix.'

It was a statement, not a question.

'And you enquired about him when you were in Vichy in the summer of '41.'

'You are well informed. He was described to me as a bit of a loose cannon.'

'And you have had further dealings with him since, here in Bordeaux.'

'We had lunch together one day.'

'After which, I believe he lodged a complaint against you.'

'So I've been told.'

'But nothing came of it?'

'Nothing.'

'Quite so. But I must tell you there was some anxiety – I won't say actual suspicion, but anxiety – in Vichy. If Edmond de Grimaud hadn't vouched for you, the matter might have been more thoroughly investigated. But he did. So it passed over. What do you know of Félix's activities here in Bordeaux?'

'Very little. He talked at length but not specifically. He was interested in a murder case which had come my way. But it had nothing to do with him, a purely domestic crime. One of my inspectors was certain from the start that it was what he called "a pre-war crime". I was doubtful at first, but in fact he was right.'

'So you've solved it?'

'I believe so.'

'And there is no aspect of it that might interest me or my department?'

Lannes picked up his glass which he had left untouched, sniffed the brandy and took a sip.

'How can I tell,' he said, 'what might interest you? Or your department since I don't know what that is. There was a suggestion it might involve the Resistance, whatever form that may take, but there was nothing in it. Nothing at all, no public aspect of the death.'

Fabian struck a match to relight his cigar which had gone out, the way Toscani do.

'You haven't asked me why I'm here.'

'I'm assuming you'll tell me. When it suits you to do so.'

'Careful again. I like that. What did you learn of Félix's activities here in Bordeaux?'

'Very little. He spoke at length but wildly. Of the necessity for Vichy, among other things. He talked loosely, at random. Frankly he bored me. He also insisted, repeatedly, that he was a patriot.'

'And what did you reply to that?'

'I had no reason to doubt him.'

'Who do you think will win the war?'

'What sort of question is that? I can hope only that France will come out of it less damaged and less divided than seems likely.'

Fabian smiled. He leant back in his chair and swung his right leg over, resting its ankle on his left knee.

'You're a pessimist, superintendent?'

'It seems the best thing to be.'

'Félix is dead. Killed. A shot in the back of his head. Does that surprise you?'

Lannes held his glass up.

'I won't drink to it,' he said, 'or to his memory. But, no, it doesn't surprise me. Why should it? Deaths are common these days. I thought him a fool and a meddler. So, no, I can't say it surprises me.'

'And you know nothing of it, of course?'

'Why should I?'

Fabian drew on his cigar, but it had gone out again, and he struck another match, rotating the flame around the tip of the cigar.

'A bullet in the back of the head,' he said. 'An execution perhaps?'

'Perhaps.'

'Or intended to look like that?'

'It's possible,' Lannes said. 'Depends who might want to kill him, I suppose. Do you have a candidate?'

'There are possibilities. The Resistance, naturally – he was reporting on their activities. One of our Occupying friends? That's possible too. He was attempting – against orders, I may say, but then he saw himself as a lone wolf – to try to compromise a German officer. I believe you know something of that?'

'Do I?'

'There was a liaison officer, name of Schussmann – Félix wrote a report about him. Then he shot himself. You knew him, didn't you?'

'Certainly,' Lannes said. 'He seemed a decent chap, all things considered. But I can't say why he committed suicide. It was of course no business of mine.'

'But you were required to carry out an investigation. There was a question of blackmail, I believe. On account of his proclivities. You know what I mean. There's no need to fence with me, superintendent.'

'Fencing?' Lannes said. 'Not something I've ever practised, not since I was a boy reading Dumas for the first time and we played at being the Musketeers and the Cardinal's Guard, with sticks instead of swords. But of course I know what you mean. There was talk of what Schussmann's successor – Kordlinger his name was – called "degenerate boys". I was required to look into it. But nothing came of it.'

'Quite so. For the best, doubtless. But then Kordlinger arrested you, and beat you up, I believe?'

'Not the pleasantest experience.'

'And,' Fabian smiled again, 'you turned the tables on him, by divulging information which would have compromised him, information given you by a friend in Vichy, a colleague of mine as it happens.'

'Yes,' Lannes said. 'That was fortunate. But what has this to do with Félix?'

'Nothing at all, I suppose, unless he was killed by one of these degenerate boys, or another one. You knew that he was homosexual?'

'Should I have?'

'Oh, I think so, don't you? Not that we would want to bring this into the light. For his family's sake, you understand. His father is a man of some standing in Vichy.'

'I know nothing of that,' Lannes said. 'In any case, it doesn't concern me.'

'I'm glad to hear it. Do you know, superintendent, I think I'll take a chance with my liver and have a glass of your doubtless excellent brandy. It's years since I've drunk any. Just a small one. Your health!'

'Your health!'

They met each other's eyes, and this time Lannes returned Fabian's smile.

'I'm the man called in to see about the trouble,' Fabian said, 'and this time my role is to sweep it out of sight. It would, frankly, be awkward to ask questions about this death. Awkward and even futile. Besides, as you will have gathered, I'm sure, the man was a nuisance. No reason why he should be an even bigger one in death than in life. You understand?'

'Perfectly,' Lannes said.

'Out of sight, out of mind. By the way I think you have another son besides the charming boy I met in Vichy?'

'Yes.'

'And he is where?'

Lannes raised an eyebrow and turned down the corners of his mouth.

'I see. I trust all is well with him. These are difficult times for adventurous youth.'

'For all of us,' Lannes said.

XVII

Duvallier would be taken to Bracal as soon as he had signed young René's record of the interview. Moncerre was doubtful.

'You've given him too much rope,' he said. 'The tail I put on him reports that he went straight round to the girl Marie's home and looked in a state when he came out, no doubt because her mother told him that a policeman had spirited her away. He'll be alarmed.'

'So he should be,' Lannes said. 'That's how we want him, isn't it?'

'But what makes you think he'll keep his appointment here?'

'His vanity. He's still sure we have nothing on him, and he'll easily offer an excuse for trying to get hold of Marie. Besides, not to keep the appointment would seem to him more dangerous, even an admission of guilt. I'll add your tail's report to the papers I send through to the judge. And I'm also advising him to make an order to require the doctor to produce a financial statement. I'm pretty sure Gabrielle was blackmailing him. It's the obvious motive.'

'If you say so, but I still think you should have held him yesterday.'

'No,' Lannes said, 'we've given him that little bit more rope. There's nothing to worry about, my old bull-terrier. And congratulations by the way. You were right from the start, and I was wrong. It's a genuine pre-war crime.'

'There's one thing I still don't understand,' René said. 'How did he persuade her to take her clothes off? They weren't lovers, were they? And anyway you said she was a lesbian. It doesn't make sense to me.'

'It wasn't meant to,' Lannes said. 'Moncerre here was right about the sort of crime it was, but I was right too in thinking the set-up was all wrong, intended to distract us. You're right too, René, in questioning it now, but of course all the stage management stuff was put in place after he killed her which he did when she was still fully clothed. To suggest a crime of passion, which it wasn't. He strangled her, probably when she was counting the money – the latest payment – he had handed to her. Then he carried her through to the bedroom, stripped her, and knocked over the bottle of scent, deliberately of course, before arranging the set-up in the salon. I wouldn't be surprised if he actually sat there, drinking the bottle of champagne, taking care to pour some into what we were supposed to think was her glass, and even smoked the cigar. He probably enjoyed it – he's a cold-blooded bastard. And he would do all this wearing surgical gloves.'

Moncerre laughed.

'Maybe, maybe not. But it'll do. So we've all got it right? Makes a change, don't it?'

'A nice change,' Lannes said. 'When you've delivered him to the judge, join me at Fernand's.'

'A celebration lunch?' Moncerre said. 'I don't believe it.'

When he was alone, Lannes took the envelope old Joseph had given him on arrival, and slit it open. There was a single sheet, a one-line message on notepaper with a German heading which he didn't trouble to identify.

I'll be where we met before, at eleven o'clock this morning. K.S.

*　　*　　*

Schuerle rose to greet him, extending his hand which Lannes accepted.

'At last,' he said, 'a beautiful morning. I hope it hasn't been inconvenient for you to come here.'

'Not at all.'

'I wanted to say goodbye.'

'Goodbye?'

'Yes, I've been ordered home to Berlin.'

'Promotion?'

'Perhaps, perhaps not. I'll be sorry to leave Bordeaux. You may not believe me but it's been restful being here, and agreeable.'

'And Berlin?'

'Won't be.'

He smiled. Lannes hesitated, unsure what to make of that smile.

'It has pleased me,' Schuerle said, 'to think we have understood

225

each other, even to suppose that in other circumstances we would have been good friends. You don't need to reply to that, super-intendent.'

Lannes looked across the gardens where a wintry sunshine was flickering on the bare wet branches of the trees.

'We're losing the Battle of Stalingrad. There's no question of that,' Schuerle said. 'It's the turn of the tide, perhaps the beginning of the end. Only the end is still a long way off, unless . . . '

'Unless those friends you spoke of . . . '

'Precisely.'

'And you expect to see some of them in Berlin?'

'Hope to, anyway. You understand me.'

'What are their chances?'

'Slim. Very slim. The regime is still strong. And, of course, how do you define patriotism?'

'I don't know,' Lannes said. 'Here in France, the Marshal is a patriot. But so is de Gaulle.'

'And the Communists?'

'In their own fashion. But they don't object to seeing France suffer.'

'Perhaps if we both survive the war, we may meet again and make sense of it all.'

'What are the odds on that?' Lannes said.

'In your case, my friend, I don't know. You don't object that I call you "my friend"?'

'Not at all. And in yours?'

Schuerle smiled.

'You fought at Verdun, My father was killed there. That's a sort of bond between us. As to your question, what can I say? Some of my friends assure me that Right must prevail.'

Lannes said, 'There's a boy my daughter is in love with. He's brave and foolish, and has been led by a man he admires to join this Legion of French Volunteers against Bolshevism. I tried to prevent him and failed. I can't believe she will ever see him again. It's the madness of war.'

'Yes. From what I hear Stalingrad is as terrible as Verdun. The madness of war.'

XLVIII

Because it was nearby and because he felt guilty, Lannes went to call on Michel's grandfather, the retired Professor of Literature who looked like a colonel. The elderly maid answered his ring, and said, 'The professor's not well, he shouldn't have visitors, but he wouldn't be pleased if I turn you away. He was speaking of you only yesterday. Wait here, will you, please.'

The hall with its tiled floor was cold as everywhere in the city was now, and there were several bulbs dead in the electrolier, so that more than half the space was in deep shadow. A piano was being played somewhere. Anne-Marie, he supposed, a tune he recognised but couldn't name, perhaps because she was playing it so slowly, picking the music out note by note. It was a piece she was learning, he supposed, and was still some way from mastering.

The professor was sitting in the chair from which he rarely moved now, and Lannes had the impression that the maid had disturbed the half-sleep which the old and weary drift in and out of. He rubbed his eyes with the back of his mottled hand. There was a rug wrapped round his thin legs and his pince-nez dangled on a black ribbon. Lannes apologised for intruding on him.

'I've been asking myself,' the professor said, 'where I went wrong. Was I too indulgent with the boy? I'm afraid I spoilt him, let him have his head, should have kept him on a tighter rein.'

'I would think he was an easy boy to spoil,' Lannes said. 'It's the fate of those who have charm.'

'Fate?'

'The wrong word perhaps, but I can't think of a better.'

The professor rang the little bell that stood on the occasional table by his side, and asked the maid to bring them sherry.

'I still have a few bottles,' he said to Lannes. 'I won't live to drink them all. How is your daughter?'

'Miserable, she's afraid she will never see Michel again.'

And even if she does, he thought, he'll be so marked by whatever he is going to experience that he will be a different person. But there was no point saying this to the old man.

'I would be happy if she was to come to see me,' the professor said. 'And so would Anne-Marie. She's lonely, poor child.'

'I tried to discourage him,' Lannes said, aware how feeble the words sounded.

'Oh yes, but he had the bit between his teeth.'

The music had stopped. There was no sound in the salon but for the ticking of the black marble clock that stood on the mantelpiece. The little fox-terrier woke and scratched himself and went back to sleep. The maid brought in the decanter and gave them each a glass. The professor turned his round between his fingers.

'There's nothing to drink to, is there?' he said.

'A safe return,' Lannes said. 'It's what we must hope for.'

For all of them, he thought. Surviving, that's the only true war aim. Nothing else matters. All these young people will see terrible things, do terrible things, learn what they are too young to know. He thought of Schuerle returning to Berlin and of what he himself had learnt at Verdun.

The professor coughed and put a white-spotted red handkerchief to his mouth. He leant back exhausted, struggling for breath. Lannes looked away. His visit was futile. He didn't know what he had hoped to achieve. He put down his glass and prepared himself to go.

The professor said, 'I have something on my conscience. That's another reason why I am pleased to see you, superintendent. I had a visit two days ago, from an old Russian, an aristocrat, he said, before the Revolution, who served subsequently in our Foreign Legion and now runs a gymnasium here in Bordeaux which Michel attended, and where he taught him to box – Michel was passionate about boxing, collecting photographs of that "noble art" as they call it. The old man was distressed, told me he loved Michel – "with a pure love", he insisted, and I dare say he was speaking the truth – but was now consumed with guilt because, as he said, he had filled the boy's head with nonsense. He had tried – too late – to dissuade him from the course he has taken. He spoke in that exaggerated manner we are all familiar with from Russian novels, and I confess it embarrassed me, no matter how I admire such effusions in Dostoyevsky.'

He paused to light a cigar and Lannes saw that his hand was shaking.

'So?' he said.

'He spoke at great length about his sins, which I confess bored me. And then he said it was another man who had been Michel's evil genius. I think you may know who he was referring to.'

'I believe I do.'

'And then he said he would kill him, and went away, still in tears, still sobbing. What do you make of it, superintendent?'

'I don't know,' Lannes said. 'I've never read the Russians you speak of.'

XLIX

'Something's gone out of me,' Maurice said. 'I don't know what exactly, but . . . how do you feel, Dom?'

It was night. They were sitting in the stone-flagged kitchen of a château in the mountains. The kerosene lamp on the table flickered as the wind blew through a broken pane, and each was huddled in a greatcoat to protect him against the cold. The troop of boys for whom they were responsible had been dispatched to sleep on the floor of the improvised dormitory in what had once been the salon of the half-ruined building. The flickering light threw weird shadows on the wall. The litre bottle of red *vin ordinaire* was almost empty, and since neither of them usually drank much, both were conscious of being a little drunk.

'I don't know,' Dominique said. 'Perhaps it's just that this present bunch is a poor lot. A year ago most of the kids were enthusiastic. Now they seem sullen and reluctant. They don't want to learn anything.'

'And isn't there a reason for the change?' Maurice said. 'Mightn't it be because we ourselves no longer believe in the value of our work, and our disillusion communicates itself to them?'

'You mean we no longer believe as we once did in Vichy or the National Revolution?'

'Well do you?'

'I don't know.'

'One of us had to say it.'

'And if we don't, if we have lost faith,' Dominique said, 'what then?'

'I don't know. It's beastly cold. There's a real gale blowing up. And I think it's going to snow.'

'The kids'll be frozen up there.'

'I suppose they will,' Maurice said. 'We might as well finish this bottle, don't you think? It's not just us, you know. The mood in Vichy's changed. Even my father's on edge. Before we set out, he said goodbye to me in a way in which he has never said it before, almost as if he thought he might never see me again. He kissed me on both cheeks and held me close to him. I felt for the first time that he loved me and also that he's afraid. I've never known him like that, though, actually, there was nothing unusual, let alone dramatic, in our parting – we were only about to set off on this trip which is now routine for both of us, and he is just off to Bordeaux, on family business, he said.'

Dominique picked up his glass and swirled the wine round.

'There's something I have to tell you,' he said.

'That's an ominous opening, it usually precedes bad news.'

Maurice smiled and lit a cigarette.

'Go on, then,' he said, 'No secrets between us, we agreed long ago, didn't we?'

'You know François, don't you?'

'I know several. Which one?'

'Mitterand, he was in the camp with me. We met him with your father once, didn't we?'

'Oh,' Maurice said, 'that François. He's rather a pet of Papa's, one of our rising intellectuals, he says. I never know how serious he is when he speaks like that. There's usually mockery in the background. What about him?'

'He's forming a network, asked me if I'd like to join, a network of ex-prisoners-of-war, he said.'

'For what?'

'What does it sound like?'

'Resistance?'

'Yes. He didn't spell it out, but . . . '

'And?'

'I said I didn't know, which I don't. I said I'd have to think about it, talk it over, with you, I said. We do everything together, I said. All right, François said, bring him in, the more the merrier.'

'I wasn't a prisoner of war.'

'Doesn't matter, apparently. What do you think?'

'I don't know.'

There was a knock on the door. A small boy stood there, shivering.

'I want to go home,' he said. 'I'm afraid.'

Dominique got up and put his arm round him.

'It's all right,' he said. 'We're all afraid sometimes, and sick for home. It's all right.'

*   *   *

The girl kissed Léon on the mouth for the first time.

'Did that surprise you?' she said.

It had of course, but he wasn't sure which answer she expected, or hoped for. So he said nothing and smiled.

'You didn't want it, did you?' she said. 'I know you don't really like girls.'

'What makes you think that?'

'I can always tell. I kissed you because I'm afraid.'

'We're all afraid,' Léon said. 'Or we should be. Being afraid keeps you wary.'

It was what he wanted to believe, but being afraid also made it more likely you would give yourself away. That morning, when he had stepped out of the metro at the Odéon station and a policeman had asked for his papers and stood examining them and frowning for what seemed like minutes before he nodded and handed them back, he had almost wet himself. He couldn't tell the girl that.

'I can't sleep these days and I can't eat either,' she said. 'I put the food in my mouth and chew and chew and I can't swallow. When's it going to end?'

'We just have to keep going,' he said. 'Give me the stuff.'

'Here it is. I'm glad to be rid of it. If you're caught with it . . . '

'I know. Transcribe, send and burn. That's my orders. That's what I do.'

'Do you think we're doing any good?'

'Yes, of course. We must believe that.'

'It's a pity you don't like girls. I'd like you to fuck me.'

'No, you wouldn't. Not really. I'd better be going.'

This was the danger moment. Crossing Paris with this paper in his pocket. If he was stopped – but he wouldn't be, he had to believe he wouldn't be.

'I'm sorry,' he said. 'But you'll be all right. Go and have a glass of wine. That'll set you up. I'm really sorry. It's just nerves, you know.'

He kissed her on the cheek, gave her a hug, as if they were indeed lovers parting for the moment, saying goodbye.

Two hours and he would be free of it. Then dinner with Chardy at 'a little restaurant I know where they're understanding'. His attentions were becoming pressing, but he would hold him off, 'nothing doing' he would say, politely. He wondered where Alain was, as he did several times every day. And at night. Of course at night, always at night, every night.

*   *   *

Alain lay in the ditch. His leg stung. The bastards had winged him as he crashed through the trees. There had been just a moment when the policeman had relaxed his grip, and he'd torn himself free, kicked him on the kneecap and ran. Now there was silence. The cars had driven away. Or he thought they had. Couldn't be sure, might have been other cars. He held himself as still as possible, trying not to breathe. Silence, blessed silence. They'd been betrayed. That was obvious. Who had chosen that house for the meeting? It was crazy, a building with no back exit. The Gestapo were ready for them; their cars had driven up within minutes of the meeting starting. Bastards.

'You can come out now. It's safe. They've all gone.'

He raised his head. An old man with a beard, wearing a dirty raincoat.

'I was gathering sticks in the wood, broken branches, for fire-wood. I saw it all. You were lucky.'

Alain got to his feet. No reason not to trust the man.

'Thanks,' he said. 'That was a close one.'

'You're wounded.'

'I'm all right. Just a flesh one, I think. In the calf. That's all.'

'Lot of blood, though. Are you sure you're all right? I'd take you home with me, only my wife, you understand?'

'Course I do.'

'You should get away in case they come back to search for you. It'll soon be dark, and then there's the curfew. You don't want to be stopped in the street, and you bleeding. Bound to be suspicious.'

Thanks for stating the bloody obvious, he thought.

'You're right,' he said.

'Know where you're going, do you?'

'Yes,' he said, 'of course I do.'

But he didn't, he hadn't thought about it, he didn't know where it was safe to go. They might know where he was lodging. They probably didn't, but they might.

'That's all right then,' the man said. 'I'll collect my firewood and be off. Take care. I don't know what they want you for, but I wish you well. Terrible times.'

Walking hurt, each step. He hadn't thought of that. He was cold too, and wet, there had been a couple of inches of water in that ditch. He would have liked to go into a bar and get a brandy, but the way he looked there would be questions. Bound to be. When he was back in the city, he tried to quicken his step. It was still cold, a wind blowing from the mountains, but he was sweating too, and felt dizzy. Twice he stepped into the shadows of a cul-de-sac when he heard a motor. Only the Germans or the Vichy police had wheels.

He found himself in the Place Bellecour, where he had met Raoul 'under the horse's tail'. It was Raoul he had heard shout 'run' when he broke free from the Boche. Where was he now? Were they torturing him already? Or would they keep that for the morning? He walked on trying to look like a boy going home from work. There was a bicycle leaning against a wall and he was tempted to steal it. But he didn't dare. In the morning if he got through the night he would go to that bistro in the Place Morand. The patron knew something of what Raoul was. He might be willing to help him, put him in touch with another Resistance group, or at least get him out of the city.

He recognised where he was now and knew his destination. He climbed the stairs – no concierges in Lyon as the girl had said – and banged on the door. He hoped she would be alone. If she wasn't . . .

'Who's there?'

'It's Richard. Remember me?'

She had a torch in her hand.

'The electricity's failed,' she said and shone the light in his face.

'Oh,' she said. 'You look awful. What's happened? I knew you were trouble.'

'It's nothing,' he said, 'nothing important. Are you alone? May I stay the night?'

*   *   *

'Do you know what proves that God – if He exists – has a sense of humour? It's the male genitals. They're so ugly, so grotesque, even repulsive, and yet they afford us such delight.'

Jérôme looked at what he had written, and giggled. It was what Guy, the Englishman who had picked him up in that pub in Poland Street, had said just before he passed out in his flat in Mayfair, and he had been able to slip away into the blackout, happy that nothing had happened. But he couldn't write that in his novel. It was too absurd. Besides he'd given the line to the priest who was possibly trying to seduce his young hero, himself really, though he wasn't yet sure how far he would have him go, and in any case they were words he couldn't possibly have spoken without stepping out of character. This was the problem – his novel kept darting off in wrong directions. It's because too much is happening to me, too quickly, he thought; I'm not really ready perhaps to write what I want to write. He tore the page out of his notebook and crumpled it up. He'd found Guy interesting with his talk of Berlin in the Twenties, but he'd gone home with him only because the blond sailor boy he'd arranged to meet hadn't been there. He had left a message for him with the barman, so there was still hope.

L

Edmond de Grimaud was elegant as ever in a grey suit of English flannel, a cream-coloured shirt and blue white-spotted bow tie. His black shoes were highly polished, and when he stretched out to take a cigar from the box on the table beside his armchair, there was a glint of gold from his cuff-links. They were in the little room off the back of the hall where they had first talked in the spring of 1940, a month before the Battle of France, and Edmond had wanted to be reassured that Lannes' investigation into Gaston's murder wouldn't involve, or compromise, his son Maurice, who had been Gaston's pupil.

'It's good of you to come,' Edmond said.

Lannes nodded, and looked over Edmond's shoulder at the vast still-life painting behind him, a painting featuring more dead birds and animals – a couple of hares and what might be a roe deer – than seemed decent.

'I had dinner with Maurice and Dominique before I left Vichy. They're well, you'll be glad to know, in good form.'

'It was a pleasure having them both with us for Christmas,' Lannes said.

The house in the rue d'Aviau was more like a mausoleum than ever. He wondered if Jean-Christophe was sitting in what had been the old Count's chair with his bottle by his side.

'Their work is appreciated, you know,' Edmond said. 'It's worthwhile and they are growing up to be fine young men. I wish I could say that it's a credit to both of us as fathers, but I have to confess that I have myself too often been negligent of my paternal duties. Doubtless that's not the case with you. From what Maurice tells me you are a close-knit family.'

Lannes made no reply. He watched Edmond clip the end of his cigar and apply a match to it. This talk of family, he wondered if Edmond would speak of Sigi's ridiculous suggestion that the old Count had been his father and that they were half-brothers, Edmond and Jean-Christophe, and Sigi and himself as the Count's bastards. Surely not. Nevertheless, something was different in Edmond's manner; it was as if their relationship had changed, as if what had been at best armed neutrality was easing. He had never doubted that Edmond had authorised that attempt on his life in the summer of 1940 and yet now they seemed to be meeting almost as friends. And, according to the man who called himself Fabian, Edmond had 'vouched' for him in Vichy when Félix had lodged that complaint.

'Did you listen to the Marshal's speech at Christmas?' Edmond said. 'When he told us to look up at the stars in the sky? Some thought that a reference to the American flag. Was that your impression?'

'It didn't occur to me.'

'That's interesting. I would have thought it might have.'

'No,' Lannes said. 'If the old man was making an appeal to the Americans he should have flown to Algiers when he had the chance.'

'You think so? Do you believe the war is lost?'

'Which war?'

'A good question. They're on edge in Vichy. I don't mind telling you that if only because I have no doubt you will have guessed that this is the case. As it happens, I was speaking to Monsieur Laval only last week. Would you like to know what he said? That there are only two people who can save France. One is himself – of course – the other is de Gaulle. It depends, he said, on who wins the war. What do you think of that?'

Lannes took a packet of Gauloises from his pocket, tapped out a cigarette and lit it. He inhaled, blew out smoke, and said, 'I know very little of these things, I'm only a policeman who tries to do his job, but I'm prepared to believe he may be right. Is that the answer you're looking for?'

'Oh my dear fellow, I wasn't looking for any particular answer.'

He's beginning to wonder if he has backed the wrong side, Lannes thought, and whether he can extricate himself. Of course he'll probably have friends in London himself. He had always suspected that Edmond had belonged to the Cagoule, the secretive right-wing conspirators who had worked before the war to undermine and destroy the Republic, and though it was probable that most of the Cagoulards were in Vichy, others were rumoured to be with de Gaulle, one reason why the Left distrusted the rebel General who belonged to a Catholic and Royalist family.

'It's a mess certainly,' Edmond said. 'We'll all be lucky if we come out of it alive. You had a visit from a friend of mine the other day.'

'Did I?'

'There's no need to fence with me, superintendent. A man calling himself Fabian, a very distinguished officer.'

Edmond paused, seeming to examine the nails of his right hand.

'You impressed him,' he said. '"A careful man." That's how he put it. "One who knows when to say nothing."'

'As I recall, I had nothing to say.'

'Not about that shooting? Nothing to say?'

'Nothing. It wasn't my case.'

'Fabian accepted what you said.'

Edmond switched his examination to the nails of his other hand.

'But of course he didn't believe you,' he said. 'Neither do I.'

'As you like,' Lannes said.

'The man Félix was a nuisance, I give you that. He was also – you won't deny this – someone with whom you had, as one might say, crossed swords. I've seen the photographs, superintendent – the photographs of you with a boy and of the same boy with the German officer – Schussmann, wasn't it? – who shot himself, the boy whom Félix was attempting to use to compromise him. What do you say to that?'

The blue-grey smoke of Edmond's cigar hung between then, then dissolved.

'I would say it doesn't amount to anything.'

'Of course it doesn't, but, as it happens, I've an excellent memory for faces, and when I was in Paris last week, I came upon the boy. He was dining at Lipp with an old friend of mine, the novelist Joachim Chardy. What do you make of that?'

'What should I make of it? So the boy's in Paris – assuming you are right and it's the same boy. A mildly interesting coincidence. I don't see the relevance.'

'Chardy, Schussmann, Félix, all of the same inclination, and the same boy. Only an interesting coincidence?'

'I wouldn't know. I've never read any of your friend's novels.'

Edmond smiled.

'I don't expect you'd like them. Clever but trivial. Naughty schoolboys and tales of the seminary. Dumas is more to your taste, I think your son said. So who killed Félix?'

'How should I know? As I said, it's not my case. But a bullet in the back of the head, I'm told. Sounds like an execution. So: the Resistance perhaps.'

'That would be convenient. For everybody. For you, especially, superintendent, these photographs, you know.'

Edmond got to his feet. He stood with his back against the mantelpiece.

'I don't care about Félix,' he said. 'We all agree he was a nuisance. We're well rid of him, we can agree about that too.'

He drew on his cigar, crossed the room to a table by the bookcase and poured two glasses of wine from a decanter. He passed one to Lannes.

'Your health, and farewell to Félix. More than a year ago, super-intendent, I helped you when the advocate Labiche was trying to destroy you or at least your career. You won't have forgotten, I'm sure. I'll go further and do you the courtesy of believing that you are grateful to me. I won't say you're in my debt, nevertheless . . . well, things are changing; the wind's shifting, that's obvious. It may be that I will need your help, not immediately, but some day, even if it's only to put in a word for me. You understand, I'm sure. I don't need to spell it out. Meanwhile we can agree that the Resistance, or some element of it, executed Félix. That anyway is what I shall report to my superiors. Nobody else will question you about it. I guarantee that. What do you say?'

Lannes lifted his glass.

'That sounds all right. Your health.'

Edmond turned away. With his back to Lannes, he said, 'How's my Jewish stepmother?'

'Safe, I hope. And in return as it were, how did the boy look when you saw him in Paris?'

'How did he look? Just my friend Chardy's type, I'd say. What Chardy would call "a juicy little piece". His novels are thin stuff, but he wrote some intelligent essays for my magazine. How long ago that seems.'

'Like everything pre-war,' Lannes said, and got up to take his leave. 'One other thing, however. Is your friend, nephew or whatever, Sigi, in Bordeaux?'

'No, he's in Paris. Why do you ask?'

'Tell him to stay there. There's a man in Bordeaux who is threatening to kill him. It probably doesn't mean much, but you never know. The man's a Russian émigré, a veteran of the Legion.'

'And do you suppose the threat is serious?'

'How should I know? It's only words, only words, but . . . '

*   *   *

The light was fading as he turned away from that house which old Marthe had told him was full of evil, but his spirits lifted. He remembered that exchange in the *Vicomte* which now, in middle age, was his favourite Dumas novel; how d'Artagnan's servant Planchet had said he was a man whom God had so formed that he found everything good that accompanied his season on earth, and how d'Artagnan, sitting by the window, had found that the old man's philosophy had seemed solid to him. Well, there were moments he could persuade himself it was true. Léon was in Paris, safe for the moment, and so he might allow himself to hope that Alain was safe too. And Félix was dead, executed, to everyone's satisfaction, by the Resistance.

He came to the river. The sun was declining in the west and there was a red glow rippling on the water.